Hope for Tomorrow

Hope FOR *Tomorrow*

PATTI BERG

Guideposts
New York, New York

www.guideposts.com
(800) 932-2145
Guideposts Books & Inspirational Media

Cover design and illustration by Lookout Design, Inc.
Interior design by Lorie Pagnozzi
Typeset by Aptara

Printed and bound in the United States of America
10 9 8 7 6 5 4 3 2 1

For my dearest Aunt Lola, who will live in my heart forever.
Thanks for many things, especially bologna,
white bread, mayonnaise and love.

And, as always,
for Bob.

Hope FOR Tomorrow

Chapter One

ONDAY MORNING'S DEEP PURPLE CLOUDS were skittering away by the time six o'clock rolled around, leaving behind a sky tinged with pink and orange as the first hint of sunlight peeked over the top of Hope Haven Hospital.

What a glorious October morning.

In spite of the chill, Elena Rodriguez leaned against her forest green Jeep Liberty and—as she did at the beginning of almost every workday—inhaled the clean autumn air of Deerford, Illinois, population 7,821, give or take a few, depending on how many babies had been born during the night.

She refused to think about the birth's antithesis. One event was blessed; the other a given, and she saw far, far too much of the other. That, unfortunately, was one of the drawbacks of caring for patients in the hospital's Intensive Care Unit.

Of course, there were also some pretty amazing benefits to being a registered nurse. Except for a few cranky souls and those who were perilously weak, most patients and their loved ones laughed and talked and even shared an awe-inspiring story or two with Elena as she comforted them and tried to ease their pain.

"Father, be with me as I care for my patients today," she whispered. A wisp of wind fluttered across her face and for one moment wrapped her in its oddly warm embrace before scurrying back to the maples, where it began to shake amber and crimson leaves from their branches.

Smiling, Elena offered a quick but heartfelt *amen* and hitched up the tote bag carrying the lunch and snacks her husband Cesar had packed for her, along with a notebook full of ideas, contracts, proposals and cost estimates for the Bread of Life Harvest Festival—a charity event she was coordinating for her church and two others. Instead of heading for the staff entrance, she meandered through the hospital grounds toward the front of the hospital. It was too beautiful a morning to shut out the outside world just yet.

The floribunda roses lining the walkway no longer bloomed with yellow, pink and scarlet blossoms, but after sixteen years at Hope Haven, where she'd started working at the age of thirty, their sweet scent was fixed in her mind. The green grass was rapidly turning the color of wheat, storing all its energy to survive winter and the snow that would come all too soon— but hopefully after the Harvest Festival to be held the Saturday before Thanksgiving.

On the day after Thanksgiving, members of the hospital staff would hang twinkling lights in the trees and decorate the reception area with glittering trees and wreaths and a menorah or two.

Elena was more than ready. The holiday season was her favorite time of year.

The dried leaves crunching under Elena's baby blue clogs reminded her that she needed to head to Cavendish House one day soon to gather the biggest and best leaves for harvest decorations.

Cesar would laugh, of course. "I've been raking leaves around the house for weeks now. Couldn't you have picked some of ours?" Elena would explain once again that they had to be somewhere close to perfection—the right size, the right shape and color—and those could only be found on the grounds of the 1850s Greek Revival mansion that was owned by the Deerford Historical Society, which rented it out for weddings and other special occasions.

The maple and beech trees the Cavendish family had planted a hundred and fifty-some-odd years ago were the absolute best for fall color—just right for decorating.

As she neared the front of the hospital, she was mentally compiling a few things to add to her to-do list besides gathering leaves—recruit two people willing to decorate kids' faces for free, design a maze to be built out of hay, finagle free hay from Jim Ireland—when she heard raised, angry voices coming from near the hospital's main entrance.

She heard Albert Varner's familiar baritone drifting toward her, and she stopped dead in her tracks to listen.

She'd recognize his voice anywhere. The chief executive officer of Hope Haven had a friendly smile and encouraging words for everyone on the staff. He also sang in the choir at Elena's church. She'd never heard or seen him annoyed, let alone furious, until this moment; nor had she ever seen him storm across the hospital grounds, looking like he would punch a fist through the glass doors; but they slid open just in time, and he disappeared inside the hospital.

Maybe this wasn't going to be such a glorious morning after all.

A moment later, Hope Haven's wealthiest, surliest board member, Frederick Innisk—whom Elena had nicknamed Scrooge—stepped into view, his face red with rage as he fiddled with the knot in his tie and smoothed his hands through his thick silver hair. He looked around the grounds as if searching for busybodies who might have overheard his argument with Mr. Varner. When his gaze settled on Elena, she wanted to run.

He marched toward her, the rage on his face hardening into animosity. Scrooge had loathed the Wall of Hope fund-raiser idea she'd dreamed up several months back as a way to raise money to help keep the hospital open. He'd fought her tooth and nail, and he and Elena even had a somewhat heated discussion about it in front of hospital staff, which had only raised his ire.

Adding fuel to the fire was the fact that the rest of the board would not abandon the idea, not after Elena had contacted each board member to state her case for the Wall of Hope. In the end, Elena won, and Frederick Innisk had seemed to be out to get her ever since.

He's probably gunning for me right this moment, she thought when he stopped in front of her. She didn't need to get on his bad side, not when she already had one big strike against her.

A gust of wind whipped Elena's long, dark brown hair into her face, covering the smile she offered him. Unfortunately, she could easily see his downright churlish glare.

Be nice, she thought.

"Good morning, Mr. Innisk. It's a beautiful day, isn't it?"

"Too windy for my liking." He looked at his watch and frowned. "Shouldn't you be at work by now? As far as I know, we don't pay you to lollygag or to stand outside listening to private conversations."

Elena hadn't been late a day in her life, and if Varner hadn't been yelling, she wouldn't have stopped. She wasn't one to argue, but the mere fact that he was one of the hospital's board members didn't give him the right to be an uncivilized boor.

"Actually, Mr. Innisk, my shift doesn't start for another hour. Now, if you'll excuse me," she said, skirting around him, "I have a meeting to get to."

Elena pulled her scarf up close to her face to fight off the wind and Scrooge's scowl. She rushed off, feeling the heat of Mr. Innisk's glare on her back until she disappeared through the hospital's sliding doors.

"Dear Lord," she whispered, "please let that be the last encounter I have with Frederick Innisk for a good long time. Amen."

Elena walked past the gift shop, which was dark inside and locked up tight. It wouldn't open until seven o'clock, when the hospital came to life. At this early hour, there were only two people walking through the reception area, probably on their way to day surgery. Hap Winston, one of the hospital's custodians, was busy vacuuming the carpeted area.

Hap was skinny and scrawny and had a ruffle of white hair at the sides and back of his head, which was bald and shiny on top. A fixture at Hope Haven for at least forty years, he had been named "Employee of the Month" more times than anyone could remember.

Elena waved hello, but Hap was too deep in his work to notice. She hung a right into the administrative area, just in time to see Mr. Varner shove through his office door and slam it behind him.

What on earth was going on?

It seemed odd that the chief executive officer and one of the board members would be at the hospital at the crack of dawn, arguing and slamming doors. Unless . . .

Elena frowned. The hospital had suffered through financial woes a few months ago. Was it in dire straits again?

Elena had too much on her plate to worry about what was going on behind the hospital's closed doors, but she had to think about her job, her future.

All the upheaval would gnaw at her nerves until she learned the truth.

She hoped she could get to the bottom of it during her meeting with Quintessa Smith. Quintessa was serving as the festival's financial coordinator, and—most importantly—worked as the executive assistant to Chief Financial Officer Zane McGarry. She was privy to just about everything that went on behind the hospital's closed doors. Quintessa was the height of decorum and confidentiality, but if Elena could work the argument between Innisk and Varner into their conversation about donations and sponsors, Quintessa might let something slip.

Walking into Quintessa's office was like stepping into a calm oasis of comforting colors—dove gray, mauve and pale jade—dotted with lush green plants that flourished in the artificial light and the soft music Quintessa played on a hidden stereo. The music reminded Elena of the Sarah McLachlan and Cranberries CDs Quintessa often had playing in her car.

Quintessa was like a calm oasis too. Tall and svelte, her skin was the color of warm cocoa, and her eyes were dark brown, big and expressive, reflecting her intelligence as well as her warmth. She and Elena had become good friends when they worked together on last year's hospital Christmas decorating committee. Elena had been in charge, but Quintessa was an idea person, too, and they'd made a terrific team. Naturally, Quintessa was the first to step up to bat when Elena said she needed help with the festival.

She was on the phone, seated behind an antique mahogany desk, the top neat as a pin. One corner of the desk, plus the credenza behind her, was devoted to photographs of her family—her twin brother, Dillan, a technician in Hope Haven's lab, her mom and dad, plus a host of nieces and nephews.

The desk itself was one Quintessa had rescued from a storage room in the hospital's basement. She'd found it hidden behind an assortment of old chairs and file cabinets, and while restoring it to its former glory, learned that it had once belonged to Hope Haven's founder, Winthrop Jeffries, a minister and doctor who had established the hospital in 1907 because he longed for his patients and those of other doctors in the area to receive care, not only for their bodies, but for their spirits as well.

The desk was the find of the century.

"I'll be another few minutes," Quintessa whispered to Elena, her hand over the phone's mouthpiece.

"No hurry," Elena whispered back, wondering if she'd hear more slamming doors or more raised voices coming from Mr. Varner's next-door office while she waited.

Elena dropped her coat, scarf and tote on one of the guest chairs, taking a load off...and listened, but it was only Quintessa's voice she heard.

"Let me put it this way, Mr. Welsh," Quintessa said, speaking succinctly into the phone. "If you look closely at the proposal, it's up to you to come up with a viable way to . . ."

The conversation was all Greek to Elena. Money was not her thing, and her mind wandered to her ever-growing to-do list: taking her granddaughter Isabel out for a girls' lunch and then to the zoo or the art center, and what she planned to fix for dinner that night.

"Wait a minute. We discussed—"

Elena stiffened when she heard the angry voice reverberate through the wall, nearly drowning out Quintessa's conversation. There was definitely a battle going on in Mr. Varner's office.

Elena leaned against the wall, hoping she could pick out a few phrases from the conversation, but it was all rather garbled and all she could do was guess at what they were saying.

Had the directors finally decided to vote Mr. Innisk off the board?

Was Varner being fired?

Could there be a huge malpractice suit on the horizon?

If only she could hear more.

"It can't be helped. You know that better than anyone." Board President Bernard Telford's familiar voice filtered through the wall.

What can't be helped? Elena frantically wondered.

The door slammed. She heard coughing and throat-clearing and then recognized Frederick Innisk's voice. "I don't see the need for any further discussion on this matter."

"You might not see the need, Frederick, but you haven't been around here 24/7. You—" Mr. Varner's beyond-exasperated voice was cut off by Zane McGarry's, but his words were muffled, impossible to understand.

And then, unfortunately, Quintessa hung up the phone. "Sorry to keep you waiting so long."

If only she'd been a little longer, Elena might have heard more from next door. Even though she knew Quintessa wouldn't divulge any secrets, she couldn't help but ask, "What on earth is going on? What's with all the door slamming?"

Quintessa's pretty brown eyes darted to a packet of papers on her desk that she suddenly seemed interested in. "I haven't heard even one slamming door." Quintessa was being much too coy.

And then another door slammed.

Elena's eyes widened. "Don't tell me you didn't hear that?"

Quintessa laughed lightly as if it were no big deal. "If you spent eight hours a day here, five days a week, you'd hear that a lot. It comes with the territory."

Elena wanted to dig deeper, to see if Quintessa would divulge anything, but all this crazy intrigue was pulling her away from her number one priority right now. She was the queen of multitaskers, but she already had enough on her plate without getting completely caught up in the Hope Haven hornet's nest.

Not right this moment, anyway.

Elena pulled a file folder from her bag. "Here's the list of local businesses and those in the surrounding area that I came up with to contact about possible donations." Elena handed a copy of the list to Quintessa, plus a CD containing an electronic copy of the form.

Quintessa scanned the list quickly. "I know two women who are great at sales and love talking on the phone. I think we can crank out these calls before the end of the week."

"That would be wonderful," Elena said, tucking a wayward strand of her wind-blown hair behind her ear. "I have a meeting with the pastors from Holy Trinity, Good Shepherd and Riverview Chapel in a couple of days. They might feel a little more reassured that the festival's going to go off without a hitch once I tell them you're handling the donations."

Suddenly, Albert Varner's shouting once again reverberated through the wall. "I'm out of here. Find someone else to do your dirty work."

Elena tensed, her breath catching in her throat, as the door slammed in Varner's office.

Quintessa turned her head away from Elena, picked up a stack of papers, like she had something important to get to, but Elena had seen the tears beading up in her eyes. No doubt about it, Quintessa knew exactly what was going on and hated every minute of it.

Elena put a hand on her friend's arm. "I can't possibly ignore that, Quin. You might say it's nothing, but something bad's going on. If it has to do with the hospital's finances, if there's more talk about our closing down, of my losing a job I love, I need to know."

Elena placed her file folder on Quintessa's desk and headed for the door.

"Don't go out there, Elena," Quintessa called after her. "There might be heads rolling."

"Then they might be in need of a good nurse."

Unfortunately, all Elena saw when she threw open Quintessa's office door and stepped into the hallway was Albert Varner's back as he disappeared into the hospital's main reception area; when she turned to see if anyone was going after him, she saw the tear-stained face of Mr. Varner's executive assistant, Penny Risser. She was known as the Dragon Lady, the CEO's faithful, fearless and brusque guardian. Tears were something one never saw on Penny's face, confirming that something dreadful had happened.

"Is there anything I can do?" Elena asked.

Penny's slender shoulders drew back. Her long neck stiffened, and Elena was sure that if Penny could breathe fire, she'd do so right this very minute.

"What you can do," Penny stated, "is pretend you didn't hear a thing, that you didn't see a thing. And I strongly suggest that you keep this incident to yourself."

With that, the rather tall, gangly woman with a tight curl in her short hair, stepped back into her office and slammed the door behind her.

Mind my own business? That's impossible.

Hope Haven was Elena's home away from home. She was like a mother hen when it came to protecting those she loved.

She was going to peck away at this situation until she got to the bottom of it.

Chapter Two

ELENA TOOK A BITE OUT OF A CRISP FUJI APPLE, savoring its sweetness as she sat at the desk in the ICU nurses' station, enjoying the first few moments of peace and quiet she'd had all day. She'd discharged two patients, admitted one and put up with a thirty-nine-year-old, tall and somewhat obese real estate investor—Harrison Fogarty. He'd been a hairsbreadth from dying when he was admitted two days ago; now he was quarrelsome and obnoxious.

"Hey, you. Cinderella." Mr. Fogarty's shout echoed through the Intensive Care Unit hallway. "Where's that extra pillow you promised me a good hour or two ago?"

As if his voice wasn't loud enough to catch Elena's attention, Harrison Fogarty continued to hit the "I need you now!" buzzer mounted much too close to his trigger finger.

How many pillows could one man possibly need? Elena thought, taking one last bite out of her apple. Already today she'd fluffed his pillows three times and along with taking his vitals, changing his IV bag and spoon-feeding him strawberry gelatin—the first solid food the doctor had allowed him to have—she'd changed his sheets because he thought they were lumpy.

"Did you flunk bed-making in nursing school?" he'd asked, aiming his implacable blue eyes at his nurse. "I'm paying good money to stay in your hospital. The least you could do is provide me with a comfortable bed."

Fogarty's grumpiness had not been the best followup to Frederick Innisk's blunt behavior this morning.

Why me, Lord?

Never had a patient—especially a man knocking on death's door—been such a pain.

Well, maybe he wasn't the worst she'd experienced in her sixteen years at Hope Haven, but he was close.

Elena spun away from her desk. Her few minutes of peace and quiet were over, but at least she'd been able to eat half of her chicken salad sandwich and most of her apple while reviewing patient charts and ordering medications from the pharmacy.

Standing, she scooped her hair up into a ponytail and smoothed a crinkle or two out of the pink and blue Cinderella scrubs she'd chosen to wear today, the ones that had given Harrison Fogarty reason to call her Cinderella all day long.

Most patients liked hearing Elena's story about her five-year-old granddaughter Isabel's having picked out the fabric for a lot of Elena's scrubs. "This one's pretty, *Buela*," Izzy would say, using a shortened form of the Spanish word for grandmother—*Abuela*—she'd started using as a toddler. "Your patients will like this."

Harrison Fogarty couldn't care less about Elena's stories, her granddaughter or what her scrubs looked like. He was ornery that way.

Irritable sourpusses seemed to be her lot in life today.

Elena washed her hands, grabbed an extra pillow from a storage closet, slipped it into a crisp, clean and perfectly ironed pillowcase, and stepped into Mr. Fogarty's room not a moment too soon. His trigger finger was just about to hit the button again.

"It's about time you showed up. My back's killing me and you've got so many contraptions shoved into my arms and up my nose and every other orifice you could find, that I can barely move."

Elena's gaze shot toward heaven. *Oh, dear Lord,* she prayed silently, *grant me patience.*

"Let's see if we can make you a little more comfortable, Mr. Fogarty," Elena said, untangling the jumble of tubes and catheters trailing from his body.

"You said that earlier this morning, and you didn't have much success, did you?"

If he was trying to get her dander up, he was doing a good job. But quarrelling with patients wasn't in her job description. Better to win him over with kindness—if at all possible.

"I know it's not easy lying in bed for days on end. Maybe—"

"I told the doctor I wanted to go home," he interrupted, drawing his shoulders back, perhaps hoping that might ease some of his pain. "Told my wife to get me out of here. But no one's listening."

Elena pressed a button on his bed rail, and as the head of the bed rose, she said, "You lost a lot of blood, you've just had surgery and you're weak. I know how much you want to go home, but your wife and your doctors want you healthy, which means staying in bed for another day or two and letting me and the other doctors and nurses take care of you."

"I don't have the time to lie around—sick or not. I've got work to do. Money to make. A family to provide for."

Elena wanted to tell him he might drop dead if he left the hospital—and who'd provide for his family then?—but she bit her tongue. She grabbed the pillow from the foot of his bed and wedged it under the small of his back. "How does that feel?"

"Lumpy."

Elena stood back, hands on hips and gritted her teeth. She would not yell. She would not get angry. "You know . . . ," she declared, forcing herself to smile at the man who had too many chins, was sprouting a thick white beard and was beginning to look a lot like Tim Allen getting hefty in *The Santa Clause.* Unfortunately, he wasn't as jolly. "It's possible that that bed could be part of your trouble. I'll see what I can do about getting you a different one, but for now, let me get a foam-rubber waffle pad that'll make it a little softer. Do you think that might help?"

"Maybe."

At least he didn't bark "I doubt it." She was making some headway.

"I can adjust that pillow again and bring you a warm blanket."

Harrison Fogarty glared at Elena.

Elena smiled back.

Slowly, ever so slowly, as if he were contemplating his options—continue to complain or be nice for a change—he pushed himself up in the bed.

"Okay, you win. Readjust my pillows . . . please."

Elena fluffed and then stuffed two of the hospital's less-than-plump pillows behind his back. At the rate he was going, every hospital pillow would be in this room in another day or two. "How's that?" she asked.

Mr. Fogarty wiggled around. "Much better."

Elena walked to the sink just a few feet away from his bed, soaked a washcloth in cold water and wrung it out before going back to Mr. Fogarty and gently wiping his brow.

"How's everything else feeling—on a scale of one to ten, with one being not so bad and ten being horrid?"

"Somewhere between a four and five, I suppose, except for my big toe, which is a twelve." He attempted to smile. In spite of being a grump, he had been a very sick grump who'd needed eight units of blood. If he'd been older, he'd probably be standing at the Pearly Gates right about now.

Elena walked to the end of the bed and lifted the covers, caring for him as gently as she would any other patient. "What's wrong with your toe?"

"Don't laugh. I think I might have gangrene."

"I think you're in luck," Elena said, inspecting the inflamed tip of his big toe. "It looks like the blankets have rubbed it raw while you've been lying here. I'll get some antibiotic ointment and a bandage and fix it right up. And if you'd like, we can put a little something at the end of the bed to make a tent for your feet, so the blankets don't rub on your toes any longer."

"Thank you. I'd like that."

Elena smiled. "Why don't you close your eyes and try to rest. I'll be back in just a bit. And if you think I'm taking too long or you think I've forgotten you, just trust me. I've never forgotten a patient yet."

The hospital's first-floor conference room was strewn with colorful pillows and mats as pregnant women practiced their breathing techniques with their labor coaches—husbands, sisters, or friends. Candace Crenshaw breathed with them as she strolled around the room, the gold and copper highlights in her short, wavy brown hair shining under the conference room's strong lights. She watched each team and offered individual advice if anyone needed help.

A registered nurse in the Birthing Unit at Hope Haven and a certified childbirth instructor, Candace taught an evening class four times a month. The hospital administrators had recently asked her if she could add an afternoon class, and she'd loved the idea.

Candace was tranquil and reserved, and through years of teaching, she'd fallen into a relaxed routine that put everyone at ease—not always the easiest accomplishment when working with pregnant women and their almost-always nervous husbands.

"When most of you were born, and long before that," Candace said, her voice warm and comforting, "most childbirth classes focused simply on breathing techniques to cope with the pain of labor. But we've learned so much more in the last twenty years. Nowadays, we teach—"

The conference room's door burst open. Frederick Innisk—short, hawk-nosed and the only frightening member of Hope Haven's board of directors—made a grand entrance.

What's he doing here? "Mr. Innisk, I have a childbirth class going on," Candace said, walking toward him, her five pregnant students and their labor coaches forgetting all about their breathing exercises as they watched her approach the intruder. "I hope there wasn't some kind of mix-up on the conference room schedule. I've had this room reserved for over a month now."

Even though he was short, he towered over Candace's five foot one frame. "No mix-up," he said, his voice reeking of condescension. "I'm here to watch your class."

Oh, great! Candace wanted to put her hand on his arm and persuasively lead him out of the room. His presence could make her students uncomfortable, not to mention making her totally ill at ease. She'd heard him arguing with her friend Elena Rodriguez months ago about the Wall of Hope, and she didn't want to suffer through a similar experience. Unfortunately, he was a board member, and she couldn't tell him to leave.

"I have some videotapes of actual birthing classes, if you'd like to see what I teach and how the students respond. I have some books too," Candace offered. "I'd be happy—"

"It's not my intention to get in your way." His beady eyes canvassed the room, his glare resting on one pregnant woman after another. Was there something more he wanted to say? "I've heard talk about these classes you teach." He cleared his throat. "Now I want to see you in action."

Oh dear.

Frederick Innisk headed straight to the back corner of the room, turned and folded his arms over his chest. He stood motionless, watching Candace, ready to listen to her every word.

Her initial reaction was to run; but if Dean—her late husband—had been here, he would have told her to fight on. "Quitters never prosper," Dean had said more than once. She wished he were standing by her side now, supporting her. But he'd been gone for three years, a sudden brain aneurism leaving her a widow with two young children.

Dean's death and the fact that she hadn't been able to say good-bye, hadn't been able to tell him she loved him, still tormented her; but she refused to let Mr. Innisk's pugnacious glare torment her as well.

She drew in a breath and turned away from Mr. Innisk, as if she'd been able to blink him out of her life and out of the conference room. Smiling at her class, pretending nothing was wrong, that Innisk's presence was normal, she said, "Let's breathe together one more time. Inhale deeply and slowly through your nose."

Candace watched her students as they inhaled. "Great. Now, let it out through your mouth. Slowly. Slowly."

All eyes turned to Candace at the end of that exercise. She'd done these classes so many times that she knew her script by heart, but Mr. Innisk was making her nervous, making it impossible for her to concentrate. Why was he watching her? Bothering her? Had she done something wrong? Had one of her students complained about her?

She refused to sigh and let Frederick Innisk know that he was driving her crazy. The thank-you notes in her personnel file proved she was a good instructor. Everyone knew that she loved teaching. She could not and would not let Frederick Innisk dampen her enthusiasm.

Leaning against the edge of a table, she picked up one of the pamphlets she'd planned to hand out to her students at the end of the class, hoping it would help her focus again. Fortunately, one of her students raised her hand, giving her a reprieve.

"You said the breathing will help us relax," the student at the back of the room said. "Will it take away the pain too?"

"Actually," Candace said, smiling at the flame-haired woman, "breathing the right way will help you cope with the pain. It'll help to calm and relax you during labor."

"Will it help calm my husband?"

Candace laughed, looking from the *Hi, my name is GINGER* sticker on the redhead's turquoise sweater, to her labor coach. Wearing a *Hi, my name is STEVE* tag, her husband looked to be in his midthirties, like his wife, an age that was becoming more and more common for first-time parents. "If you're nervous, Steve—"

"It's not that I'm nervous, ma'am," he said, his deep, Southern accent edged with concern. "It's just that I might be on duty. And if I get called out on a fire, Ginger will be on her own."

"You're a fireman?" Candace asked.

"Yes, ma'am. I've been with the Deerford Fire Department since February. We lived in Orlando before that."

"We'll take good care of Ginger, whether you're able to be here or not," Candace said, smiling at the nervous father-to-be.

"Since you're new in town, there's something you should know about Deerford—we're a close community. We like to take care of our own. And if Ginger goes into labor while you're out fighting a fire, we'll take every step imaginable to get you here so you can be at her side."

"But she'll be alone if—"

"She won't be alone," Candace said. "Don't you worry about that."

"I've been telling him that," Ginger added, squeezing her husband's hand, "but he worries about me."

"When are you due?" Candace asked, although she could pretty much tell from the size of her belly that Ginger was somewhere in her third trimester. She liked getting to know a little bit about each of her students; and, if she was on duty when they gave birth, she enjoyed helping them through the process.

"Right around Thanksgiving," Ginger said, without any trace of her husband's Southern accent. "We've got the nursery ready and my suitcase is packed and—oh dear, I'm talking too much. I have a tendency to do that on occasion."

"If talking gives you comfort," Candace said, moving about the room, looking at her other students, making sure they were taking in her words, "remember . . . you can talk all you want in Labor and Delivery. You can talk to your baby, to your husband, to the doctors. You can even sing if you'd like. Giving birth is as normal as breathing. Your body will know what needs to be done. You just need to relax and let it happen."

A phone rang, startling Candace out of teaching mode. She'd gotten so wrapped up in her talk that she'd forgotten Frederick Innisk was standing at the back of her class, leaning against the wall, watching her, even as he pulled his cell phone from his pocket and said hello.

"Uh-huh." He paused, turning toward the windows that looked out on the tall, leafless trees surrounding Hope Haven. "I see." Another pause, this one even longer. "No!" His voice rose to shouting level. "Absolutely not."

Shutting his cell phone and gripping it in his fist, Frederick Innisk stalked out of the conference room as loudly as he'd stormed in, making an impression on her students—and not a good impression, at that.

Thank goodness he's gone!

"Now," Candace said, drawing everyone's attention back to her, once again pretending nothing at all had happened, "why don't we practice some massage techniques."

Nearly every woman in the room sighed. This was the part of class her students, especially the mothers-to-be, always liked best.

A nice massage was something Candace had always loved. She missed them. She missed Dean. And not for the first time, she wondered if she'd ever get used to his being gone.

With her reading glasses perched on her nose, Anabelle Scott stared at the computer monitor, proofreading one of the myriad administrative documents she had to submit each week. Life had been simpler when she was strictly a registered nurse at Hope Haven. Since she'd become nurse supervisor in the Cardiac Care Unit, the number of reports she'd had to prepare each week had increased at least tenfold, keeping her from spending as much time as she'd like with patients. Still, she enjoyed supervising the other nurses, offering advice, making suggestions on patient care and attending advanced training so she and her staff could offer the best care imaginable.

When she was satisfied the report was perfect, she hit one simple key and sent it off to Human Resources. She wasn't all that crazy about the computerized system that had been installed in the hospital a few years ago. She much preferred writing everything by hand. But sending reports electronically was much easier and, fortunately, didn't waste paper.

With just another few keystrokes, she logged off the computer—and it was only a quarter past three. For a change, she was ending her shift almost on schedule.

Tucking her glasses into the pocket of her lab coat, she grabbed her purse out of the bottom drawer in the desk behind the CCU counter and put her hand to her mouth, hoping no one would notice her yawn. She might be nearly sixty-three and gray-haired, but she didn't have any plans to retire, and she didn't want anyone to think that working full time was too taxing for her.

Standing, she pressed her hands against the small of her back to stretch out the kinks. She'd worked hard today, putting together a request for an extra registered nurse and sending it to the nursing administrator, Leila Hargrave, even though she doubted it would be okayed considering all the recent budget constraints.

Waving good-bye, Anabelle headed out of the CCU, planning to go straight home. Her husband Cameron had called an hour ago to tell her he had picked up a roasted chicken and a loaf of fresh Italian bread at the store.

As she walked down the hall, her mind wandered to the quilt she and the other ladies in the quilting guild were going to make for the Harvest Festival and the pink or blue baby blanket she planned to make for Ainslee's first baby—her first grandchild. She rounded the visitor's lounge, heading for the stairs, when she nearly collided with board member Frederick Innisk.

"Excuse me, Mr. Innisk, I—"

"You weren't watching where you were going," Innisk interrupted, his arrogance as pronounced as his frown. He stared at the name tag pinned on Anabelle's white lab coat. "I believe there are rules about not rushing through the hallways, Nurse Scott. You could have run into a patient, opening the hospital up to a possible lawsuit."

There were times to argue a point and times to accept criticism, even when it was delivered in a condescending tone. She didn't care all that much for Frederick Innisk. His superior attitude and the way he brandished his wealth totally annoyed her. Unfortunately, he was right. She might not have been rushing, but her mind had been somewhere else. She definitely could have collided with a patient, and the last thing the hospital needed after suffering through financial troubles just a few months before was a lawsuit.

Anabelle wouldn't apologize, though. Instead, she hoped she might be able to find out what he was up to. Board members were rarely seen on the second floor. "Is there something I can help you with?" she asked. "Someone I can help you find?"

He gazed at his large gold watch. "Is your shift over, or are you just going on duty?"

This wasn't a question she wanted to hear, not when she was tired. "I'm on my way home."

His brow rose. "And you'll be back here—in the CCU, if I'm not mistaken—at seven in the morning?"

Anabelle could only nod. The word *yes* seemed stuck in her throat. She wasn't frightened or cowed by anyone, but Frederick Innisk was temperamental and wielded great power around the hospital. If she wasn't careful, her job—her entire department—could end up in jeopardy.

"Then I'll see you tomorrow."

With that ominous pronouncement delivered, Mr. Innisk turned away from Anabelle and headed for the elevator. Anabelle turned the other way. It seemed like a good time to take the stairs on the opposite side of the second floor. Getting away from Mr. Innisk before she said something she might regret was a wise idea.

Climbing the steps to the third floor, her mind spun with concern. What was going on? She didn't need Frederick Innisk lurking around the CCU. It was a busy place. There wasn't time to answer questions from a stuffy board member who had miserly tendencies.

When she entered the staff lounge, her friends Candace and Elena were gathering up lunch bags from the refrigerator and getting ready to go home. Perfect. Someone to talk to about Innisk.

Anabelle dropped into one of the lounge chairs. "You'll never guess who I ran into in the hallway!"

"I hope it wasn't Frederick Innisk," Elena said, blowing a strand of dark brown hair out of her face.

"Yes," Anabelle said with a frown. "How'd you know?"

"I had a run-in with him this morning and it wasn't the least bit pleasant."

"He must be making the rounds," Candace added, closing the refrigerator door. "He spent time in my birthing class this afternoon. Made me a nervous wreck until I decided that's probably what he was shooting for."

"Probably looking for any old reason to put a black mark in someone's personnel file, in case he decides to go hunting for people to can," Elena added, her usual smile gone from her face.

"You can all rest easy. He won't be in your wards tomorrow morning. He'll be in mine," Anabelle said, shaking her head in dismay, "which means I won't get an ounce of sleep tonight. I'll be too worried about what he's up to—not that I have anything to hide."

"Then I suppose I should tell you what happened this morning." Elena sat down across from Anabelle. "I overheard Innisk arguing with Mr. Varner outside the hospital, and that argument turned into an all-out war in Varner's office a little while later, with Zane McGarry and Bernard Telford getting into the act."

Candace frowned. "What were they arguing about?"

"I don't know, but they were shouting and slamming doors and . . ." Elena dragged in a deep breath and blew it out. "Mr. Varner stormed out of the hospital saying, 'I'm out of here. Find someone else to do your dirty work.'"

"Did Mr. Varner quit?" Anabelle asked, shocked that such a thing could have happened. She liked Mr. Varner. Hospital administrators came and went—but he was one of the good guys that no one wanted to see depart.

"I don't know if he quit or just needed to get away," Elena said, "but I hope it's the latter."

"I'm surprised we haven't heard any rumors yet." Anabelle normally didn't like gossip and rarely approved of it, but this was different. It could affect her and her unit.

"We're bound to hear something soon," Elena said. "I doubt that I'm the only one who heard doors slamming right and left or saw Penny in tears."

Anabelle ran her fingers through her short gray hair. "I imagine I'll have nightmares about all of this tonight. But rest assured, when Innisk shows up in the CCU tomorrow, I'll find out what he's up to."

Chapter Three

*T*HE TIMING COULDN'T HAVE BEEN WORSE. Leila Hargrave, Anabelle's supervisor, showed up in the CCU at 7:30 Tuesday morning to talk with Anabelle about the justification she'd included with her request for two half-time registered nurses. Five minutes later, Frederick Innisk walked into the nurses' station, hands behind his back, and hovered over both women like a vulture. Making it worse, Leila was all business, and she didn't seem to understand that there could be a problem discussing this issue in front of Innisk.

"We send our nurses to training on a regular basis, Anabelle." Leila lowered her short, plump body into a chair next to where Anabelle was sitting. "If they're not learning how to deal with stress and burnout from the experts, you need to coach them."

Keep your cool, Anabelle thought. This was too important to be completely direct and assertive. It would take finesse to acquire the new staff—especially with tightwad Frederick Innisk listening in. "My daytime RNs have worked here for years, and

Hope Haven couldn't ask for more dedicated nurses—they know how to handle stress. But our caseload has increased in the past year or so."

"Is that in your weekly reports, Scott?" Frederick Innisk asked, addressing Anabelle by nothing more than her last name, which thoroughly irritated her.

Anabelle wasn't going to give Innisk the satisfaction of standing over her. She stood, stepped around her chair, and grasped the back, squeezing it tightly. "I could print out a graph if you'd like, showing you the month-by-month increase and how that number goes even higher at holiday time."

"Print it up and have it sent to my secretary," Mr. Innisk said. Anabelle had thought he'd take her word for it, but that had obviously been wishful thinking. "I'd like to see it before the end of the day."

"I haven't had the opportunity to look at Anabelle's graphs yet," Leila said, turning her gray-eyed gaze toward Mr. Innisk. "Let me take a look at them, and I'll have them sent over to you."

"There were hourly charts with my report too," Anabelle added. She'd been thorough, knowing that her justification would be completely dissected. "They show the busiest times of the day, which seem to occur early in the morning, right around shift-change time, and again in the afternoon at shift change, when patients are getting out of surgery. That's why I requested two half-time positions, so they can overlap during shift changes."

Anabelle wanted to add that if she weren't required to do so much paperwork, she'd have more time for nursing, which would help immensely. But complaining about the amount of administrative work hadn't helped any of the hospital's supervisors. Paperwork had become a fact of life.

"Do you think having eight extra RN hours per day will be enough?" Leila asked, taking Anabelle by surprise. She sounded like she might agree with Anabelle that the half-time positions were needed.

Innisk immediately shut down Leila's curiosity. "Nurse Scott asked for part-time help. I suggest you not offer or even recommend anything more. This request is already excessive."

"Stress is a grave problem for nurses," Leila said, "especially those working in Critical Care Units. Inadequate staffing has been a problem at hospitals around the country."

"Provide me with reports on this problem. I want to see statistics, recommendations and what has been done in these other hospitals you say are experiencing problems."

There were dozens of reports. Anabelle had them stored in her computer, and she could easily print out hundreds of pages on the subject—or take Mr. Innisk to a meeting of the American Association of Critical Care Nurses. Let him hear firsthand what stress and burnout were doing to the men and women who dedicated their lives to caring for critically ill patients. But it all came down to finances for him. A nurse's health and well-being didn't seem to enter his narrow frame of reference.

"I want this information by the end of the day." Innisk stared down his nose at Leila. "And contact my secretary to set up a meeting to discuss this further. Tomorrow would be good."

He didn't even bother to say good-bye before leaving the CCU, which was probably a good thing. Anabelle might have said something she'd regret.

"I'll give you a call after I look at the charts," Leila said, pushing herself out of the chair. "But convincing Innisk of something when his mind's already made up is nearly impossible."

Anabelle took a sip of her coffee, which had grown cold during the impromptu meeting. It tasted awful, but she needed something to help her swallow the bitter lump in her throat.

"Have you ever worked in Intensive Care or Cardiac Care?" Anabelle asked Leila, not that she really wanted an answer. "The work is never-ending. The nurses rarely take a break; and more often than not, they work through their lunch hours. They're constantly on the alert, watching monitors, changing IVs, administering medications—and then there are the emergencies, when everyone comes running and controlled chaos takes place."

"I've been there, Anabelle. I know what you're going through." Leila bit her cheek, looking like she was contemplating saying something more. Apologizing for bringing up the staffing request in front of Innisk, maybe?

Anabelle liked Leila. She was a tough lady and a good administrator, but she knew as well as Anabelle that the hospital operated on a tight budget.

"I'll take a thorough look at your request, Anabelle, and I'll see if I can set up a meeting with Zane McGarry to discuss finances before meeting with Innisk."

"What about Albert Varner? Shouldn't he be in on a meeting like this?" Anabelle hoped she might learn a little something about the argument between Varner and Innisk. "Mr. Varner's fair-minded. He understands stress and—"

"He's not in the office today, and I don't know if he'll be in the office before we meet with Mr. Innisk. Mr. McGarry's fair-minded too. I'll state your case as best as I can. I'll fight for the extra staff. However"—Leila shrugged—"I wouldn't count on getting extra help, not even for a short period of time—like the holiday season."

Leila's parting comment pretty much spelled doom.

Anabelle took another sip of cold coffee, picked up her stethoscope, draped it around her neck and headed off to check on one of the patients. There wasn't time to mope around in the CCU, and she wouldn't let the nurses she supervised know that she was upset. They didn't need the added stress.

Anabelle didn't need it either. But it came part and parcel with the job.

Chapter Four

BUNDLED UP IN A NAVY PEACOAT AND AN AUTUMN-colored scarf one of her patients had given her a few years back, Elena walked out of the hospital at three thirty Wednesday afternoon, half an hour after her shift ended. She needed a good, brisk walk to get rid of the tension that had been building up inside her the past few days. Even though the sun was hidden behind a sky full of ominous gray clouds, she decided to head uptown. With luck it wouldn't rain, and she'd come back for her car later.

Slinging the handles of her tote bag over her shoulder, Elena strolled along the path leading to Bureau Street. It was only a few blocks to Once Upon A Time, the store where Anabelle's daughter worked. She hadn't seen Ainslee in a few weeks and wanted to find out how she was feeling—if she was suffering morning sickness, or if her pregnancy had been a piece of cake so far. Of course, while there, she planned to see if the owner would donate a gift certificate or some other item for the festival's auction.

She might even treat herself to something pretty or fun—if the price was right.

The usual traffic was making its way up and down Bureau Street. It was a far cry from heavy—no honking horns, no road rage—but there were enough cars traveling through this part of town that the city council had finally declared it imperative that WALK and DON'T WALK signals be installed at all the cross streets surrounding Hope Haven.

Not one to do anything slowly, Elena dashed across the street the moment the green WALK light flashed. She hustled endlessly on her job, never took an elevator when she could take stairs, and she and Cesar jogged five miles a minimum of twice a week, weather permitting. The exercise, the sun, the wind and even the rain and snow helped to clear her head and could relieve almost any tension she stored up.

Shopping calmed her nerves, as well. And, of course, scoring a bargain was as exciting as watching Cesar, her police officer husband—still good-looking, still fit and trim at forty-eight—slam-dunk the basketball or run for a touchdown when he played with the guys.

Ten minutes after leaving the hospital, Elena ducked into Once Upon A Time, a kitschy vintage shop filled with fashions and accessories that had been all the rage from the twenties to the sixties. It sat in between the ultradecadent Chocolate Garden, which made the most scrumptious dark chocolate and raspberry truffles this side of heaven, and Clyde's Donuts, where she and Cesar often stopped when they took a morning jog. Cesar would have plain old black coffee and two maple bars. Elena ignored the pastry, but would order a tall cup of café mocha, with extra cocoa stirred in for good measure, plus a fat dollop of whipped cream to lick off before taking the first sip.

When she entered the store, a recording of Perry Como crooning "Don't Let the Stars Get in Your Eyes" could be heard in the background, and she found herself humming along with one of her grandmother's favorite singers. Elena looked around for Ainslee or the owner, but the only person she saw was a tall young girl with bleached blonde hair waving about her face in a Veronica Lake do, wearing a post–World War II blue velvet pantsuit.

With no one to talk with about the donation, Elena headed straight to the fifties nook, looking for a sweater set with a Peter Pan collar or something similar, hopefully in pink and carefully preserved for over half a century. Something that would go perfectly with skinny black pants. But nothing jumped out at her, except for an adorable twinset that might fit a size 2. Elena was much closer to a 10.

Oh well, someone else would have to score a bargain on that lovely sweater.

Walking about under the sparkling light from the pink crystal chandelier, looking at a host of other fun items, she recalled the pink poodle skirt she'd gotten here several years back, when she and Cesar attended a party with a bunch of his fellow Deerford police officers. She'd found decently priced pedal pushers here, too, which were much cuter than the new-style capris she'd seen elsewhere.

Her mother was a child of the fifties, but it was Elena who'd gravitated toward that period. Lucy Ricardo could have stepped out of the TV set and been perfectly comfortable in Elena's retro home, with its starburst clock hanging above the fireplace and the chrome dinette set in the kitchen she and Cesar had remodeled almost five years ago, with a black-and-white checkerboard vinyl floor and turquoise stove, dishwasher and fridge.

The house might not be big or fancy, but it was her dream home.

When none of the clothes begged to be worn by Elena, she moved on to the accessories, eyeing the chunky Bakelite bracelets, earrings and pins. Most of it was too expensive. Basic, cheap plastic was more her style; but every once in a while, a really good deal would pop up, and then she'd have angst over buying it. She worked hard and Cesar never begrudged her a thing, but reality usually ruled the day. Tucking money into Izzy's future college fund or the Cesar-and-Elena-travel-the-world-in-retirement piggy bank was more important.

"Find something you can't live without?"

Elena spun around to find James Bell walking toward her, eyeing the jewelry as he got close.

"If I were rich, I wouldn't live without it." She slid a bangle bracelet on her arm and admired it in the chandelier's glowing light. "Unfortunately, I'm far from rich."

"That makes two of us, but I need a gift for Fern." James, a good friend and one of the RNs in the Medical/Surgical Unit, flinched as he looked at the price tags affixed to a few of the more expensive pieces of jewelry on top of the display counter.

"Lucky woman. I can't imagine Cesar shopping in here for me. He'd rather hit up the local hardware store."

James laughed. "That's my idea of shopping, too, but coming in here should take my mind off Frederick Innisk."

Elena found herself rolling her eyes. "Don't tell me you've had a run-in with him too."

"The man spent a good half hour loitering around the ward, listening to every conversation I had with my patients and looming over my shoulder while I changed IV bags. I wouldn't be surprised to find him checking the staff lockers to see if any of us are absconding with cotton balls or tongue depressors."

"We've already had one fiscal scare this year. I don't want to go through another one anytime soon."

James shrugged, and as if the thought of another financial crisis didn't bother him, he took a gaudy black felt hat covered with purple sequined orchids off its stand. He held it over his head, checking himself out in the mirror.

"I hate to tell you this, James, but that hat doesn't go with green scrubs."

"Think Fern would like it?"

"No," Elena said flatly. She knew James's wife too well to think she'd go for that hat or any other.

James put the flashy hat back on the stand. "You know, if the hospital ended up in another monetary mess, I wouldn't send out résumés again. Instead"—he grinned—"I think I'd stick around and give Frederick Innisk a hard time, plotting an intrigue here, a mystery there, little things to make his head spin."

James wrapped a blue feather boa around his shoulders. "There was a big part of me that wanted to stick around the ward this afternoon, maybe lead Innisk on a wild-goose chase, making him think I'm doing things I shouldn't be doing, just to get his goat. But my shift was over, and Innisk would probably frown on my putting in for overtime. Besides, I really do need to get something for Fern."

Elena tried on the tacky black hat, checking it out in the mirror. "Do you have any thoughts on what you'd like to get her?"

James leaned his tall, solid body on the glass display case, looking totally out of place in such a kitschy shop. "Not a clue. Something to make her smile," he said, removing the feather boa. A multicolored rhinestone peacock brooch caught his attention. "Gideon said her physical therapy was a bear this morning. She's sick and tired of using the walker, which is the only way she can get around right now, and . . ." He sighed heavily. "I don't want to bore you with the details."

"I'm a detail person. You know that."

Elena flicked a speck of dust off the hat and put it back on its stand, probably the only place it would ever look halfway good.

The Veronica Lake look-alike stepped behind the counter. "Why don't I show you that brooch?" she said to James.

It was probably just as well that she'd interrupted their conversation. James wasn't one to complain about his job, all the extra work he had to do when he was home or to moan about Fern's multiple sclerosis, which had to have been a challenge for their family.

The blonde clerk handed the brooch to James. "It's beautiful, isn't it? Nineteen thirties Art Deco from the estate of Princess Lucinda Alexandrovna. She wasn't a real princess, of course, but her third husband was an exiled Russian prince who had a title and no money whatsoever." The girl's sales pitch was absolutely impeccable, although it was probably going to get her nowhere.

"Princess Alexandrovna had two more husbands after her exiled prince, and several of them died under mysterious circumstances, but that makes this brooch, which the princess wore in almost all of her photographs, all the more interesting."

"And all the more expensive, I imagine," James added, while studying the peacock's every nook and cranny.

Elena watched the way James held the brooch with his big yet gentle hands, before handing it back to Veronica Lake and moving on to the less expensive Bakelite jewelry.

He was a guy's guy, who looked like he'd be more at home on the range or chopping trees in the woods than dressed in green scrubs with a stethoscope hanging around his neck. Rugged as he appeared, he could easily get lost in a crossword puzzle. He was a homebody whose wife and sons meant the world to him, who loved cheering on the kids competing in a spelling bee as much as he did playing basketball with the guys.

Fern, on the other hand, was a petite little thing, standing just a fraction of an inch over five feet tall. She was one of the sweetest women Elena had ever met. Why something like MS had to hit a woman with so much to offer the world was a huge question in her mind. Elena knew God had a good reason for everything, and she tried not to question His decisions, but why Fern? Why the mother of two great sons? The wife of a man who had been a medic during the Gulf War, who'd dodged enemy fire to bring aid and comfort to fellow soldiers and who now gave his all to care for the sick.

Trust Him, Elena told herself. *Have faith and pray.* That's all she could do for James and Fern right now. Of course, she might be able to help James out of his current shopping predicament.

"You know, James, I saw a fabulous twinset a few minutes ago, one I would have loved for myself, but it's too small—more Fern's size than mine. It's a lovely peach color and has rhinestones sewn into a pattern of embroidered flowers and—"

She took hold of James's hand, dragged him across the shop, riffled through the rack of clothes and pulled out the twinset, which she knew would look fabulous on Fern, *if* James decided to buy it. It just might brighten her spirits too.

"What do you think?" Elena asked, holding the twinset up for James to see.

He frowned, deep in thought as he studied it. "I don't know. I usually buy her jewelry or candy."

Typical man, afraid to think outside the box.

"Trust me, James." Elena smiled. "She won't be disappointed."

After leaving Once Upon A Time, Elena popped into the Chocolate Garden to buy herself a dark chocolate and raspberry truffle before heading to the hospital parking lot. The clouds had cleared just enough to let a patch of blue show through. She was thinking about the harvest princess costume she was designing for Izzy when she heard the siren. An ambulance raced up Bureau Street. It slowed for the red light at Jeffries. The driver made sure there were no cars or pedestrians to collide with, and then he made a left turn and then another right into the hospital's emergency entrance.

Abandoning her plans to climb into her car and head for home, she sprinted across the road as soon as the light turned green, raced across the lawn and made it to the back of the ambulance just as the gurney was pulled out.

A child, a boy of maybe five or six, lay motionless, his face covered with scratches, his eyes closed.

If there'd been more than one patient, she would have gone into the ER to see if she could help, but the doctor and nurses who were on duty were some of the best around. They wouldn't need her. Not this time.

She stood back as the EMTs wheeled the gurney into the hospital. A moment later, a minivan squealed into the emergency lot and parked cockeyed in a slot reserved for the handicapped. The driver's door flew open and a young woman, with blonde hair pulled back in a ponytail, tore out of the van. Tears streamed down her face as she rushed to the ambulance.

"Are you Mrs. O'Mara?" the driver asked, slamming the back doors of the ambulance closed.

"Where's Caleb? Is he okay? I need to see him."

"He's just been taken into the ER." The driver touched the woman's arm lightly, although Elena knew from experience there was no way to comfort the mother of a child who'd been injured, who could be dying. "Come on. I'll go in with you."

Over the years Elena had become accustomed to emergencies, but she wasn't numb to emotions. Long ago, in her early twenties and fresh out of nursing school, she had believed she'd get used to other people's grief, but her throat still tightened when it played out in front of her.

And now, worried about the little boy and his mom, Elena did what she so often did when she was alone. She silently prayed.

You know, Lord, I certainly understand that You move in mysterious ways, that You have a plan for all of us, but please, with the holidays so close, could we end the year with a miracle or two?

As she prayed, a mud-splattered police car pulled to a stop behind the ambulance. The driver's door opened, and Cesar climbed out. He wasn't wearing his Smoky the Bear hat, which he normally wore when working. His short black hair was wet, looking like it did when he stepped out of the shower. His uniform was wet too—the navy winter-weight wool sticking to all five foot ten inches of his athletic body. He headed for the emergency doors but then spotted Elena standing beside one of the columns supporting the covered portico.

Elena hadn't noticed dark circles beneath his eyes this morning, but they were there now. He looked exhausted as he switched directions and walked toward her.

"The little boy," he said, his words choked. "Is he going to be all right?"

"I don't know," Elena said, caressing away a drop of water that had slipped from his hair and ran down his cheek. "The ambulance—and his mom—arrived right before you. Do you want to go inside?"

Cesar shook his head. "Not right now. I'll come back later, though, after I change uniforms and get my weapon dried out." He pressed a kiss against Elena's forehead. His mouth was cold, and taking hold of his hands was like gripping a block of ice.

"You're chilled to the bone, Cesar. Why don't you let me take you up to ICU, get you some coffee or cocoa and a few warm blankets."

"Thanks, hon, but I've gotta get back to the station and write up my report."

"You'll catch pneumonia if you don't get out of those clothes now and get warmed up."

Cesar managed to chuckle, even through the anxiety that was written all over his face. "That's an old wives' tale, and you know it."

"Maybe, but that doesn't keep me from worrying about you."

"I'll be fine. It's the boy we should both be worried about."

"He's in good hands, and they'll medevac him to Children's Hospital in Peoria, if necessary."

"I'd rather he stay here so I can keep an eye on him."

Elena wished she could tell her husband that he cared too much, that he'd done his job already—that it was now time to let go, to let the doctors and nurses care for the child. But Cesar didn't let go, not when it came to kids. That was one of many reasons she'd fallen in love with him.

"Can you tell me what happened?" Elena asked.

Cesar leaned against the column Elena had been standing beside, his gaze trained on the Emergency Room door. "He and a friend were playing on the railroad trestle that runs across Lincoln Creek—you know, up near Starvation Point. Crazy kids must have skipped school, thinking they'd have a little fun instead, and then the boy—Caleb—lost his balance, I guess, and fell into the creek." Cesar shook his head. "I never saw the need for kids that age to have cell phones, but maybe I've been wrong, 'cause Caleb's friend called 9-1-1 just a minute or two after Caleb hit the water."

Cesar shivered, and Elena wanted desperately to take him inside, but she knew he wouldn't go. He was too stubborn, and she could tell that right this moment he simply wanted to talk.

"I wasn't all that far away when the call came in on the radio, but the creek was high after the storm we had last month and it was flowing fast and . . ." Cesar ran a hand through his hair, his gaze darting from the ER doors to Elena. "Took me a good half hour to find him caught in a log jam of downed tree branches. It took a long time to swim out to him, and even longer to get him untangled from the limbs."

Cesar inhaled deeply, then let the breath out as a sigh. "He wasn't breathing, and I had to get him back to the shore when I heard the sirens. I was giving him CPR in the water and . . . I was never so glad to see the paramedics."

"You've got to let go now," Elena said. "Let God take over."

"I wish I could, but—" Cesar shrugged. "I can't put all my faith in God. Not the way you do."

"You could if—"

"Let's not go there, Elena. You know my reasons."

She did know, and it broke her heart. His mother had died when Cesar was just a boy. He'd sat at her bedside, praying for God to make her cancer disappear, praying for a miracle that never came. "I believe in God," he'd once told Elena, "but if He doesn't answer prayers, why bother?"

She'd tried to help him find the answer to his question, but he resisted. He wouldn't even go to church with her and Izzy. Cesar Rodriguez was a stubborn man. A good man—but tough as nails sometimes. Surely God had a plan, and she'd just have to wait it out.

"I'll tell you what," Elena said, slipping her fingers around her husband's chilled hand. "I'll pray and—for now—you can put your faith in the ER team."

"I wish I had your optimism." Cesar gave Elena another quick kiss.

In twenty-seven years of marriage she'd never tired of his kisses, even when they were fleeting.

"I've got to get back to the station," he said, heading for his patrol car. He swung open the door and put one foot inside before calling out to Elena, "Don't forget I'm coaching at the Y tonight, so I'll be home late."

"What about dinner?"

"I'll grab a hamburger or something—not to worry."

Elena watched Cesar's patrol car as it pulled out from behind the ambulance. She spotted his pitch-black eyes in the rearview mirror, peering at her as he drove toward the parking lot's exit. A second later his flashing lights went on; so did his siren, and he was off again to another emergency, still dressed in a soaking wet uniform in forty-degree weather, if it was even that warm.

She sighed heavily. *Worry? Me?*

Always.

Cesar was a cop, a good cop who did risky things to save the lives of others. Unfortunately, worrying about her husband came part and parcel with the wedding ring and the marriage vows.

Love and honor through the good, the not so good . . . and the dangerous.

Chapter Five

*J*AMES FELT LIKE A TEENAGER DRIVING THROUGH town on his way to pick up his date for the prom—the pretty girl he'd been keen on since junior high; the pretty girl he'd vowed to someday make his wife. Instead of a pink carnation corsage, though, he had a fifties twinset wrapped in brightly colored paper sporting pictures of a leather-clad Elvis Presley. And James wasn't wearing a white sport coat and a black bow tie, just a pair of green scrubs and a red and black Chicago Bulls hoodie.

No one would ever accuse him of being a fashion plate or ingenious when it came to picking gifts for his wife. Thank God he'd run into Elena. If Fern fell in love with the sweater set, he just might hire Nurse Rodriguez as his personal shopper.

He turned onto McCleaf Street, where he and Fern had bought and started to remodel an older but comfortable brick home a couple of years before her MS had brought their we-can-do-anything-together life come crashing down around them. Today, he couldn't help but notice the well-kept lawns stretching out in front of every house but his.

What was it he'd said to his sons, Gideon and Nelson, when he'd left for work this morning? "Rake the front yard as soon as you get home . . . then do your homework . . . after that we'll shoot some hoops."

Obviously his words had fallen on deaf ears.

Sadly, the Bell front yard was a sea of autumn leaves. Mountainous gold and orange waves washed over the flower beds and crested against the house and pooled beneath the ancient elm that shaded the house in summer, when it was lush with leaves, at least half of which were now obliterating the lawn.

And then there was the rake. James shook his head, sighing heavily. The lethal tool lay in the middle of the yard, sharp metal tines sticking straight up, ready to massacre the first person absentminded enough to step on it.

It was time for a little talk.

Gideon and Nelson were shooting hoops in the drive, oblivious to the fact that their dad had to park at the curb because he couldn't get to the detached garage that sat at the back of the yard. James wasn't one to get angry. He wasn't one to lecture. His own dad, although he was a good man and a hard worker, had been prone to criticizing. He'd pushed and prodded till James knew not to break the rules.

Gideon and Nelson knew right from wrong. They were great kids. Gideon was a fifteen-year-old freshman; Nelson was thirteen and in eighth grade. They'd more than handled the responsibility thrust upon their shoulders, rarely complaining when they had to help their mom and dad with a lot of chores around the house.

But they couldn't ignore simple directions, unless they had good reason—not if they wanted to be successful in life.

Throwing his battered backpack over one shoulder, and grabbing the gift for Fern, James climbed out of the minivan and slammed the door shut, only then catching his sons' attention.

"Hey, Dad!" Gideon shouted, dribbling the ball around his body and between his legs. He was the spitting image of James, with the same blue eyes and wavy brown hair. He might only be fifteen, but Gideon had already shot up to five feet ten inches, just an inch shorter than his dad; and Fern and James fully expected he'd tower over James in another year, if not sooner. That meant, of course, a lot more trips to the mall to buy jeans and sports shoes.

How on earth could a fifteen-year-old already wear a size 13-D shoe?

"Got time to shoot some hoops?" Gideon asked, lobbing the ball at his dad, who caught it easily in one large and skillful palm.

"After dinner and after your mom and I look over your homework . . . *maybe*. And"—James nodded toward the leaves shrouding the lawn—"neither one of you are getting a bite to eat until those leaves are raked up."

"Aw, Dad," Nelson whined, "what good does it do to rake them up? They'll all be back tomorrow."

James shot a meaningful glance at the dark clouds above. "And tomorrow they could be soaked with rain, and each rakeful will make you feel like you're lifting a ten-pound sack of cement.

Get to it now, and once that's done . . . you might want to give your homework a shot, since I'm assuming you've managed to overlook that too."

"Good grief, Dad," Nelson groaned yet again. He was smaller than Gideon, which, thankfully, didn't seem to bother him a bit. He'd gotten the short gene from his mom, who was a petite bit of a thing. If Nelson grew to be five foot six, they'd all be surprised.

Nelson tramped across the yard, ignoring the fact that his brother was kicking leaves at him, soccer style.

Gideon was the tough guy, enrolled in ROTC and playing sports, to boot. He'd even been recruited by the high school soccer coach to play on the junior varsity team at the beginning of the year.

Nelson, on the other hand, had inherited his dad's brainy tendencies. James liked words and languages; Nelson was a gifted student and played saxophone, along with being active in Boy Scouts. He had more than seventy merit badges ranging from astronomy to weather, which he'd earned after they'd spent a weekend together last spring making a hygrometer, an instrument to measure relative humidity.

Although Nelson wasn't all that much into team sports, he excelled in the individual sport of swimming. He'd gotten his technician amateur radio operator license when he was ten, thanks to Fern's father, who'd been showing Nelson the ins and outs of radio since he was little. His report cards might show nothing more than a B-minus in PE, but he'd scored a lead role in a school play and he had straight As in math and science.

Both boys made their mom and dad proud.

Of course, neither kid was any good at raking leaves; but good or not, they'd get it done sooner or later.

James gave the ball a one-handed lob toward the acrylic board on the portable basketball backstop and watched it roll around the ring three times before dropping through the basket.

"Good shot, Dad, but I think I can do better," Gideon said, still kicking leaves and annoying his brother.

"Not when the ball's locked away in my bedroom closet." James retrieved the ball and tucked it under his arm as he headed up the concrete path toward the front door. "Now get to work."

James jockeyed the basketball and Fern's gift around in his arms and listened to the screen door squeal when he pulled it open. Just what he needed. Something else to put on his to-do list. Ignoring it for now, he pushed open the front door and headed into the kitchen, where he dropped the basketball and his backpack on the counter. He hadn't realized how heavy it was until the weight was off his shoulder, but he had some good bedtime reading inside—the New Testament written in Greek, a Greek-English lexicon, to help him with the words he was a little rusty on, and an early piece of Christian literature, also written in Greek.

Put him in front of a TV watching the Super Bowl or give him books written in Greek, Latin or Old English for Christmas and he was in seventh heaven.

There'd been many a night during Desert Storm, when Scud missiles were being launched right and left, that he'd fallen asleep reading the original Old English version of *Beowulf.* He'd played football in the sand with his buddies, running for more touchdowns than anyone else in his unit, but his taste in literature had given them an opportunity to laugh, when there hadn't been much to laugh at in the Persian Gulf.

There'd been a time when he thought Fern would laugh at his preoccupation with old languages, especially when she'd find the books strewn across the sofa or their bed. But then he'd read to her, translating as he went along, and she was mesmerized.

Now he hoped he could mesmerize her, even raise her out of her doldrums, with a fifties twinset.

The house was warm inside; the brightly burning fire crackled in the fireplace that separated the kitchen and family room. Had the boys started the fire for their mom? Had Fern's sister done it after taking Fern to physical therapy or had Fern managed it on her own? If his wife had done it, had it completely exhausted her?

And what if . . . James tried to shake the thought out of his head, but he couldn't. Fern's balance was precarious. If she'd gotten weak or fallen while lighting the fire, she could have burned herself, even set the house on fire.

Worry was his on-again, off-again companion. Off—or close to off—when they were together; on when they were apart and she was alone.

Dear Lord, keep Fern safe. She's the light of my life. My heart and soul.

James smiled when he spotted Fern stretched out on the couch in front of the big picture window, a crocheted afghan warming her from neck to toe, and Sapphire, their Maine coon cat, curled up in her lap.

"Have you been sitting there long?" James moved toward his wife, the brightly wrapped gift box in his hands.

"An hour or so. I was watching the boys play basketball, remembering what it was like when they were toddlers and we'd rake the leaves into one big mound and then dive into them like they were snowdrifts."

Fern combed her fingers through the silver-streaked smoky black ruff around Sapphire's neck. "If I'd had a better day and if the wind weren't so cold, I would have sat out on the front porch and cheered them on."

James's left brow rose and a smile tugged at his lips. "Before or after their chores and homework?"

"They were having fun, and I didn't want to spoil that. Life's too short, and . . . you never know what might come along to interrupt your ability to enjoy life."

James kissed his wife softly. "Bad day at physical therapy?" He sat on the magazine-strewn coffee table in front of her and pulled one of her chilled hands into his, tenderly massaging some heat into her fingers and palms.

"I hated every second of it."

There were times when James wanted to tell Fern to buck up, that if she continued to let herself have bad days, if she didn't stick with her therapy, the MS could take a bigger hold on her, even cripple her for life. But today wasn't the day for that, not when the circles beneath her eyes were extra dark and she looked exhausted.

Multiple sclerosis was a horrible disease, already destroying the protective lining of her nerves, often distorting the signals sent from her brain to her spinal column. Some days she felt okay;

others, she might stumble, her words might slur. And then there were those days, probably like today, when she felt too weak to move.

And there was nothing he could do for her. "Want to tell me about your day?"

She smiled. "I'd rather see what's in the box."

James shook his head. "Not until you spill your guts and get what's bugging you out in the open."

"You shouldn't have to listen to my whining."

"I'm your husband, and I'm pretty good at listening—so whine away."

Fern pulled the afghan closer to her neck, disturbing Sapphire, who jumped from her lap and headed for parts unknown—more than likely somewhere in, under or near their bed.

"We've decided to give yoga a try." She picked up the present James had set next to him on the coffee table. She shook it a couple of times. "This is too big and too heavy to be a piece of jewelry or even chocolate candy."

"I took a risk this time, but you're not going to find out what it is until you stop changing the subject and tell me what the problem is with yoga."

"Well," she said, toying with the package's colorful ribbon, "Dr. Chopra and Greg Clement, my *new* therapist—not that there was anything wrong with my old therapist—seem to think yoga might be just the thing for me."

"And you disagree?"

"Of course I disagree. The whole experience was awful. I couldn't sit on a floor mat, like a real yoga enthusiast, because I'd never be able to get up again. So I had to sit in a chair and I've never felt so ridiculous in my life. There was a time when I was great at gymnastics—so good that if I'd been more devoted, if I'd been able to train with a great coach, I could've gone somewhere with it. Now I have to do yoga sitting in a chair, and I felt like a giant jellyfish drooping over the seat. I couldn't even lift my arms or legs because I was exhausted from getting in and out of the car on the way to the clinic."

"You're too hard on yourself."

"I want to be normal again." Her eyes welled with tears. "I couldn't do any of the easy bends, and I'm talking *easy*, James— bends a hundred-year-old person could do without any trouble. When that proved a disaster, we switched to deep breathing exercises to strengthen my diaphragm, and all that seemed to do was slur my speech and make my hands and feet go numb. I was so embarrassed—"

"You've nothing to be embarrassed about."

"How would you know? You're perfectly healthy. You can shoot hoops with the boys and jog with them, and you don't have days when someone has to cut your steak or lift your food to your mouth because you don't have the strength to do it yourself, or because you're trembling so badly that you might cut yourself with your knife or jab yourself with your fork. And yes, I know I'm feeling sorry for myself but . . ."

James slid onto the couch next to Fern and pulled her into his arms, cradling her head against his chest, pressing a kiss against the wavy brown hair of her pixie cut. He could feel her heart pulsing rapidly. Her sobs beat against his palm, which rested lightly on her back, and tears fell from her cheeks.

He whispered, hoping his words would offer some comfort. "We've weathered storms before and we'll survive this one too.

You just have to remember how many people are cheering you on, how many friends you have praying for you. And God's with you as well. He's watching over all of us, making sure we get through this one way or another."

It took a moment or two, but at last Fern lifted her head, attempting a smile. "You think so?"

"I know so. Remember what David said in Psalm 23. 'Even though I walk through the valley of the shadow of death, I will fear no evil, for thou art with me.'"

"That's pretty easy to forget when you're mired in self-pity."

"God's pretty forgiving." James kissed her again. "Now open your present, babe, and I hope you can forgive me if I've blown it."

A smile radiated on Fern's face as she carefully removed the ribbon and Elvis Presley paper, which James knew from experience she'd use again someday. Fern's resourcefulness had gotten them through more than one rough time.

Slowly she lifted the lid, wanting to savor each suspenseful moment, just as she had taught the kids and James to do on Christmas morning. There was no ripping paper off boxes and tossing lids in the Bell household. They took their time—and Fern was doing that now, making James sweat.

He'd never seen her in a twinset, especially something that had been worn by another woman half a century ago. If she hated it, it would be one more disaster added to her day.

Fortunately he didn't have long to worry. Fern peeled back the pink tissue paper and her pretty brown eyes sparkled. "Oh, James." She lifted the peach-colored sweater that glittered with rhinestones and inspected every inch of it. "It's beautiful. I've got photos of my mom wearing a twinset like this when she and my dad were first married, and I always hoped they'd come back in style so I could find one to wear."

"This one's a good fifty years old."

A smile burst out on Fern's mouth as she dropped the sweaters and cradled James's five-o'clock-shadowed face in her hands. "You're a good fifty years old."

"And getting a little worse for wear."

"No, sweetheart, you just keep getting better and better."

Forty-five minutes later the Bell family gathered around the dining room table, the fettuccine Alfredo and chopped salad James had prepared—following Fern's expert instructions—ready to be devoured.

"Would you say grace for us tonight, Nelson?" Fern asked, folding her hands and bowing her head.

"All right, Mom." Nelson folded his hands and lowered his head. "Here's a little ditty from Robbie Burns, Scotland's favorite son.

O Thou, who kindly dost provide
For every creature's want!
We bless thee, God of Nature wide,
For all thy goodness lent:
And if it please thee, heavenly Guide,
May never worse be sent;
But, whether granted or denied,
Lord, bless us with content! Amen.

Amen was repeated all around the table before the boys grabbed the bowls of pasta and salad, heaping loads of each on their plates. They'd eat Fern and James out of house and home before long. Still, both boys were a blessing.

"Hey, Dad." Nelson's mouth was too full of pasta to be talking, but James let it slide. One crackdown on manners during dinner was more than enough. "Mr. Fischer's decided being our scoutmaster's going to be the death of him. His words, not mine. So he's quitting."

James had a forkful of pasta halfway to his mouth. "You've got to be kidding. He's the best leader I've ever met."

"It's obvious that you haven't spent much time at meetings."

True, unfortunately.

"Mr. Fischer doesn't quite know how to work a compass, and he wanted to give us refresher courses on knot-tying once a month like it's something we didn't all master years ago. At this rate, I'll never make Eagle Scout."

"Has anyone volunteered to take his place?" Fern asked, picking at her salad, rolling a cherry tomato from one spot on her plate to another.

"Nope, it's the same old, same old. Everyone's too busy."

"So what's the plan?" James asked out of curiosity, not that he planned on volunteering, since he fell into the same old, same old crowd.

"Someone from the Boy Scout Council is having a meeting next Monday at Mr. Beckwith's house, six o'clock sharp, to talk with all the parents. You'll come, won't you?" Nelson aimed critical but loving eyes at his parents. "Both you and Mom?"

Fern finally lifted a shaky fork full of salad toward her mouth. "I'll try, Nelson . . . if I feel up to it."

Nelson gave his eyes a quasi-roll, even though he knew his mom's health was unpredictable. They had an unwritten rule about not making Fern feel guilty, but he was only thirteen—a precocious thirteen—and sometimes he slipped. Fern and James also had another rule: The boys were allowed to be human and getting frustrated once in a great while was A-OK.

Gideon shoveled another heaping mound of pasta onto his plate while Nelson stared down his father. "What about you, Dad?"

Any excuse James came up with would sound a bit lame, so he said, "Mark it on the calendar and remind me on Sunday and again on Monday morning. I'll go to the meeting, but don't commit me to anything beforehand . . . or while we're there."

"It's not like you have to be *the* scoutmaster, Dad," Nelson stated, excitement rising in his voice. "You could volunteer for something else, like teaching first aid or giving a talk on what it was like being a medic in Desert Storm."

"I'll think about it. But like I said, don't sign me up for anything."

"Your father's worried that he's got his hands full already, working all day and taking care of me. But I'm getting better all the time, and I'm sure he can find a few extra hours a month—or maybe even a week—to help out."

James nearly choked on his pasta.

"Great! Thanks, Dad. I'll put a big note on the fridge so you won't forget."

James gave his wife the *look*, the one that asked, "What are you doing to me?"

He just couldn't take on more commitments, even though Fern was looking at him with gentle, loving eyes that said, "Thank you, hon," and Nelson was already rambling on about next year's Jamboree and how much fun they would have camping out . . . with spiders and snakes and maybe a bear or wolf or two.

Never, James thought, as he swallowed a bite of salad.

He didn't have the time, and he had even less energy lately. He couldn't get involved or add anything else to his already big to-do list.

And there was no way he could be talked into it.

Chapter Six

SNUG AND WARM IN A SOFT FLANNEL NIGHTGOWN, pink chenille robe and furry slippers, Elena curled up on the sofa with Daphne du Maurier's *Rebecca*, her favorite book, one she'd read many times since she had fallen in love with reading as a child.

Tearing her gaze from the page—from the wicked Mrs. Danvers caressing one of Rebecca's delicate silk nightgowns, as she pointed out to the second Mrs. de Winter how beautiful Rebecca had been, trying her best to drive the second Mrs. de Winter away from Manderley—Elena looked at the clock once again. It was quarter past ten, and Cesar should have been home long ago.

She tried not to worry, tried to bury her mind deep in her book, to allow the writing to transport her from her home in Deerford to the Cornwall coast, to a gothic mansion overlooking the rough-and-tumble ocean.

But the scents of peanut butter and chocolate swirling about the kitchen and family room, the delectable aroma of the cookies she and Izzy had baked earlier in the evening blended with wafts of evergreen from the pine logs sizzling on the hearth and kept her firmly planted at home.

She put down the book. Rising slowly, she stretched the kinks out of her back and walked into the kitchen. Taking a freshly baked cookie from the cookie jar, she leaned against the counter, waiting to hear the diesel engine on Cesar's truck rumble up the drive.

As so often happened, Elena looked around the kitchen and family room, her favorite part of the home she and Cesar had shared since shortly after their wedding twenty-seven years ago, and wondered if there were any more changes needed, any future remodeling they could do. But everything appeared perfect.

This was where she baked cakes and breads, canned fruits and vegetables, made tamales from her mother's secret recipe and created frilly dresses for Isabel, almost always in pink, with streaming ribbons and lots of ruffles and lace. Her designs were terribly old-fashioned—just like the interior of her home—cut from half-a-century-old McCall's and Simplicity patterns; but that didn't matter to Isabel. No Hannah Montana rocker outfits for Isabel Rodriguez. No sirree.

Isabel, with her curly, waist-length black hair and striking, wonder-filled light gray eyes, was long asleep, tucked into bed at eight by her dad—Elena and Cesar's son, Rafael. Izzy was one of a kind. The best kind—independent, precocious and the apple of her grandparents' eyes.

What a blessing it was to have Isabel and Rafael living under their roof, even when Rafael was making way too much racket in the basement downstairs practicing his music, as he was doing right now.

As much as she wished she and Cesar could have their home all to themselves, as much as she wished twenty-six-year-old Rafael could find a good woman to love and marry and create even more wonderful grandchildren to spoil, Elena loved sharing their home with Rafael and five-year-old Isabel.

Elena took a bite of cookie, remembering how quiet the house had been when Rafael had lived on his own, before he'd met Sarah and before Izzy was born. He'd struggled as the bass player and backup singer in a band that played a lot of weekend gigs in Chicago; but he'd found a one-bedroom fixer-upper that he could afford, and with Elena and Cesar giving him a lot of hand-me-downs, he'd had a pretty decent place to call his own.

And then he'd met Sarah.

Elena heaved a sigh, thinking none-too-fondly of the pretty and petite girl who'd wrapped Rafael around her little finger, before getting pregnant three months later.

That wasn't completely Sarah's fault, of course; but once Elena had found the drugs in Rafael's apartment, once she'd learned that Sarah had a problem and wouldn't stop using, even though she was expecting, Elena couldn't stop worrying about the health of her first grandchild.

Now she mostly remembered the five-pound-eight-ounce newborn with a hefty scream and a 100 percent healthy body, and how she'd fallen in love with the curly-haired baby long before she was swaddled in a pink blanket and placed in her arms.

Sarah had worried that she'd be a lousy mom. She'd been afraid of hurting the baby, not intentionally, of course; but she admitted that drugs were a problem for her, and she didn't want to go to rehab, in spite of Rafael's encouragement.

A few days after Isabel's birth, Sarah disappeared, leaving a note for Rafael saying he and Isabel would be better off without her in their lives.

Rafael hadn't agreed, not in the least. At first he was angry, then resigned to the fact that he'd be raising their daughter on his own. A month later he and Izzy moved back to Deerford, back into the home where he'd been raised.

For Cesar and Elena, having Izzy in their lives, living under their roof, was like having the second child they had always wanted, but couldn't have.

Elena was just about to grab another cookie when the kitchen door opened, the cold breeze ruffling the black-and-white gingham curtains and blowing Cesar and an abundance of autumn leaves into the house.

It wasn't often that Elena threw her arms around her husband, but he'd barely closed and locked the door before she was smushed up against his chest, feeling his heart beating in time with hers.

"I thought you'd be in bed long before now." He planted a lingering, feel-good kiss on her forehead.

"Too many things on my mind."

"The Harvest Festival?" Cesar pulled away and dropped his duffel bag on one of the dinette chairs.

"That and . . . you."

Cesar winked. "Nice to know I fit into your thoughts on occasion."

Although there was laughter in his voice when he uttered those words, she knew at the back of his mind that Cesar sometimes felt excluded from her life, what with work, helping to care for Isabel, all of her projects—like the Bread of Life Harvest Festival—and the Bible study group she attended each Monday evening, not to mention church.

They'd argued about the time she gave to everything but their marriage more than once. Elena thought she was always there for Cesar, but since she'd returned to church, since she'd brought God back into her life after a long absence, he'd told her more than once that he felt neglected.

This, however, wasn't the night for a long and meaningful conversation about their marriage. She loved him; he loved her. Somehow they'd get beyond the bump that had arisen in their lives.

"I suppose the festival is consuming a bit more of my time than I'd expected," she said, "but this is something new for the community, and I've had to start from scratch."

"You take too much on your own shoulders. You need volunteers."

Cesar—now wearing jeans, a sweatshirt, and athletic shoes instead of his uniform, and looking much younger than his forty-eight years—stripped off his jacket and tossed it over a hook in the laundry room, just off the kitchen. He turned and walked into the kitchen.

"Quintessa and some of her friends are going to call potential donors, which is a huge help." Elena watched Cesar open the fridge, take out a carton of milk and fill a tall glass.

"Want some?" he asked.

"I'll share yours," she said, smiling. "As for the cookies, I ate half a dozen while waiting for you to get home. Did you have to go back to the station after coaching at the Y?"

"Yeah. Had some hefty reports to write and a hit-and-run court case tomorrow that I needed to get ready for."

"I suppose that means tomorrow's going to be as tough as today?"

Cesar shrugged, taking everything in his stride. "I don't get paid to do the easy things."

"But it's not every day you jump into a raging river—"

"It was a creek, hon, running high and a little too fast."

"You saved a little boy. That's the only thing that matters."

"If I hadn't, someone else would have."

Again he opened the fridge and rummaged around. "Any tamales left from last night?"

Elena scooted in between Cesar and the refrigerator that was almost bursting with leftovers, soda and milk and fresh vegetables. "Rafael ate half of them with dinner tonight, but I saved some for you just in case. Sit down, and I'll warm them up."

Cesar sat on one of the gray vinyl dinette chairs and stared at the stacks of paperwork Elena had left on the table. "I take it this is festival paperwork?"

Elena nodded. "Lots and lots of to-do lists."

"Think you're going to make enough money to buy furniture for all three Habitat for Humanity homes?"

"If we don't," Elena said, sliding the thick, corn husk–wrapped pork tamales she'd made onto a plate and setting them in the microwave, "I'll be hitting up every doctor at the hospital for a hefty donation, and I'll give a shout out from the pulpit of every church in town asking people to reach a little deeper into their pockets."

"The economy hasn't been all that great lately. Maybe you should curb your expectations."

Elena crossed her arms over her chest. "That would be like asking you to shoot for the hoop without trying to score a basket. I've never gone hungry. I've never lived on the streets. The people getting these houses have worked hard, day and night, building walls and hanging doors and windows. They've smashed thumbs learning how to use a hammer and—"

Cesar put up his hands in surrender. "Okay, I get your point. You're not going to stop until you have enough money to completely furnish each home."

"Not me. The people of Deerford. A big portion of them, at least. Can you imagine how special Thanksgiving will be for the new homeowners?"

"I can imagine the look on your face when you go shopping for sofas and chairs and pillows, although . . . you might want to go with something a little more modern than the fifties."

The microwave dinged, and Elena removed the plate of tamales. "I've got it all scoped out already." She grabbed a fork and napkin for her husband, and he pushed paperwork aside, cleaning off a spot for Elena to set the plate. "The Friedrichs— the people who own Carol's Furniture and Appliance—have promised to sell everything at cost."

"Think you could get me a new truck at cost?" Cesar asked, grinning as he dug into the tamales Elena set down before him.

"I think your current wheels will have to do for a while longer."

"I was thinking about giving my truck to Rafael and—"

"His car's fine, Cesar. I love helping him out, but I don't want to make life too easy for him. Besides, he says he's saving up for a down payment on a van that'll hold his guitars and amps."

"He could get by with a smaller car if he'd give up the idea of becoming a music superstar."

"You had your dreams, Cesar. He has his."

Cesar didn't comment, although Elena knew exactly what he might have said if they'd continued to drone on about the subject. He'd say that Rafael should get a real job. Something stable. Maybe become a cop and get a regular paycheck, health insurance, paid vacation time and retirement.

Elena agreed with her husband, but Rafael loved his music. He made enough to pay for Izzy's day care and made sure they both had good health insurance—something Elena and Cesar had insisted on. He paid them a modest amount for rent and food every month, and he was always on time.

Still, they had to be careful and not do too much, like giving him a good vehicle instead of encouraging him to save and buy his own. They didn't want Rafael and Isabel moving out, but they longed for Rafael to be independent again.

While Cesar ate his tamales, Elena imagined her son graduating from the academy, dressed in a Deerford Police Department uniform, driving a squad car and arresting the bad guys. And after a long day at work, maybe he'd go home to a new wife. And more babies.

Her thoughts came to a halt when Cesar said, "I stopped by the hospital a couple of hours ago to see how Caleb O'Mara's doing."

All of a sudden she was no longer picturing her son dressed as a cop. The snapshot in her mind was a bruised and battered little boy wedged in a pile of downed trees, their roots and limbs holding him captive, as the water from Lincoln Creek rushed over him.

"He was in ICU tonight, still in serious condition, still in a coma but holding his own—or so I was told."

"You didn't get to see him?"

Cesar shook his head. "His mom and dad were there, and I figured it would be best to stay out of everyone's way."

"You should have introduced yourself."

"And I suppose you would have liked for me to tell them that I saved their son?"

"I know you'd never do that, but—"

"You're right. I wouldn't." Cesar winked. "And I wasn't about to barge into the room, either, not with his mom crying and his dad sitting in a chair, his head hanging down, looking like his world had come to an end."

"I can understand that, but if Caleb's still in ICU tomorrow, will you come by and let me introduce you to his parents, if they're there?"

"Why? I don't need thank-yous. You know that."

He rose from the chair, ending the discussion as he took his plate and glass to the sink, rinsing both and putting them in the dishwasher.

Elena turned off the kitchen light and heard Cesar's foot-steps directly behind her. She turned and smiled at the man she loved, then cradled his face in her palms. "You're a good man, Cesar Rodriguez. A very good man."

"So you've told me . . . more than once."

His smile slowly turned to a frown, as if something had just dawned on him. "You know, all this 'you're a good man' talk is usually accompanied by a request for me to do something I don't want to do. Some crazy scheme you've dreamed up that's going to require a bunch of my time or, worse, something that's going to require a strong back, more than likely mine."

Elena hadn't had an ulterior motive, not at first, but one amazingly popped into her mind. "Well, now that you mention it . . ." She let her voice trail off.

Cesar shook his head. "I'm not marching in a parade. I'm not dressing up as an ear of corn or a scarecrow for this Harvest Festival of yours."

"Actually, it's the dunk tank I have in mind."

"Oh no. I'm not getting dunked in cold water when it's forty degrees outside. That swim I took today was enough of a soaking for a while."

"Come on, Cesar. You've done a lot of good things in town, but I'm sure many of the people you've given tickets to over the years would love the chance to send you plummeting into a tank of water."

Cesar grinned, pulling Elena into his arms. "I'll do it if you do it, sweetheart."

"Naturally." Elena smiled, thinking of all the money for charity the dunk tank would make. "I wouldn't have it any other way."

Chapter Seven

THE NEXT MORNING, ELENA HAD THE PRIVILEGE OF discharging Harrison Fogarty at 9:02 AM, sending the occasionally crabby guy home to be with his family. A few hours later, two dozen yellow roses were delivered, with a thank-you note from her cantankerous patient.

Dear Cinderella,

In case you didn't notice, I hate being sick. Thanks for sticking with me, in spite of my foul temper. If you're interested in buying a new home or investing in property or buying glass slippers or finding a castle in the sky, I'm the guy to come to. I've attached my business card. Give me a call.

Harrison

Something told Elena that Harrison Fogarty would be back in the ICU within another year, his stomach once again riddled with ulcers. The guy was a workaholic, and some things just couldn't be cured.

Elena cupped one of the roses in her palm and inhaled its sweetness, such a refreshing change from rubbing alcohol and pine cleaner. With the rose's scent lingering, she slipped quietly into Caleb O'Mara's room. He was still in a coma, yet the cerebral edema—brain swelling—that had been causing intracranial pressure was reacting favorably to oxygen therapy, plus his IV fluids and medications. Elena had thanked the good Lord more than once that Caleb hadn't had to undergo a ventriculostomy, a procedure in which the surgeon cut a small hole in the skull and inserted a tube to drain excess cerebrospinal fluid.

So many things were looking good for the little boy. His mom, Christine O'Mara, on the other hand, was exhausted. According to the night-shift nurse, the boy's mother had left the hospital yesterday only long enough to go home and shower.

Christine was curled up now in a recliner on the far side of Caleb's bed, sound asleep, a baby blanket Elena assumed was Caleb's, cuddled in her arms.

The midday sun streaked through the room's window, casting warming rays and God's heavenly love on Christine and Caleb. Elena checked the level of oxygen in Caleb's blood and adjusted his respirator, enjoying the hope-filled rays herself. As she took his temperature and rearranged some of his IV tubes, Elena watched his dark brown lashes flutter just above cheekbones that had been scraped and cut and stitched. His delicate, black-and-blue eyelids quivered, and she hoped he was deep in dreams of birthday parties or Christmas morning instead of reliving the rough ride he'd taken beneath the current in Lincoln Creek.

She brushed a curl away from his eyes and wondered if he was as sweet as he appeared, or if he was all worms and snails and puppy dogs' tails, 100 percent inquisitive little boy, as her own Rafael had been.

Even after just one night, nearly everyone in the hospital had already fallen in love with Caleb. They didn't keep pediatric trauma patients at Hope Haven all that often. Usually they transported serious cases to Children's Hospital in Peoria, but Caleb had stayed, reaffirming the decision in a lot of minds that Hope Haven needed its own Pediatric Intensive Care Unit—a PICU—and a children's ward too.

There had been debate over the subject for years, and Elena was pretty sure that Hope Haven's administrators and board would make it happen, sooner rather than later—as long as they didn't encounter dissension from Frederick Innisk. Deerford was growing; many young families with children had moved to town. Even though Peoria's PICU was wonderful, and it was only sixty-five miles away, the people of Deerford had been asking the hospital to expand to provide more extensive pediatric services.

But money was obviously an issue. Albert Varner had not been in the hospital since Elena saw him storming out on Monday. Chief Financial Officer Zane McGarry, Quintessa's boss, seemed to be in charge. And Frederick Innisk had become a plague on the hospital, creeping around, showing up when they least expected him, making everyone ill at ease.

However, the hospital's monetary woes and Scrooge Innisk were the least of Elena's concerns. Caleb was her only priority—and the only ICU patient in her care at the moment, something that could change at any time.

She took a quick look at the computerized chart in Caleb's room and entered a few notations. His breathing was still a bit labored. His blood pressure had stabilized. Even the chalky white skin that was nearly hidden by his black and blue bruises was beginning to turn pink.

Elena adjusted Caleb's pillow, checked for swelling in his ankles, and when she touched toes that were icy cold, dashed out to the nurses' station, took a couple of heated blankets from the warmer and went straight back to Caleb's room.

Christine barely moved in the recliner when Elena covered her with a toasty blanket. Caleb didn't move, either, as she tucked him up all snug and warm, just as she had done with Rafael when he was a little thing.

Elena hummed softly as she retrieved a fuzzy blue bunny from halfway down Caleb's bed and curled it up where he would be able to see it when he finally opened his eyes. The bunny, a floppy bit of fluff, had been a gift from Izzy, who'd heard Elena and Cesar talking about the little boy at breakfast. It had shared her bed along with half a dozen other stuffed animals for the past year or two, but she'd wanted Caleb to have it.

"Thumperina"—the name Izzy had given the bunny— "keeps his eyes open all night long watching out for lions and tigers and bears, oh my!" she'd said, her eyes wide when she'd given the bunny to Elena that morning. "It could be awfully dark and scary in the hospital at night, kind of like being all alone in the forest with man-eating trees and flying monkeys watching you, so Caleb might like having Thumperina around for protection."

Caleb was not much older than Isabel. *He's probably just as bright,* Elena thought, *and he'll probably like slumber song, just like Izzy.*

"*Duérmete, mi niño,*" Elena sang softly. It was a lullaby she'd learned from her mother, one that Spanish people had been singing for many generations. "*Duérmete solito,*" she continued, even when Frederick Innisk peeked into the room.

She tried to ignore him, to go about her work as she sang, but for once he didn't seem to be spying on her work habits. Instead, he looked around the room, his gaze resting on Christine for a moment before looking at Caleb.

Did she see a hint of a smile trying to crack through his hard exterior? Was it even possible for him to smile?

He disappeared only a moment later, and as she sang, Elena wondered if Frederick Innisk might actually have a heart. It was definitely something worth finding out.

"*Duérmete, mi niño—*"

"What a pretty song."

Elena turned to find Christine O'Mara wiping her tear-filled eyes with a handful of tissues as she climbed out of the recliner and walked toward Caleb's bed.

"It's a Spanish lullaby. 'Go to sleep, my child. Go to sleep, my love.'" Elena moved over a bit so Christine could get closer to her son. "I could teach it to you, if you'd like. Or better yet, I have a recording of my son singing it while playing the guitar. He has a beautiful voice."

"A recording would be nice. Thank you." Mrs. O'Mara kissed her son's forehead, her fingers barely whispering over his cheeks, as if she were afraid anything stronger might further break his already battered body. "I shouldn't have fallen asleep, but—"

"You need the sleep, Mrs. O'Mara. And Caleb's doing so much better than he was last night."

"But he's still in a coma and there's no way of knowing when he'll come out of it." Her voice cracked. "If he'll—"

The tears that had pooled in the corners of Mrs. O'Mara's eyes now flowed freely down her cheeks, and she didn't bother trying to stop them with the tissues.

"You must think I'm a horrible mother," Christine said through her tears. "Oh, God, I am a horrible mother. To let him go off alone—"

"That's not what happened, Mrs. O'Mara. Please, don't be so hard on yourself." Elena slipped her hand around Christine's arm. "Caleb's friend told the police that he'd talked Caleb into ditching school—"

"He's too young to ditch school. Kids don't do that until they're older."

"Six-year-olds do it too. My Rafael did it once or twice. You can't be there every moment of every day."

"I should have kept my eyes on him."

Elena wanted to tell Mrs. O'Mara that God had been with her son, that He was watching over Caleb now, but she was careful not to tread on anyone else's beliefs. Instead, she smiled warmly and held Mrs. O'Mara close while she cried. The poor woman was afraid of losing her son, the little boy who meant everything to her.

Through Mrs. O'Mara's tears, Elena could hear the buzz and hum of monitors and a host of other medical equipment in the

ICU. She also heard the familiar gait of Pastor Tom's footsteps in the hall, heard the softness of his voice as he and Marge, the day shift nurse supervisor, said hello and smiled when he walked into the room. His sky blue eyes were filled with the compassion and deep, quiet faith that were so much a part of him, as he walked up to Caleb's bed.

Christine looked up, smiling faintly at Hope Haven's chaplain.

"Thank you for coming by again," Christine said, stepping away from Elena and pulling a handful of tissues from a box to wipe her eyes.

"You've got a tough little guy here," Pastor Tom said, placing a gentle hand on Caleb's brow. "Spending time with the two of you has been one of the brightest spots of my day."

"All I do is cry. That has to get boring after a while."

"That's much better than a frown, or you not being here at all."

Looking back at Caleb, he took hold of the little boy's hands, bowed his head and said a silent prayer.

Pastor Tom had a unique way of knowing when and where he was needed. No one had to ask for his help or advice—he just seemed to pop up out of nowhere, guided by the good Lord, he would say, if asked for an explanation.

Walking around the bed, he looked so much like a man of God in navy slacks and shirt, with a white clerical collar. He took hold of Christine's hands, holding them close to his chest. "You look like you could use some strong coffee and one of the cafeteria's special chicken salad sandwiches. I was just heading down there for an early lunch. Would you join me?"

"I can't, Pastor. I left Caleb alone yesterday and look what happened."

"Elena's with Caleb, which means he's in the best of hands. But, I certainly understand your wanting to stay with him."

Pastor Tom smiled that friendly smile that seeped right into someone's heart and soul and made her feel good inside. He also knew how to change a conversation at the drop of a hat, to help patients and their families look forward, not back—if that was needed, and in Caleb's case, it was.

"I hear Caleb wants to play Major League baseball someday."

Caleb's mother nodded. "He wants to be a catcher."

"It's going to take some time for that to happen," Pastor Tom continued. "First he's got to come out of the coma, then he has to regain his strength so he can go home and practice, and although it may not seem all that important to you right now, *you*, Mrs. O'Mara, will need the energy to help him when that day comes. So come on, please. Let's go down to the cafeteria. We can talk. And since it's so nice outside, maybe we can go for a walk . . . or go to the chapel if you'd like."

Christine looked from the pastor to Elena, and then at Caleb. "I don't know."

"Go on," Elena said. "I'll be here, and when you come back, maybe you can bring a little bit of that sunshine to Caleb."

Christine smiled at last. "He likes playing outside."

"Once he's well," Pastor Tom said, sliding a hand around Christine's arm and gently leading her from Caleb's room, "he'll be back outside again."

Elena watched them until they disappeared as she heard Pastor Tom ask, "What other sports does Caleb like to play?"

"Just about everything," Christine answered, her voice fading the further they got from the room.

Caleb was a lucky kid to have such a devoted and loving mom.

The little boy's eyelids fluttered, a positive sign, Elena hoped. She checked his vitals again and thought about the devotion the women in her family showed for each other. Her mother. Her grandmother. Her own love for Rafael. There was only one mom missing from the equation—Izzy's.

She'd prayed that Sarah would turn her life around. Prayed that Isabel could have the mother she longed for.

She didn't know if her prayers would be answered, but she held out hope for tomorrow.

Chapter Eight

CANDACE STARED AT THE ORIENTAL CARPET ON THE floor in her counselor's office Thursday afternoon, the kaleidoscope of colors swimming in front of her tear-filled eyes. She hadn't wanted to go to grief counseling. She was a nurse, a trained professional. She could deal with her grief all on her own. But her mom had nagged until Candace made the first appointment. She'd seen Lila Adams nearly half a dozen times now, but it all seemed useless.

A waste of money.

She should be home, playing with her five-year-old son Howie or taking her eleven-year-old daughter Brooke out for a special mom and daughter dinner before taking her to choir practice.

But she sat here anyway, her nose running and a lump in her throat, still suffering the loss of her husband.

"I don't want to forget Dean," she said, looking up at Lila for just one moment, then turning away from her, afraid she might see the compassion in her counselor's face turn to judgment. "But the memories aren't as clear as they used to be, and I'm so tired of looking at pictures of him when the smile that looks back at me never changes, when they don't show the real Dean."

Lila sat quite still, legs crossed, an Audrey Hepburn–like picture of perfection. She took a sip of tea from a delicate porcelain cup.

"Memories, no matter how precious they are, do fade, Candace. But that doesn't mean they leave us forever," Lila said at last. "Memories crop up when you least expect them to. An aftershave commercial on TV might remind you of a moment when Dean stood in your bathroom shaving. Maybe he nicked his chin and you blotted away the blood, or you touched his cheek and wished it always felt that smooth."

She did remember. "When we were still in college, he wanted to grow a beard," Candace said, smiling at the memory that came to her all of a sudden, "but he was still shaving peach fuzz."

"Do you remember how that made him feel?"

"I thought it would make him feel like he was less of a man, but Dean didn't have hang-ups like that." Candace wiped a stray tear from the corner of her eye with the damp tissue she'd been twisting and turning in her hands. "Howie seems to have inherited the confidence gene from his dad."

Candace crossed her jeans-clad legs, remembering the way Dean had carried Howie on his shoulders on a vacation to Walt Disney World. How they'd sat next to each other on the Dumbo ride, their hair blowing as Dumbo flew through the air. Their smiles had been so big, so happy. Except for their hair color— Dean's blond, Howie's brown and copper like Candace's—Howie would be almost a mirror image of his dad someday.

"What are you thinking about, Candace?" Lila asked. "You seem a thousand miles away."

"I was thinking about our last vacation together. We had such a great time. No work; all play. And—" Candace reached for a dry tissue and wiped away another tear, wishing the flash of memory she'd just had could have stayed buried deep in her subconscious.

"And what?" Lila asked.

Candace stared at her hands, no longer concerned about the tears streaking her cheeks. "We talked about having another baby. Maybe two more. We talked about buying a big-screen TV so Dean could watch baseball, and a bigger house for the bigger family we wanted and . . . and all we managed to get before he died was the TV."

"Are you angry at Dean for dying and bursting your dreams?"

"I'm not angry at him, I'm just angry that my life and my children's lives have been turned upside down. Brooke shouldn't have to see a psychologist and neither should I. I want Dean going to parent-teacher conferences with me. I want him sitting by my side in church. I want him holding me when I go to sleep at night. I even want to hear his lousy singing this Christmas when we gather around the piano and sing carols."

Lila set her teacup on the table beside her. "Holidays can be an awfully tough time, especially the first few years."

"You want to know what the toughest thing is?"

Lila nodded. "Of course."

"That you're the only one I can share these feelings with."

Candace stood, walked across the room and picked up one of the cookies Lila always kept at hand. She didn't want a cookie, she just needed to move. Needed to do something with her hands besides worry a soggy tissue.

Taking a bite of the cookie, Candace returned to the chair and stood behind it. "My friends rarely, if ever, mention Dean's name in front of me. My mom doesn't talk about him. His parents don't. It's like he never existed—but he did. I miss him and I'm lonely and I can't share my feelings with my closest friends because they don't know what to say. They don't know what I'm going through."

"That's why you're here, and that's why I asked you to attend my new group session."

"I went last week, but I'm the only one who even mentioned the word *grief.* I'm the only one who said anything about feeling guilty. The others simply introduced themselves then clammed up, and it's obvious none of us have anything in common—"

"But you do, Candace. You've all lost a loved one. You're all still grieving."

"So we're supposed to sit and stare at each other until one of us gets the courage to talk?"

"The first session's never easy, but dropping out can't possibly make anything better."

When Lila said those words, it was as if Dean were sitting in the room, looking at her, teasingly calling her a wimp, as he'd done so many times. *Don't chicken out, hon. Don't be a wimp.* But Dean didn't know what she was going through now. He wasn't here to hold her hand.

"Come to group next week," Lila said, her voice soft even though her insistence came out loud and clear. "We'll be meeting in my home instead of here. My receptionist should have given you a pamphlet with instructions on how to get there, the time—"

"She did, but—" Candace sighed deeply. "If I go, it'll mean more time away from Howie and Brooke."

"It could mean having a chance to let off steam with people who understand what you're going through. But it's your decision, Candace."

That was another thing that was bothering her. She had to make all the decisions by herself—and she was tired of it. So very, very tired.

Running behind schedule, Candace and Brooke dashed across the Riverview Chapel parking lot. Candace could hear children singing inside, along with the rush of water in the creek that used to meander at the back of church property, but had overflowed its banks during the big storm a couple of months before and had been flowing heavily ever since. Not much had changed at Riverview Chapel over the years. It was still small. Still intimate. Still filled with wonderful people.

Brooke rushed to the front of the sanctuary after Candace opened the front door. The children's choir director Rick Shaw was a taskmaster. He didn't appreciate anyone being late, but he didn't even nod at Brooke as she took her place in the front row. Instead, he waved his conductor's baton merrily through the air as Brooke joined the others who were singing "Come Ye Thankful People, Come."

Candace slid into a pew, joining a few other parents, a lump building in her throat as Brooke, her blue-eyed, blonde-haired little girl, sang out loudly. Three years ago, right after Dean died, Brooke had stopped speaking for a couple of months. She'd sat through counseling. She'd cried. She'd been angry. But gradually she'd healed. She wasn't quite as fragile now, but she still missed her dad.

Candace didn't want to think about how much she herself missed him. She'd thought about him enough already today. She had to move on.

Somehow.

"All right, children, that sounded pretty good," Mr. Shaw said. "Fortunately we still have a few more weeks to work out the kinks so it will sound beautiful during our Thanksgiving services. But right now I'd like to talk for a moment about the Christmas concert."

Christmas was nearly two months away. Why would he want to talk about it now?

"This year," Mr. Shaw continued, "we're going to stick with carols and hymns that everyone knows."

"Jingle Bells?" one of the children shouted out.

"I think we'll do something more in keeping with the reason we celebrate Christmas. I've printed up the words for all the songs we'll be singing, and I'd like you to start practicing at home." Mr. Shaw paced in front of the children. "We'll be working on our program, designing costumes, writing our own short plays, and—"

He stopped in front of Brooke and Candace's heart sank. Was she going to be punished for being late? Maybe left out of the program?

"Our music director and I have been talking, and we've decided we'd like a piano solo this year." Mr. Shaw smiled down at Brooke. "We'd love it if you'd play 'The First Noel' for us, Brooke."

Candace's heartbeat sped almost out of control. Happiness and pride mixed together to form a megasized lump in her throat.

The sanctuary lights shone on Brooke's blushing cheeks. "Are you sure you want me to do it?"

"Naturally," Mr. Shaw said, putting a hand on Brooke's shoulder. "Would you want to play for us?"

Brooke swallowed. A tear slipped down her cheek. She looked at Candace as if she needed or wanted her mom's approval. Candace merely smiled. The biggest smile she'd managed in three years.

At long last, Brooke looked back at Mr. Shaw and nodded. "Yes."

"Good," Mr. Shaw said emphatically. "Now that that's settled, let's practice 'We Gather Together to Ask the Lord's Blessing.'"

Candace sat in the pew beaming at her daughter, thankful that she'd been here tonight to share such a special moment.

And oh how she wished Dean had been able to share the moment too.

Chapter Nine

HAMMERSTEIN'S BOOKSTORE IN PEORIA WAS packed with people on Saturday. It was huge, a place Anabelle knew she could get lost in, literally and figuratively. Of course, she'd always preferred a small, intimate bookstore like Francie's Books & Things, that once stood in the heart of downtown Deerford. Francie Latrelle had known everything about books. She'd known her customers' likes and dislikes and constantly recommended good reads. And then the economy took a downturn, and she had to close up shop.

Kirstie and Ainslee, both dressed casually in jeans and sweaters, led Anabelle in and out of aisles—Fiction, Mystery, Romance and Fantasy, Cookbooks, Study Guides, Reference and Medical. There wasn't anything in particular that Anabelle wanted to look at, but she was happy to follow, watching her girls laugh and talk about anything and everything, just as they'd done earlier, over a big Italian dinner.

Twenty-three-year-old Kirstie led the pack toward the Architecture & Design section, her long, wavy black hair shining in the store's bright lighting. Not exactly where Anabelle would look for nursery designs, but she'd give her daughters a chance to convince her that babies should have a room decorated in something other than pink or blue.

"Let's try this one." Ainslee pulled out a hefty tome that looked anything but babylike. With mom and sister following, Ainslee dropped the book on a big square table, sat in one of the hard, straight-back chairs and opened the oversized book. Kirstie sat next to her sister, while Anabelle stood behind Ainslee's right shoulder, absently fingering her daughter's mahogany hair as Ainslee flipped from page to page.

"Does it have any urban chic designs?" Kirstie asked. "If not, I'll grab a couple of other books."

Anabelle didn't want to feel like a dunce, but she asked, "What on earth is urban chic?"

"Cool and modern," Kirstie said. "Refined elegance."

Ainslee looked up at her mom. "Geometric forms. Pure colors."

"Oh," Anabelle said, not wanting to admit that she still didn't have a clue. "Where do pastels fit into the mix?" she asked. "What about Winnie the Pooh, Peter Rabbit or Elmo?"

Ainslee spun around, frowning. "They don't fit in at all, Mother. I'm doing the baby's nursery in apricot and café au lait, although Doug would like black, camel, cream and deep taupe."

Anabelle rolled her eyes, but she refused to say anything negative. Maybe early sixties was a lot older than she thought. She certainly didn't understand the design sensibilities of twenty-something young women.

"What about flowers?" Anabelle asked, hoping she'd hit pay dirt with that designer staple.

"I've never been the flowery type, Mother." Ainslee flipped through a few more pages. "You know that."

"But this isn't your room," Anabelle said. "It's the baby's room."

Both Kirstie and Ainslee laughed. "Oh, Mother." Ainslee patted Anabelle's hand, making her feel like a child whose thoughts were unimportant. "You'll love the room when it's painted and decorated, and once the baby's born, you won't even notice the furnishings or the paint on the walls."

Anabelle pursed her lips. She didn't want to be an old-fashioned, conservative fuddy-duddy, but there were some styles that shouldn't be tampered with, and one of those styles had to do with a baby's room. But . . . she'd promised Cameron she wouldn't butt in to Ainslee's baby plans, no matter how much she wanted to.

"This book's got some great ideas that I can mix and match." Ainslee tucked the book under her arm as she stood, then looped her free arm through Anabelle's. "Let's go pay for it, then head to Country Quilters. I'm dying to see what Mother has in mind for the Harvest Festival quilt."

At last, Anabelle thought. Someone was interested in her design skills. Just wait until she showed them what perfect design looked like.

Anabelle knew Country Quilters like the back of her hand. She frequented other fabric stores when she came to Peoria, but Country Quilters gave her a discount on her fabrics and notions. And if she was having trouble determining just the right pattern or color for a quilt she planned to make, the owner would step in and help—almost always saving the day.

Ainslee quilted also, but some of her finished products didn't have that homey feel. Obviously she'd been making urban chic projects for years, and Anabelle just hadn't realized it.

Anabelle headed straight for the current holiday fabrics. There were row upon row of Christmas, Thanksgiving and other autumn and winter patterns. *This*, Anabelle thought, *is heaven on earth!*

Although Anabelle had her favorite designers, she sometimes ordered off the Internet, when she couldn't find exactly what she needed within an hour or two of home. But she didn't think online shopping would be needed this time, not when she spotted a bolt of fabric with an autumn leaf pattern in variegated reds and purples.

"Wouldn't this be perfect for the back of the Harvest Festival quilt?" Anabelle asked Kirstie and Ainslee, who were admiring some batiks.

Anabelle pulled the bolt from its slot on the shelf and laid it out on the cutting table behind her, unfolding the fabric a few times and examining it under the light.

"It's gorgeous," Kirstie said, running her hand over the fabric. "It's not exactly a neutral color that would fit into anyone's room, but it's bold and beautiful."

"Worth repainting the walls in your room for?" Anabelle asked, smiling at last.

"Definitely," Ainslee added. "I can see people paying a fortune for one of your art quilts, especially if you're starting off with a fabric like this. And if their carpet clashes with it"—Ainslee laughed—"they'll just have to install new carpeting."

Together they pulled out bolt after bolt of fabric, patterns and solids in varying shades of red and purple, sage and teal, black, russet and white, laughing and talking as they shopped. They'd spent a lot of hours in fabric stores when the girls were younger, Anabelle remembered. That togetherness was something she missed and she now wanted to enjoy what little time they were able to share.

There'd been too many years after Kirstie's accident, after she lost her leg and had to learn to walk with an artificial limb, when Anabelle's time was consumed with caring for Kirstie. If Ainslee had wanted time with her mother, she had to help out.

It might not have been fair, but Ainslee didn't regret a moment. If she did, she'd never said a word. That was Ainslee in a nutshell. The perfect daughter. Kirstie, as well.

Anabelle had been blessed.

If only they didn't have such odd tastes in baby rooms.

Chapter Ten

I T WAS WELL AFTER THREE O'CLOCK ON MONDAY afternoon, long past the end of Elena's shift, when she was finally able to get away from the ICU. Jessica Jones, one of the RNs who worked the night shift, had been late—again. She had boyfriend troubles—again. She was stressed—again. She couldn't find her car keys. She'd forgotten to feed the cat. And on and on and on.

Elena had a tough time listening to the same excuses she'd listened to for the past six months, ever since Jessica came to Hope Haven from a hospital in Chicago, which had given her a glowing recommendation. She was a good nurse, and once she was at work she could be trusted with anything. It was just getting her to work on time that was a problem.

Oh well, Elena didn't want to dwell on Jessica Jones. Marge knew there was a problem, and Marge, their RN supervisor, was dealing with it. And Jessica was only twenty minutes late today.

Usually she arrived thirty to forty minutes after her shift began. Today was a big improvement.

"I've been looking in on Mrs. Julian in room 2 every five minutes or so," Elena told Jessica. "She's having hallucinations and I was just getting ready to ask one of the aides or a volunteer to come sit with her in case she starts calling out for her husband and children again."

"I'll take care of that, Elena. Not to worry."

"And," Elena continued, "as soon as a bed is ready in Med/Surg, we can move Mr. Alcarez out of ICU."

"Sounds like a piece of cake." Jessica twisted her long blonde hair into a bun on the back of her head. "What about Caleb? How's he doing?"

"Stable. Still in a coma."

"I'll say a little prayer when I pop into his room."

"His dad's with him tonight," Elena said, slinging her coat over her arm. "His mom finally decided she needed to be home with her other children, and hopefully she'll get some rest while she's there."

"I'll send good thoughts her way too."

How could someone so nice and so totally sweet be so irresponsible away from the job? It made no sense at all. She was a creature of habit. She followed the saying that there's a place for everything, and everything in its place. Her mother had taught her that a lady was never late—for anything—and she'd never break her mother's rules.

Slinging her tote over her shoulder, Elena dashed out of the ICU, nearly colliding with an elderly male patient pushing a rolling IV stand down the hallway.

"I'm so sorry," Elena said, apologizing profusely. Her meeting with the pastors of Holy Trinity, Church of the Good Shepherd and Riverview Chapel wasn't for another hour, and she really shouldn't have been rushing. "Sorry doesn't cut it, young lady." The wrinkled man with a shock of uncombed white hair shook a finger in Elena's face, quite like one of the schoolteachers she had in fifth grade. "Hasn't anyone ever told you there's no running in the halls?"

"At least a thousand times," Elena offered with a smile, and even though she wanted to get going, she asked, "Can I help you get back to your room?"

"I'm ninety-seven. I'm not dead. I'm not lost, either. And I can very well walk back to my room all by myself."

"Well then"—Elena saluted the man; most definitely a teacher at one point in time—"enjoy the rest of your day."

As she walked away, Elena saw Frederick Innisk sitting in the visitors' lounge. Unfortunately he wasn't reading a magazine like everyone else. Sadly, Scrooge's glare was directed straight at her, clearly showing he'd observed her exchange with the elderly patient.

Not good.

The man was driving her—and everyone else—nuts, and Elena had the sneaking suspicion that he enjoyed watching the staff of Hope Haven Hospital squirm. Straightening her shoulders and holding her head high, not giving in to Mr. Innisk's intimidation tactics, Elena strolled toward the stairs, until she rounded the corner and found James, Candace and Anabelle huddled in quiet conversation in the second-floor nurses' station.

"You do know that Frederick Innisk is sitting just around the corner in the visitors' lounge, don't you?" Elena said, resting her arms on the counter.

"I wish I'd never heard that man's name," Anabelle said. "He's caused me nothing but misery, and now I'm having to find another way to get help in the CCU."

"He was hovering around Med/Surg off and on all afternoon, playing vulture, looking for fresh meat to devour." James looked up from the desk where he was sitting, pen in hand, doodling on a piece of paper with two columns headed Pros and Cons.

"I'd be paranoid," Candace said, "if I thought it was just the four of us he's been harassing, but he's been skulking around every department in the hospital. No one seems to be safe. Heath told me he's seen Innisk stalking the halls of Radiology too."

Elena and Anabelle exchanged a knowing glance at the mention of Heath Carlson, one of the hospital's radiologists. Blond and good-looking, Heath was a great guy, and as they had quietly discussed more than once, he and Candace would make a nice couple.

Unfortunately, a relationship between Heath and Candace wasn't uppermost on anyone's mind right now.

"Innisk's doing exactly what he wants to do—making us overly anxious—afraid of our own shadows." Anabelle, almost always the voice of reason, laughed. "I suggest we pretend he's invisible and do what we've always done, which is to provide the best nursing care anyone could ever want."

"Well, I, for one, am getting awfully tired of the intrigue around this place," James said.

"You aren't thinking of quitting, are you?" Elena asked, staring over the counter at the paper in front of James.

"I like my job too much to quit. I even like the three of you." James attempted a fairly lame wink.

Curious as ever, Elena asked, "Then what's the pros and cons list for?"

"Should I or shouldn't I take on the job of scoutmaster for Nelson's troop. I was hoping the cons would rule the day, but they're both pretty much equal. Con number one..." James fingered the numbers on the paper. "I don't have the time. Pro number one...I'd like to spend more time with Nelson, and this would be a good way to do it. But"—James drew in a deep breath—"I don't know if I can commit the time it'll take, and if I take on the job and blow it, Nelson will be crushed."

"How soon do you have to make the decision?" Anabelle asked, pulling her glasses out of her pocket to study James's list.

"There's a meeting tonight to discuss the whole thing," James said, pushing out of the swivel chair and tossing his backpack over his shoulder. "I'll see how that goes and decide afterward."

After a quick, "See you tomorrow," James disappeared down the stairwell.

"He'll cave," Anabelle said, looking at her friends over the top of her glasses. "He's too good a guy to let Nelson's troop fumble without a leader."

"I think we'd all cave. It's just who we are," Candace added, slipping on her coat. "I've got to dash also."

Once Candace had left, Anabelle turned to Elena. "If you have a minute, I need your opinion on something." She grabbed her purse and set it on top of the desk. "I have fabric swatches for the Harvest Festival quilt."

Elena glanced at the clock in the nurses' station.

"I have a meeting at Holy Trinity in less than an hour, but—" Elena's face brightened. "You know I can't ignore fabric swatches."

Anabelle flexed the fingers of her right hand as she dug into her bag.

"Arthritis acting up today?" Elena asked, wishing there was a sure cure for the affliction, which could make a nurse's work a trial.

"Something awful," Anabelle said, "and the medication's not doing much good right now, not with the weather turning cold. Of course, I've been doing a lot more quilting than usual, which doesn't help."

"We can get along without the quilt if making it is causing you pain."

"This is my contribution—the quilting guild's contribution, I should say—to raise money for Habitat for Humanity. What I can't do, my friends will. The wall hanging is already planned out. I bought fabric over the weekend, and we'll start putting the pieces together in the next couple of days. It's going to be beautiful. Look."

Anabelle pulled out a stack of fabric swatches, gingham patterns, florals, solids, and swirls in a multitude of colors like antique rose, dark olive, leaf green, mint, gold, cornflower blue and several shades of wine.

"The individual pieces don't look like anything special and won't until we start the appliqué and piecing everything together," Anabelle said, "but just wait until it's finished. We're calling it 'Over the river and through the woods,' which should give you a good idea what it'll look like."

"I've got half a dozen ideas already running through my mind," Elena said, "but give me a hint at what you're envisioning."

"A country cottage at twilight, autumn leaves scattered over the ground, smoke curling from the chimney—"

"And a sleigh anxiously waiting the first deep snowfall?"

Anabelle smiled. "You've been talking to someone in the guild?"

Elena shook her head. "More like the instincts of a consummate seamstress."

"I want you to see this too," Anabelle said, drawing swatches of pastel pinks, yellows and greens from her bag. "These aren't the colors Ainslee's planning for the baby's room, but I've had these at home, just waiting for my first grandchild. What do you think?"

Elena touched the soft fabrics, tracing the delicate patterns with an index finger. "I love them, but if Ainslee has other colors in mind—"

"She'll change her mind once she sees this quilt made up." Anabelle shook her head, clearly frustrated. "I don't know what it is about the younger generation, needing to be so different."

Elena frowned. "How different?"

"Urban chic. She's been home all day today sketching a layout. The nursery walls will be apricot and café au lait stripes. There won't be a duck or teddy bear anywhere in sight—and, I'm sorry, that just isn't right."

Elena came close to laughing, but she could see that Ainslee's choices for the baby's room had clearly upset Anabelle, whose idea of a nursery would come straight from the pages of *Winnie the Pooh* or Beatrix Potter.

"I'm sure the room will be beautiful, once Ainslee's decorated it," Elena said, hoping to make Anabelle feel better. "Just wait and see."

"Or she'll hate it and wish she'd listened to me when I told her that those colors wouldn't be the least bit soothing to her baby."

"You didn't say that to her, did you?"

Anabelle shook her head. "I thought it though. And Cameron's asked me not to present her with a pastel pink or baby blue quilt at any time in the future, but I just can't wrap my head around her color choices."

"She did a great job picking Doug for a husband, and you didn't have a hand in that."

"You're starting to sound a bit like Cameron now." Anabelle shook her head as she stuffed the pastel fabrics back into her purse. "I suppose you're right."

"Good. Now, I need to get a candy bar before heading to my meeting, or I'll be starving before it's over. Then I'm having dinner out with Cesar. Just the two of us."

After saying good-bye to Anabelle, Elena ducked into Hope Haven's gift shop for a candy bar, something in deep, dark chocolate with a creamy center and lots of sugar to keep her going strong until dinnertime.

Quintessa was joining her for the meeting with the pastors. They were going to discuss finances and logistics, and Elena was at the point where she could pretty much relate details about the Harvest Festival in her sleep.

She grabbed a small package of oatmeal raisin cookies and a dark-chocolate Milky Way. While waiting in line at the cash register, she picked up a beautiful dark brown teddy bear dressed in a purple leotard, fluffy pale lavender tutu and satin ballet slippers that laced halfway up its pudgy little legs.

Isabel would love it. Even now Elena could imagine it under the tree on Christmas morning, a little something left by Santa Claus during the night.

"This is adorable," Elena said to Ruth Lieberman, the clerk with dark gray hair worn in a heavy bun on the back of her head. "Could you hold on to it for me until shortly before Christmas?"

"Ah, a gift for our little Izzy?"

"You know me too well."

"I like knowing all of my customers," Ruth said. "Makes the day much brighter."

Elena and Ruth had shared many a story and many a recipe here in the gift shop. Ruth was as devoutly Jewish as Elena was Christian. She faithfully observed Shabbat, not working from Friday at sundown or at all on Saturdays, and had invited Elena to her home to learn how to make sweet, eggy challah bread, which was absolutely delicious. It was Ruth who suggested Elena make French toast from challah for Cesar, and it had become one of his favorite breakfast meals.

She owed Cesar not just a special breakfast, but a special day, as well, something more than the dinner they were sharing tonight, in between her meetings. He was right—she did take on too much and she was gone a lot. So many nights he fended for himself when dinnertime rolled around. She usually worked on his days off; he worked on hers. If they weren't careful, they could drift apart.

That was the last thing Elena wanted.

She had to stop taking on more projects.

After paying for her purchases, Elena dropped her wallet, the cookies and candy bar into her tote. Glancing at her watch and knowing she'd have to hurry, she turned and bumped into a tall, redheaded woman holding two of the fluffy teddy bears against her very pregnant body.

"I'm so sorry," Elena said for the second time in the last hour. "I didn't hurt you, did I?"

"I'm fine, really."

Elena found herself fingering the green vest on one of the bears the redhead was holding.

"This is Robin Hood," the woman said. "Cute isn't he?"

Elena nodded. "I just bought one dressed as a ballerina for my granddaughter. Are these for your children?"

She touched her protruding belly. "This is my first. As for the bears, they're creations of mine and Ruth's been kind enough to let me sell them here."

"Really?" Elena asked, an idea popping into her mind. "Would you be interested in renting a booth at our Harvest Festival and selling more of them there?"

The woman contemplated the question for a moment or two, then smiled. "I'm sure my husband would love that. My bears and some of my other creations have been running him out of house and home." She tucked Robin Hood under her arm and held out her hand to Elena. "I'm Ginger Murphy."

"Elena Rodriguez," Elena said, shaking her hand. "I've got a meeting at my church so I have to run, but I'll be here tomorrow, in the ICU from seven until three. If you want to stop by, I can give you more details about the festival."

"As long as my feet aren't swollen and I can get into the car, I'd love to talk with you."

"Great. See you then," Elena said, heading for the door.

"Wait."

Elena was going to be late if she didn't hurry, but she stopped anyway. She turned to see Ginger walking toward her.

"Mind if I ask which church you go to?"

"Holy Trinity."

"Is that the gothic church with the chimes?"

Elena nodded. If she weren't in such a big rush, she could go on and on, extolling the virtues of Holy Trinity, but she held back and merely said, "If you're looking for a church to join—"

"Actually, I was hoping to find a Bible study group, at least to start."

"It just so happens my group meets tonight at seven." Elena dug into her bag, pulled out a pen and notepad and scribbled down the address for Holy Trinity, her name and her cell phone number. "I'll wait outside for you—if you can make it."

"I'll be there," Ginger said, touching her belly. "I really do need some people to pray with."

Chapter Eleven

*T*HE OVEN TIMER BEEPED AT 5:30 PM, THE EXACT moment Candace heard the drone of the automatic garage door rising.

Right on time.

If there was one thing Candace could always trust, it was that her mother, Janet Fuller—Grammy to Brooke and Howie—was punctual.

Candace had so many things to be thankful for in her life. Her children, the sweet and precious memories she and Dean had shared and her mom's willingness to give up her own home and move in with Candace and the kids after Dean's death. She was a godsend who never grumbled about helping with meals, child care, getting Howie and Brooke to and from school and a whole assortment of other things.

As much as Candace wished she could do it all on her own— as much as she wished Dean could be there to help with their children—it wasn't possible. And Janet doted on the munchkins as much as Candace did.

She pulled a meatloaf—Howie's favorite dinnertime entrée—out of the oven. Its juices sizzled in the glass baking dish and the scent of the spices she'd added to the meat, plus the apricot preserves she'd mixed in for an extra special flavor, wafted about the kitchen. The meal was going to be delicious—and she was starved.

As she transferred the meat to a high-gloss pottery platter, one of the mismatched and colorful pieces of dinnerware she'd started collecting while in college, the children bounded through the garage door and into the mudroom. The first sight of them brought a smile to her face and extra warmth to her heart.

Even from the kitchen she could watch their movements. They dropped their coats and backpacks on the mudroom floor, because it was much too difficult to hang them on the perfectly good rack mounted on one wall.

Howie kicked off his tennis shoes, more than likely left a pile of sandbox sand on the floor and raced into the kitchen, launching himself into Candace's arms. She hugged him tightly, kissing his cold, reddened cheeks just as he kissed hers, before letting him down so he could run around the house and expend some of his little-boy energy. She hated the thought of Howie getting older and not getting three or four hugs from him every day.

Brooke, on the other hand, had pretty much outgrown kisses and hugs, unless giving them was her own idea. Candace's small-for-her-age yet beautiful, blonde-haired, blue-eyed daughter, seemed to be flirting with adolescent moodiness. She hadn't even looked at Candace when she ran into the house.

"How were piano lessons?" Candace called after her daughter as she jumped down the short flight of steps to the split-level home's family room, which was separated from the kitchen by a simple oak railing.

"You know, same old, same old." To quell further conversation with her mother, Brooke turned the television up full blast while flipping through channels for something to watch.

Candace raised her eyes toward heaven. Was this the same daughter who'd been so excited at choir practice last week? The same daughter who'd shed a few tears when asked to play a solo at the Christmas services? Candace consoled herself, thinking it wouldn't be any fun to have a kid who displayed just one mood all the time.

Janet stopped next to her daughter and said, in her quiet, calm and I've-been-through-this-before-and-you-too-shall-come-out-of-it-alive voice, "Lessons were wonderful, but she was having a bit of trouble with 'Claire de Lune,' and after her instructor watched her play, told her she was moving her thumbs all wrong."

"There's a right way and a wrong way to move your thumbs?" Candace asked as she drained the boiled potatoes for her extra creamy mashed potatoes with cream cheese, the steam rising up, obliterating most of her view.

"Yeah, Mommy," Brooke shouted over the big-screen TV. "You move your thumbs from the wrist, not from the joint. It makes all the difference in the world."

"Thanks, honey." Candace scooted around Janet, who was poking through the frozen vegetables in the freezer, and took milk and margarine out of the fridge. "Would you play something for me?"

"*Hannah Montana's* on."

"Why don't you set the table then? You can watch *Hannah Montana* when you're done."

This time she was completely ignored. Candace tried to give her daughter the benefit of the doubt. She hated to think that Brooke was just being obstinate and ignoring her.

Boy, she was a lousy disciplinarian.

Dean would have walked down the stairs, picked Brooke up and carried her to the kitchen. But Dean wasn't around. And he never would be. Ever again.

Toughen up. Go to that group session tonight and talk it out of your system.

"Peas okay?" Janet asked, pulling her head out of the freezer and dragging Candace back to the present.

"Perfect, Mom."

Janet pushed a footstool across the kitchen floor and climbed on top to retrieve a bowl from one of the cabinets. "Need one for the potatoes while I'm up here?"

"Please."

Dinner would be ready in about fifteen minutes, and the table still wasn't set. That's where toughness came in, and Candace wished she wasn't such a pushover or so afraid to upset her daughter. Still, she called out, "Hey, Brooke. I've got to leave in about forty-five minutes, so DVR your show, come set the table and you can watch TV after your homework's done."

"Leave?" Candace could hear the fear in her daughter's voice as Brooke's head whipped around to stare at her mom, a sudden fear on her still-a-little-girl face. She'd lost one parent; having another disappear in a flash struck a note of terror.

"I have a meeting to go to, honey. No biggy." It was a half-truth; not exactly a lie. She couldn't tell Brooke she was going to a therapy session. Moms were supposed to be perfect. In their children's eyes, they could handle anything and everything—or at least they should be able to. That's how they protected their kids.

Her counselor would probably tell her to spill the beans, but Candace couldn't. Not now.

"I thought you were going to be home to watch *It's the Great Pumpkin, Charlie Brown* with us." Brooke sounded disappointed.

"I already checked the television guide and it's not on until eight thirty. I've got a bowl all ready for the popcorn, and I've planned to douse it with extra butter, just like you, Howie and Grammy like it. Now come on, sweetheart, time's running out on me."

"Oh, all right."

Would it be a struggle every night until Brooke went off to college? Candace pressed a kiss to her daughter's forehead as she took silverware from the drawer. A second later Brooke had her arms around her. "I love you."

"I love you too, honey."

Brooke didn't move for the longest time. She was in her thinking mode, and not for the first time, Candace wished she could read her daughter's mind.

"What are you thinking about?"

"Daddy."

There wasn't any hint of sadness in Brooke's voice, maybe because all the grief was resting in Candace's throat, welling up, getting bigger and bigger. *Toughen up*, she told herself, caressing a hand over her little girl's cheek. *Don't smother Brooke. Don't make her cry. Don't cry yourself.*

"Mommy? Did you hear me?"

Candace nodded. "Yes, honey. What about Daddy?"

"I bet God's happy having Daddy up there with Him."

Candace felt her voice crack before masking it as if she were clearing her throat. "I'm sure He is."

"He laughed a lot."

"All the time."

"Do you think he's laughing in heaven?"

"I imagine so."

Brooke looked up at Candace's face and seemed to breathe a sigh of relief at her mom's response. As Brooke walked over to the table with her hands full of knives, forks and spoons, Candace wondered when Brooke had become so logical. So perceptive.

Was this all a fluke? Or a breakthrough? A chance for her daughter to be a happy little girl again? That's what Candace had been praying for.

Thank You, Lord, for letting me see Dean's sparkle in Brooke's eyes. I'll always have that. Always.

Chapter Twelve

AMES DID NOT WANT TO BE AT THIS MEETING, but from the size of the crowd—four other parents, including the host, and five boys—most of the other parents didn't want to be here and hadn't shown up.

"Thank you all for coming out tonight on such short notice," Ron Beckwith said, "but as you may have already heard, we've lost our scoutmaster."

James sat next to Nelson, inside the enclosed back porch at Ron Beckwith's home, and listened to the big man with a voice to match speak about how the troop had been deserted by their scoutmaster. He didn't use those exact words, but James could hear the frustration in his voice.

"Quite a number of activities have been planned for our boys," Ron continued, and James was trying not to picture himself in a scoutmaster uniform. He'd worn a uniform during Desert Storm; he didn't want to do it again. "Jamboree, of course, which will be held next summer in North Carolina as well as working with service organizations like the Salvation Army, Habitat for Humanity and the American Red Cross."

One of the parents, Bud Singh, who was leaning against the sliding glass door leading from the living room out to the porch, stepped forward. "You do plan to take over the scoutmaster position, don't you Ron?"

Nelson nudged his dad and frowned. Apparently having Ron Beckwith as scoutmaster didn't appeal to Nelson. Why? James couldn't imagine. The guy seemed perfectly fit for the job. Far more fit than he himself would be.

"No, I'm afraid I can't take over. My job sends me out of town quite often, which means I can't attend all weekly meetings. Having one person who can devote the time and energy it takes to lead the troop would be the best way to go. If we fail to find someone who can do that, we might consider having co-scoutmasters or have our sons join another troop, perhaps one in Princeton, Tiskilwa or Wyanet, until we can find someone to take over."

"That would be too far away," Bud Singh added. "Our boys wouldn't be able to ride their bikes to meetings if they joined an out-of-town troop. And neither my wife nor I have the time to drive them to meetings."

"If we can't make any of those alternatives work"—Ron shrugged—"Deerford's troop might have to disband."

"We can't let that happen," Bud Singh said. "I was in this troop when I was a kid. I went to Jamboree, did the turkey shoot with my dad at least three or four times."

"This troop's been a big part of Deerford history," James added. He'd done his homework, wanting to be prepared for this meeting. "After World War II the kids collected money to build a memorial to those who died. They've shoveled snow for the elderly and sandbagged homes during storms. I don't believe letting it die is an option."

Ron Beckwith folded his arms across his chest. "Perhaps we could merge with a troop in another town? Alternate meeting places. Carpool."

"That's better than the boys not having a troop at all," James stated, "but I'd rather see us go in search of a new scoutmaster. Put an ad in the newspaper. Post notices around town."

"Does this mean you have the time to devote to this?" Beckwith asked.

James knew he'd open himself up to extra work if he brought up the subject of advertising for a scoutmaster, but the troop meant a lot to his son. And Nelson meant a lot to him. "I don't have any more time than anyone else, but, yeah, I'll get notices sent out."

Beckwith nodded as he sighed with relief. "I'll give you the name and phone number of our contact at the council office. They were supposed to send someone out for today's meeting but he didn't show up."

"Before we launch an advertising project," James said, looking at the two other parents who'd been quiet so far, "are either of you able to take on the job?"

Heads shook a definite no.

No surprise there.

"I suggest," Ron said, eyes on James, "that you take a look at the storage shed full of gear that we've amassed over the years, before you send out the advertisement, that way you'll know what equipment we have. I can give you the key to take home with you tonight, along with our bank statements and the financial books, so you'll know about our other resources. And, of course, you'll need the pamphlets the council office sent me on the scoutmaster position and how volunteers can be an asset to our boys."

Nelson practically knocked over his folding chair in his rush to get to the literature Ron had pointed to on the patio table. All the other parents seemed to be in a rush to leave without taking anything home to read.

"Look, Dad," Nelson said, his hands full, "this one describes the scoutmaster uniform, this one talks about a background investigation—of sorts—that you have to go through before you can become a scoutmaster and this one describes how fun the job will be."

James put a hand on Nelson's shoulder. "I'm going to help find a scoutmaster," he said, "but don't get your hopes up that it'll be me. Volunteering to teach first-aid or give a talk about being a medic are vastly different from leading a troop. I honestly don't feel I have the time."

Nelson's lips pursed and he aimed his eyes at the ground as James thanked Beckwith for hosting the meeting and took the keys and troop paperwork off his hands.

Nelson was silent for most of the ride home, but James could tell that his son's mind was working hard, trying to think of a way to talk his dad into taking over the troop. Finally, he said, "I know you've got a lot on your plate, Dad, with Mom being sick so much of the time, and working so many hours a day and needing to go to Gideon's ball games. And I know how tough it is to do things you don't really want to do. I mean, I don't really like playing basketball, but I do it because it makes you happy."

Nelson was smart; attempting to get under his dad's skin by using reverse psychology. It was a good try, but James knew he couldn't give in.

"I like it when you're happy, Dad."

"Thanks, son."

Right now, there wasn't much more James could say—and they were both silent the rest of the way home.

James flopped down on the couch next to Fern the moment he walked in the door, while Nelson raced upstairs, the sound of his bedroom door shutting a bit harder than normal, reverberating all the way down to the living room. It wasn't the first time one of his sons had been upset with him; it probably wouldn't be the last.

Pretending he and Nelson had enjoyed nothing but a good time at the Scout meeting, James threw an arm around Fern's shoulders. "You're never going to believe what I did."

Fern snuggled close, hitting her husband with inquisitive brown eyes. "Volunteered to be scoutmaster?"

"I might as well have, all things considered. But no, I some-how volunteered to be chief scoutmaster recruiter." James rested his head against the back of the sofa, staring at the ceiling. "I can't believe I said yes when everyone else at the meeting was saying no."

Fern laughed. "Obviously you've forgotten that you said yes to just about everyone needing volunteers when we first got married. If someone needed help building a deck, you were there. When my dad broke his leg, you drove him to his doctor appointments, you built a ramp so he didn't have to climb the stairs getting in and out of the house and—"

"That was a long time ago. Our lives have changed since then."

"*My* life has changed," Fern said. "I know that's had a big impact on you, but you've given up too much of your own life to take care of me."

"Someone has to do it."

Fern twisted around on the sofa. Her eyes narrowed, her jaw tightened, and he wondered if he'd said the wrong thing.

"You know, James, there's always the possibility that I could do more if you didn't jump in and do things like cook and clean and do the grocery shopping before I've had the chance to try it on my own."

James pushed up off the sofa and walked across the room, holding his hands in front of the fire burning on the hearth. They weren't cold, but he needed a moment to let Fern's comment register. Never before had she even hinted that he was getting in the way, that his help was an annoyance, that it was hindering her ability to do things on her own.

Running a hand through his hair, James faced his wife. "So what is it you want me to stop doing?"

"It's not so much that I want you to stop doing things, just give me the opportunity to do them first and if I fail, then you can take over."

"What if you fall? What if—"

"If I fall I figure out how to get back up or stay on the floor until someone comes along who can help me get up. If I have trouble chopping vegetables, I'll find new recipes that are easier to make."

James walked across the room and sat on the cluttered coffee table where he could face her and see what emotions played across her face. Did she really mean what she was saying?

"Have I complained about helping?" he asked. "Is that what this is all about?"

"You don't complain about much of anything. You don't even complain about my complaining."

"You're my wife. Seeing the agony in your face when you're in pain nearly kills me. I don't want you getting overly tired or—"

"Or nothing. I don't want to spend the rest of my life bored to tears or moping around because I hurt or I'm afraid of looking stupid. And I don't want you giving up your life and the things you used to enjoy before I got sick."

"I haven't given up all that much."

"You used to spend more time with Nelson and Gideon."

"They understand."

"I'm sure they do, but that doesn't make it any easier. They want their dad to hang out with them once in a while and . . . Nelson really wants you to be his scoutmaster."

"I just don't have time—"

"If you want to do it, you'll find the time." Fern reached out, caressing his cheek with the palm of her hand. "I'm not going to tell you that you should take on the job. That's a decision only *you* can make, but don't use me as an excuse to get out of it if it's the thought of camping trips and spiders crawling into your sleeping bag that's turning you off."

"I hadn't given spiders in my sleeping bag much thought," James said, pulling a folded piece of paper out of the pocket in his jacket. He unfolded it slowly. "I suppose I should add that to the con side."

"Let me see that list." Fern snatched it out of his hands. She stared at the two columns. "This is looking a little lopsided."

"You know me. Mr. Analytical, looking at both sides of the argument and trying to make the right decision."

"Mind if I make a suggestion?" Fern smiled softly, a look he'd fallen in love with over twenty years ago. "Quit thinking so hard about this and listen to your heart."

Chapter Thirteen

ELENA AND CESAR SAT ACROSS FROM EACH OTHER IN a cozy booth at Baldomero's, an authentic Mexican restaurant in downtown Deerford owned by Elena's mother Camila Baldomero. A Luis Miguel CD played in the background, mixed with a little mariachi and some boleros, the music romantic at times, lively at others.

Elena was out of her scrubs for a change, wearing jeans, a red turtleneck sweater, and a pair of simple diamond stud earrings Cesar had given her for Christmas several years back. Cesar was on his dinner break, still in uniform, looking handsome as always. Someday their schedules might mesh, making it easier to spend long, leisurely hours together.

"I think the chef has added a few extra spices to the *pollo en mole* recipe." Elena took a bite of the tender chicken in a spicy, chili, nut and Mexican chocolate sauce.

"You don't like it?" Cesar stuffed a steaming flour tortilla with *carne asada* and rolled it up like a small burrito before taking a bite.

"I do, but I've always thought the recipes my mother gave me were perfect, handed down from generation to generation of women who loved to cook." Elena reached across the table and took a small forkful of Cesar's *carne asada*. "Is this as good as mine?"

Cesar's dark brown eyes sparkled in the glittering candlelight. "It's okay, but nothing like yours. And sitting here, even with you, is nothing like eating at home, just family, with all of us making a mess in the kitchen and not worrying about fancy tablecloths, candlelight and music."

"I never expected you to be a homebody when we got married."

"You were nineteen and I wasn't much older. Fast food was a good meal back then."

Cesar dug his fork into a mound of garlicky white rice and mixed it with his refried beans. "How did your meeting go?" He'd asked the same question when he picked her up at Holy Trinity, but her answer had been interrupted when a car skidded off the road in front of them, and he'd stopped to make sure everything was okay, then called for a tow truck.

Too many of their conversations were interrupted by one thing or another.

Elena picked a chip out of the basket between them and dipped it into a bowl of salsa. "I was afraid the meeting would go on for hours, especially when I saw the long list of questions each of the pastors had, but we were prepared, especially Quintessa. She had charts and graphs, and she wowed everyone with the numbers of donors she and her friends have lined up and the quality of the auction items." Elena bit off a corner of her tortilla chip. "It's all pretty amazing."

"You make it sound like she did the whole thing."

"I did my share." Elena smiled. "I gave a presentation on the Web site I've been creating with the help of Hope Haven's webmaster. Then, of course, we had to talk about all the mundane logistics. Tables and chairs for exhibitors, the layout for the festival and the use of Good Shepherd's kitchen facilities, gym and their grounds and play areas."

"That's it?"

Elena took a sip of cherry cola. "Everything else is even more mundane."

Cesar rolled another carne asada burrito. "You didn't volunteer for anything extra, did you?"

She'd expected that question to come up, and even though she hated to see the face he was going to make, Elena looked her husband straight in the eye. "I'm going to make a few costumes for the Harvest Festival."

Cesar glared up at the ceiling. His jaw tightened. "How much more can you put on your plate, Elena?"

"It's just a few costumes. I'm already making one for Izzy and something for me. It's not that much more work to design and sew a few extras."

"You're already cutting short the number of hours you sleep at night."

"I've never needed a lot of sleep. You know that."

"I also know how tight your neck muscles have been getting when you sit at the sewing machine for hours on end."

"I love to sew as much as you love to play basketball."

He closed his eyes and shook his head, frustration getting the best of him. "I don't want to argue about this."

"We're not arguing. We're getting this thing that's been coming between us out in the open."

"I could write a mile-long list of things that are coming between us."

"I don't need it in writing. Why don't you tell me right now and let's talk about all these things of mine that are bothering you."

"All right." He pushed his plate off to the side and folded his arms on the tabletop, leaning toward Elena. "When we got married, we said that Sunday would always be our family day, that the only thing we'd let come between us doing things together, like going for a picnic or boating or to a ball game—something recreational where we could get away from home—would be our jobs. And now—"

Cesar stopped, but she knew what he'd been planning to say. "I go to church on Sunday."

"That's right. You go to two church services on Sunday mornings, and in between them, you help out in the nursery or make coffee for the other parishioners, and you spend Saturday making banana bread or muffins or some kind of cookies for everyone to eat."

Elena smiled, reaching across the table to place her hand on top of Cesar's. "I make banana bread and muffins for you too."

"That's not the problem, Elena."

"Then what is?"

"I'm losing you."

Elena frowned as a lump formed in her throat. "That's crazy. I'd drop everything if you needed me."

"Maybe, but the truth is, Elena, you've stopped needing me."

"That's not true."

"It is. There was a time when we used to sit on the couch together and talk about our day, or talk about the future or what was bothering us. Now you do that with your Bible study friends or your pastor. And sometimes I hear you talking to God, telling Him what's bothering you, and I realize that you haven't shared those things with me."

Elena stared down at her plate, pushing black beans around with her fork. Had she really stopped talking with Cesar? Had she shut him out of a big part of her life?

"I don't fit in any longer, Elena," Cesar said. "I've heard you praying, asking God to bring me back to the church, to restore my faith. And then I think: Am I not good enough just the way I am?"

Elena fought her tears, but they slipped down her cheeks anyway. She tried to wipe them away with her napkin, but they continued to come. "I didn't realize I was making you feel that way, but you should know that nothing could ever come between us."

"How could I know when you make a point of filling your life with anything and everything to keep us apart? To keep us from having the time to talk like we used to?"

"What do you want me to do? Give up going to church? Give up my volunteering?"

"That's not my decision to make." Cesar put his hand over Elena's. "I want you to be happy, Elena, but I don't want to lose you in the process."

Elena stood in the chilly night air just outside Holy Trinity's chapel, waiting for Ginger Murphy to arrive. Why, of all nights, was it absolutely necessary that she attend Bible study tonight? It wasn't that she didn't want to go, that she didn't want to introduce Ginger to her friends, it was just that—she sighed, her breath forming a foggy cloud in front of her face—she wanted to be sitting inside Cesar's patrol car, riding around with him, talking if they could. Or at home, trying to figure out where she'd gone wrong.

Digging her cell phone out of the oversized purse carrying her Bible and a study guide, she dialed Cesar's number, hoping he wasn't out of the car. It rang and rang and just as she was about to hang up, Cesar answered. "Hi, hon. What's up?"

He sounded so normal, as if everything were right in their world.

"I forgot to ask what time you'll be home."

"Ten. Ten thirty. Shouldn't be any later than that."

She could hear his radio in the background, knowing that he could get a call at any time, that a thief or a drunk or a street fight could drastically alter the time he'd arrive home. But somehow or other, they had to make time to be together, even if they were just watching a movie.

And then an idea sprang into her mind. "I was thinking, why don't you stop at the video store and pick up a movie? If you have time."

Cesar was silent a moment. He was either listening to a call on the radio or trying to figure out what she was up to.

"Do you want a movie for me or for you?"

"For both of us. For tonight—when you get home. I thought I'd make the pistachio flan that you like and—"

"Hold on, hon."

As happened all too often, their conversation was cut short. Elena heard him talking on the radio and wondered if he'd forget she was on the cell phone, but a moment later she heard his voice in her ear, the tender voice she'd fallen in love with so many years ago. "Flan sounds good, hon. See you later."

Elena smiled as she closed her phone and dropped it back in her purse. A movie and flan wasn't the greatest start to mending her marriage, but it was the best she'd been able to come up with on the spur of the moment. Tomorrow, if she could find a few extra moments in her busy day, she'd figure out how she could weed out her to-do list.

She didn't have a clue what she could give up, but she'd start crossing off things immediately.

Wrapping her arms around her chest to ward off the cold, Elena was beginning to think that Ginger wasn't going to show up. It was already five after seven and the other women in her Bible study group had shown up and gone into the classroom at least fifteen minutes ago.

Another few minutes flew by and Elena was just turning to go into the church when an older, dark blue Chevy Suburban pulled into the parking lot. Even in the dim light from the streetlamps, Elena recognized Ginger's wild red hair. Waving, she walked toward the vehicle, glad that Ginger had come.

When the driver's door opened, a very pregnant Ginger slid out, dressed in a dark teal maternity tunic, black stretch pants and, Elena laughed, fuzzy green house slippers.

"Let me guess," Elena said. "Your feet are swollen."

"I tried squeezing them into real shoes, but only the slippers fit, and I so wanted to come tonight."

"Well, I'm glad you're here."

"Me too, of course, I hadn't planned to be so late," Ginger said, tugging her coat from the back seat and throwing it on over her tunic, "but I must have left the eggs or soda out of the first batch of muffins I made and they refused to rise, so I had to whip up another batch. There was no way I was going to come tonight without bringing a little gift."

"You didn't have to, but—"

"Oh, it was nothing." Ginger reached into the car again and pulled out the loveliest basket, its handle decorated with ribbons and bows in varying shades of orange, and an orange and white gingham cloth tucked beneath a pile of scrumptious-looking muffins.

"I've discovered this wonderful new recipe that uses Friendship Batter for its base," Ginger said, as Elena took the basket from her and they headed toward the wing of classrooms at the back of the church. "If you've never had a starter of Friendship Batter, I'll give you a jar. It's absolutely the best and these muffins—oh my!—they're terribly fattening, but they're also chock-full of nuts and fruit and oatmeal, and I throw in just a bit of peanut butter."

Elena could smell the aroma of cinnamon and sugar. She didn't have to bite into one of the muffins to know she'd be indulging in manna from heaven.

"Our group will love these," Elena said, slowing down when she realized Ginger was having trouble keeping up. "And let me give you fair warning, the ladies have a tendency to cater to pregnant women. Be prepared to be treated like a queen."

"As long as I can put my feet up I'll be happy. Hopefully that'll make the baby happy as well. This little one of mine has been kicking up a storm for hours now. I believe she's a bit unhappy with me for some reason."

"Maybe you were standing on your feet too long. I know you wanted to make the muffins, but—"

"My mama told me long ago that you never go to a party empty-handed, that it's absolutely imperative that you take a little something to your hostess, so I had to make the muffins, even if it meant standing when I should have been sitting. Of course, it could be all the broccoli I've been nibbling on that's making her do somersaults. Steve's positive our baby's going to be green."

Ginger chatted all the way to the meeting room, her voice filled with laughter, her smile never leaving her face.

Elena introduced Ginger to everyone—seven ladies tonight—and they swarmed around her, making her at home, setting her down in the comfiest chair and finding a stool to put beneath her feet.

Helen Mitchell served coffee, Belinda Boyd passed out napkins as she passed around the basket of muffins and each woman shared a quick story about herself before begging Ginger to divulge all her secrets.

"There's very little to tell, really, other than the fact that I was born and raised on a farm in Kansas. We had our own chickens and cows and a huge vegetable garden. My mother, who's a miracle worker in the kitchen, says I started baking and making crafts before I could walk. Not that that's true, of course. I think I was around three when that started."

Elena told the group about Ginger's teddy bears, raving about the costumes Ginger had made for them, and took a moment to promote the Harvest Festival and remind everyone that all the proceeds would be going toward furniture for three Habitat for Humanity homes.

Judy Clemente, a longtime member of Holy Trinity and the leader of their prayer group, walked across the room, sipping from a fresh cup of coffee before sitting. "Are you new to Deerford?" she asked Ginger.

"We've been here since the first of the year. Steve and I were in Orlando, Florida, which I dearly loved the five years we were there, except for the heat and the never-ending humidity and, of course, there was always the threat of snakes and gators. And then, well—"

Ginger sighed, pinched off a bit of her muffin and looked at Elena, her eyes filling with tears. "I'm so sorry. I didn't mean to talk your ears off."

"Don't stop." Elena took the young woman's hand. "What were you about to say?"

"It was nothing. Really."

"I know you've just met us," Judy said, leaning forward, clasping her coffee cup in both hands. "But we're good listeners, and we're here to support each other as much as we're here for Bible study."

"Well"—Ginger placed a hand gently on her belly—"this isn't my first pregnancy, or my second or third." Her voice quivered as she held back her tears. "I hope you'll pray for me and Steve and for our baby, because"—she dragged in a deep breath—"because I've had three miscarriages. This child's lived the longest and I love her already and . . . and I can't bear the thought of losing another child."

Several women tried to sniff back their tears.

"I hope you don't think I came here just so you'd pray for me," Ginger said. "Steve's a fireman and he's away from home a lot, and I've been awfully lonely not knowing very many people in town and—"

"Even if you had come just so we'd pray for you, that would have been okay." Elena squeezed Ginger's hand. "We'll pray for you every day, whether you decide to come back or not."

"But we want you to come back." Judy smiled. "And not just because your muffins are heavenly."

Through her tears, Ginger managed a smile. "I make wonderful brownies too."

"Just bring yourself next week. You need to start resting a bit and, besides, it's Helen's week to bring cookies," Judy said, and then she bowed her head.

"Heavenly Father," Judy prayed, "Ginger and her dearest husband Steve have entrusted to Your care a life conceived in love. May Your blessing come upon them now—all three of them—and be with them always. We ask that You remove all anxiety from their minds and strengthen this love so that they may have peace in their hearts and home. And we ask, dear Lord, for You to smile upon the baby Ginger is carrying, and bring the child into her arms, healthy and full of love. We ask this in Jesus' name. Amen."

"Thank you ever so much," Ginger said, looking about the room at a host of women who would be her friends through good times and bad, the way they had been for Elena. "That means so much to Steve and me . . . and our baby."

And suddenly it dawned on Elena. "Do you have any family here besides Steve?" If not, someone would have to plan a baby shower. She'd do it herself, but . . . but she needed to cut things from her to-do list, not add to it.

"We left everyone behind in Kansas, I'm afraid. None of our family wanted to follow us to Orlando, which is probably a good thing because I'm sure they would have hated the snakes and gators and insects just as much as me."

Ginger took a bite of muffin, her free hand resting on her belly. "Poor Steve, he wanted so much to stay in Florida, but he wanted me to be happy even more, and after the third—"

She wiped a tear from her cheek and forced a smile. "He wanted me to be happy so he began applying for other fire department jobs and, lo and behold, we wound up here in Deerford, which doesn't—thank the good Lord—have swamps. And I suppose that's the long version of what should have been a short answer. No, Elena, we have no family."

"Well you do now. All of us."

Ginger smiled again, and as pregnant women were prone to do, she once more began to cry. Seven women sprang from their seats to offer her a tissue, then settled down again with the most delicious muffins they'd ever tasted and opened their Bibles.

Chapter Fourteen

THE WIND BLEW A SMATTERING OF GOLD AND burgundy leaves down on Candace's car as she parked her black Honda CRV at the curb in front of Lila Adams' home. Would she and the others in the grief counseling group feel more at ease meeting here? Candace wondered. Would they open up and talk instead of staring at their hands, too afraid to share their feelings?

Candace leaned back in her seat, not yet ready to get out of her car, and watched two tabby cats batting at leaves on the Victorian's front porch, a picture-perfect place straight from a Thomas Kinkade painting, sitting far back from the wide, tree-lined street, surrounded by extensive lawns, lush landscaping and other beautiful homes built in the late nineteenth century.

She and Dean had driven up and down this street time and time again when they'd first gotten married. They'd dreamed of living in this part of town, even in a fabulous Queen Anne–style house, although she might have painted their home a semidark seafoam green with all the gingerbread and trim painted a creamy white, rather than the pale salmon, wine, black and white of Lila's.

In the summer, she and Dean would have sat out on the porch, drinking lemonade or iced tea; and from Thanksgiving until New Year's Day, the house would have been aglow with twinkling lights and a giant star mounted on top of the roof to show all their friends the way to their home. Candace sighed. She and Dean would never live in a home like this, not now. What little money they'd saved for a down payment on a bigger and more beautiful home had been spent instead on a funeral and was now paying for grief counseling, which seemed senseless.

She didn't want to forget Dean.

She reached across the car, wanting to slip her hand into his and feel the calluses worn into his skin from doing remodeling work on the only home they'd been able to afford, but his hand wasn't there. Only thin air. No comfort. No smile.

Candace wrapped her arms over her stomach, willing away the desolation, wishing for sweetness to fill her again. Tears slipped down her cheeks, the lump in her throat swelled and every muscle in her body tightened with grief. She allowed herself to sit in the empty car, crying until she had no more tears. Until her chest hurt.

Until she realized that there was no one in that car who could give her comfort—no one but herself. But there was a grief counseling group inside.

"You can share with them, Candace," Lila had said. "They, too, are dealing with the loss of a loved one. They'll understand what you're going through."

The car's engine was still running and for one moment she thought about putting the car in drive and leaving. She could go shopping for an hour, long enough to make her mom think she'd gone to her counseling session, and arrive home just in time to watch Charlie Brown, to eat heavily buttered popcorn, made the way her mom and the kids—and Dean—liked it.

Oh, bother! Just go inside and get it over with.

Candace turned off the engine, threw open the car door, climbed out and marched up the cobbled walk and around the house to the back door, remembering the instructions Lila's receptionist had given her on how to find the meeting place.

The gentle atmosphere and light strains of Chopin wrapped around her the moment she stepped into the reception room at the back of Lila's home. After hanging her coat on a Bentwood rack next to a large potted palm, Candace opened the door marked Group Session Inside and, swallowing back some of her fear, walked across the hardwood floor to sit with the small group of women she'd met a week before. No one said a word. One crocheted. One read. One stared at her hands.

Maybe I shouldn't have come after all, Candace thought, but she'd made it this far.

She sat in one of the mismatched chairs, hers decades old but comfy, gathered around an Aubusson carpet, decorated in a mass of mauve, sage and cinnamon swirls, with open-winged doves at each corner.

It must have cost a mint. If Candace had been wealthy, she might have bought one just like it.

As she waited for Lila to show up, Candace studied the room, afraid to look straight in the eyes of the women around her. Everything was warm and comforting, so different from the clinical atmosphere of Lila's office. Framed prints hung everywhere, mostly pre-Raphaelites like Rossetti and Hunt—romantic, heroic and beautiful. She could get lost in the paintings, if the group was as quiet as it had been last week.

At seven on the dot, according to the tall and ornate grandfather clock sitting in one corner of the room, Lila walked in, carrying a plate of cookies—snickerdoodles, it looked like—which she set on the coffee table just a few feet in front of Candace. It was a stunning table, at least four feet square, made from a stained-glass window mounted atop a sleeping stone lion. Was this one of the pieces Lila had told Candace about during one of their sessions, made from bits and pieces she'd found at salvage yards?

Lila had so many talents, among them taking lost and forlorn items and making them useful again, giving them new life.

Could she do the same thing with the people gathered together tonight?

Lila sat directly across from Candace, a picture of perfection in flat black ballet shoes, skinny charcoal pants and what looked like a terribly expensive cashmere sweater in the same color. Her hair was a luscious brown, in a pixie cut. Oh what Candace would give to have a face structured like Lila's so she, too, could wear her hair in a non-fussy style. Totally wash and wear, so she could spend more time with the children in the morning, talking with them a bit, making a big breakfast before rushing off to work.

Someday. Maybe.

"Grief can't be measured," Lila started. "It knows no bounds and it can hit anyone, at any time. We're not here to 'get over' anything. We're here to make peace in our hearts and rediscover the little joys in life." Lila took a cookie from the plate and leaned back in her chair, calm and cozy, like a storyteller. "We're here to support each other. You don't have to climb into a shell. You don't have to be alone."

For the longest time, everyone was silent. Then Olive sighed heavily. "I don't know if I can open up," she said. "I don't know if I want to come out of my shell, to talk about Clarence dying. I don't want to talk about colon cancer or how much pain he was in or . . ."

"Then let's start somewhere else," Lila said. "You'll probably shed a lot of tears, but our hope is that there will eventually be laughter as we share the sweet memories, cherishing them instead of feeling saddened by them. That may seem like a tall order right now, but we'll get there."

Lila smiled gently. "Tell us about yourself, Olive. What do you do—or what did you do—for a living?"

Olive unclasped her hands and attempted to smooth out some of the wrinkles in her long denim jumper. "For over forty years now I've been making pottery vases and coffee mugs and bird feeders—with my own unique touches—and selling them at Renaissance fairs and harvest festivals."

"Sounds like a wonderful life," Lila said.

"Rather nomadic." Olive smiled, the age and laugh lines in her face deepening. "At first Clarence and I traveled the country in a Volkswagen van and when we finally had a little money saved up we bought a battered and beaten 1980 motorhome. We—" Olive stared down at her hands. "*I,*" she corrected, "still have the motorhome; I still travel from city to city, but it's not the same with Clarence gone. Nothing's the same."

Silence again, a silence Candace knew all too well.

Lila didn't intrude on Olive's thoughts. Didn't ask questions. She just waited, her years of working as a counselor, as a police negotiator before that, having taught her when to speak and when to wait.

"I'm no good without Clarence," Olive said at last. She looked from one woman to another, swallowing hard, her eyes begging them to understand. "I don't know one day from the next anymore. I don't know the time, don't know where I'm supposed to be when, and . . ." Olive began to cry.

Red-haired Jazz sighed. She looked like a 1940s librarian, a homelier version of Shirley Jones in *The Music Man*. "I lost my mother five months ago." Jazz fidgeted with the paperback in her lap. "I miss having someone to care for."

Verla Parker piped up. "I cared for my Carl for fifty-five blessed years and had hoped for a good ten or fifteen more." Her jaw then set in anger. "Until that drunk driver swerved into us." Verla had to be close to eighty, with beautiful white hair that waved about an aged face that might have seen good times but now showed only tragedy. Tight fists clenched the cane she held across her lap. She swiped at a tear. "He wasn't supposed to die, not before me. I begged him not to die before I heard the sirens, but I don't think he heard me. He just held my hand."

Verla let go of the death grip she had on her cane and twisted her plain golden wedding band. "And then he was gone."

The back door slammed and a beautiful woman Candace had never seen before rushed into the room. Was she a patient of Lila's?

"Sorry I'm late," she said, breathing hard, her face red from the wind. Or had she been crying?

The woman dropped an obviously expensive handbag on the floor beside the wing-backed chair she sat in. She wore jeans, furry boots and a thick turtleneck sweater that would have made fairly slim Candace look like a blimp. The stranger, however, looked like she weighed little more than a breath of air.

"I'm so glad you could make it, Megan," Lila said, then introduced Megan Gallagher to the rest of the group.

"My son called and then I couldn't find my car keys which is crazy, because I'm always organized, and then . . ." She took a long, deep breath, then broke down in tears. "I'm sorry," she said, rising from her chair, "I don't want to be here."

Candace clasped Megan's hand. "Please. Don't leave. You don't have to talk. It's okay to cry."

Megan's tear-filled eyes looked down at Candace. She glared at Lila. "I've got to go."

Megan grabbed her bag and took off just as quickly as she'd come in, both doors slamming behind her.

"Aren't you going after her?" Candace asked Lila, her heart beating heavily, understanding exactly what Megan was going through.

Lila shook her head. "She'll come back. Probably not tonight, maybe not next week, but she'll come back. We all have to deal with grief in our own way, in our own time. Megan's just not ready yet."

Lila picked up another cookie and continued on like they hadn't been interrupted.

"There is a wonderful eulogy engraved on a headstone in Ireland. It's nearly hidden by deep grass and a rambling rose has wound its thorny vine and pink buds all about the time-marred piece of granite. Yet"—she smiled at each woman—"you can still read the eulogy: 'Death leaves a heartache no one can heal, love leaves a memory no one can steal.'"

Lila took a bite of her cookie, giving everyone time to absorb the words on the headstone.

"Some of our memories are small, almost infinitesimal," she continued at last, "memories that crop up when you least expect them to, like . . . favorite foods. Such a simple thing can trigger emotions—"

"My mother liked liver and onions," Jazz stated. "No, she didn't just like liver and onions, she loved it."

"My grandmother fed Dean liver and onions the first time they met and somehow he gagged it down, pretending to enjoy each mouthful." Candace laughed. "They bonded over that abominable meal."

Lila was right. Something as simple as food could conjure up a host of warm memories. It could even bond a bunch of strangers.

"The thing is," Jazz continued, "I hate liver and onions, but I cooked it for my mother every Wednesday—and now I cook it for me. I don't know if I do it out of habit or because it makes me feel my mom is still alive, still sitting at the kitchen table." Jazz sighed heavily. "Maybe I should stop making the liver and onions."

Lila passed a box of tissues to Jazz. The redhead took one and dabbed at the tears streaming down her face.

"Your feelings aren't silly," Lila said, "and don't let anyone tell you they are. More importantly, don't tell yourself how to feel. You're grieving for the loss of that closeness you felt with your mom. You're missing the time you spent together in the kitchen."

"But it's been five months."

"Experiencing grief and the mourning time that follows involves many changes. There's no on and off switch for grief. Adapting takes as long as it needs to take."

Lila picked up the plate of cookies and walked from one woman to the other, helping them help themselves.

"It's important," Lila continued, "to accept the fact that we do not get over a loss, but that we learn to live with the loss. It's one of the journeys in life that we all have to take." Lila sat back in her chair and crossed her legs. "Your grief is your own. It's okay to be angry, to cry or not to cry. It's also okay to laugh, to find moments of joy and to let go when you're ready."

Candace held on to Lila's last sentence all the way home. She felt better than she had in months, as if she'd finally been given permission to laugh and cry without feeling guilty.

She hugged and kissed Brooke and Howie when she breezed into the house, laughed and cried with them and her mom while watching *It's the Great Pumpkin, Charlie Brown* and drank in wonderful memories, little ones and big ones, to hold on to forever. Someday, twenty or thirty years from now, something small, like a piece of heavily buttered popcorn or a photo of

Snoopy or Charlie Brown might trigger a memory of this night and the special time they'd shared.

Later, when all the lights were turned out and she'd tucked Howie and Brooke under warm down comforters, Candace went into the room she'd shared with Dean and sat on the edge of the bed.

Gone was the sound of Dean's footsteps coming up the stairs. She could no longer imagine him sitting down on his side of the bed or the sound of his breathing during the night. Some of the most intimate things that she'd promised herself she'd never forget didn't come to her anymore. Not during the day while she was at work. Not at night when she was all alone.

Outside a gentle breeze blew, whooshing easily through the near naked branches of the trees. Last fall she'd heard Dean's voice in a similar breeze; now she only heard the wind.

He was slipping away.

And she knew she had to let him go.

Chapter Fifteen

THE HEAVENLY AROMA OF STEAMING MOCHA LATTE with a dollop of whipped cream and cinnamon on top wafted about Elena as she paid the cashier at Cuppa Coffee. She went extra heavy on the cocoa today, hoping to fight off the fact that she and Cesar had stayed up way too late last night.

Even though it was just past six o'clock, Anabelle and James were already seated at a small table, sipping coffee when Elena joined them. She saw Candace at the counter chatting with Heath Carlson. Heath was talking as Candace laughed, her eyes sparkling. Their fondness for each other was apparent, and as she did every day, Elena prayed for Candace to find peace in her turbulent heart.

Turning her curious gaze away from Candace and Heath, Elena said "Good morning" to her friends as she unwrapped the turquoise scarf from around her neck, slipped out of her coat and hung both over the back of a chair.

"You're late," James said, emptying a packet of sweetener into his coffee, a plain old-fashioned cup of Colombian, made good and strong. He was already in green scrubs and wore a Chicago Cubs blue and white hoodie. "This is a first."

Elena looked at her watch, while stifling a yawn. "Only two minutes, give or take a few seconds. Cesar and I stayed up way too late last night watching *The Man Who Shot Liberty Valance*."

"John Wayne did it," Candace said, joining her friends as Heath left the coffee shop. "Everyone thought it was Jimmy Stewart who shot Liberty Valance, but no, it was good ol' John Wayne."

James cocked one brow. "One of your favorites?"

"One of Dean's. He loved anything with John Wayne or Jimmy Stewart."

"I'm more a Cary Grant kind of girl," Anabelle added, a wistful smile on her face. "Charming. Tall, dark and handsome." She sighed.

"Does Cameron know you have this fixation on Cary Grant?" Elena laughed lightly before taking another sip of mocha.

"Fortunately for me, he doesn't have a jealous bone in his body."

For a good ten minutes they talked and laughed, as they often did before heading to the hospital and the busy day ahead.

Anabelle swirled the vanilla latte around in her cup. "How did your meeting about the Boy Scout troop go last night?" she asked James.

"Real good, for everyone but me."

"Did you agree to be scoutmaster?" Anabelle folded her arms on the table. "You'd be great, I'm sure, but you've got too much on your plate already."

"That's what I keep telling Fern and Nelson. But Fern's insisting I should get out more, that she's perfectly fine on her own, but—"

"But what?" Elena asked.

"I'm worried about Fern. I'm worried about time constraints. I'm worried my heart's just not in it to be a Scout leader, but I don't want to disappoint Nelson. Plus I'm fifty-two years old when most of the other dads are in their thirties."

"If that's what's bothering you," Candace said, "it shouldn't. You've got more going for you than most of the thirty-year-olds I know. If Howie were old enough for Scouts, he'd love to have a scoutmaster like you."

"You would be terrific," Elena said. "Cesar was a scoutmaster when Rafael was a kid and he loved it."

"Maybe he'd like to take over Nelson's troop." James pushed up out of his chair and filled his cup from the thermal pump pot, then grabbed another packet of sweetener when he sat down.

"You know, James," Anabelle said in all seriousness, "your children are only young once. When they get older, they don't always want to spend a lot of time with you. They have families or friends of their own, and most of the time they do their own thing . . . without you. How old's Nelson?"

"Thirteen."

"Three more years and he'll have his driver's license," Anabelle added. "When that happens, you'll cease being the most important person in his life."

"A moment ago you were reminding me how much I have on my plate."

Anabelle, with her elbows resting on the table, lifted her usual cup of vanilla latte, holding it close to her mouth. "True, but then I was just thinking how much I enjoyed having my children at home. Not that I don't love Cameron and I having alone time, but I miss that special closeness I had with the girls. Kirstie has a boyfriend now. Ainslee's going to have a baby. It's not the same. In a few years Gideon and Nelson will be on their own, too. And trust me, that time sneaks up on a person all too quickly."

"Talk to Cesar," Elena said. "He'll give you the scoop on how time-consuming he found it. He'll also let you know if he thought it was worth it or not."

"Thanks for the support," James said. "I haven't ruled it out yet, but I haven't ruled it in, either."

Elena was downing the last bit of her mocha latte, listening to Anabelle as she chatted about the art quilt for the Harvest Festival, when her cell phone rang, something it rarely, if ever, did at half past six in the morning.

As organized as she was, she had to dig to find her cell phone and noticed the familiar number for ICU. "Hello," she said, and when she heard the words on the other end of the line, learned that a near miracle had occurred, her throat tightened.

"I'll be there in less than five minutes."

Elena wadded up her cup and lobbed it into the recycle bin. "Caleb O'Mara came out of his coma. He's talking. Smiling."

Even with James helping, Elena couldn't get her coat on fast enough. She grabbed her tote, threw her scarf around her neck and sprinted out the door, calling Cesar as she ran down the street.

Cesar's groggy voice answered the phone, but she didn't think he'd mind being wakened out of a sound sleep. Not for this.

"Caleb's out of the coma."

If she said anything more, she wasn't sure what it could have been. She was in too big a hurry to get to the hospital.

She caught the WALK signal at Bureau Street and ran at nearly full speed toward the hospital, through the front doors, past Frederick Innisk who frowned at her—what was he doing in the hospital so early?—took the stairs two at a time and almost slid to a stop at the ICU nurses' station.

Out of breath but smiling, she tore off her coat and scarf, shoved her bag under the desk and quickly pulled her windblown hair into a ponytail. Then, trying not to burst out in tears, she walked into Caleb's room.

Dr. Wanda Hunnicutt, one of the physicians who specialized in neurology, leaned over Caleb's bed. Using an ophthalmoscope, she examined the interior of his eye, checking movement and reaction, while Caleb's mom and dad hovered nearby, holding each other.

Elena could only wonder what was going through their minds. Was Caleb going to be okay? Would he slip back into a coma again? Even Elena wondered those things, and she dealt with it all the time.

Tears streamed down Christine O'Mara's face, and she let them fall, not bothering to wipe them away. There were far too many. Her husband looked shell-shocked. Happy. Scared. Wishing he could do something for his son, rather than standing by feeling powerless.

Elena gave Christine a quick hug before stepping in to help Dr. Hunnicutt and Gloria Main, one of the RNs who worked the night shift, if they needed her assistance. And, like the doctor, she wanted to observe Caleb's movements, wanted to catch a glimpse of a smile from the little boy who'd been so close to death.

Dr. Hunnicutt was thorough. She wanted an MRI stat and a few other tests, and Gloria left the room to order the work.

With Caleb's eyes opening and closing, falling in and out of sleep, Dr. Hunnicutt, rather imposing at six foot one, with blue-black waist-length hair plaited into a thick French braid, turned to Mr. and Mrs. O'Mara. She smiled warmly.

That had to be a good sign.

"Caleb's looking pretty good," Dr. Hunnicutt said, "which I imagine is just about the best thing you've heard in days."

Mr. O'Mara took a deep breath. "He's going to be all right then?"

"I've ordered more tests, and I'm not in any big hurry to move him out of ICU, but I'd say our worst fears are over."

Christine attempted to smile through her tears. "Can his brothers and sisters come see him?"

Dr. Hunnicutt shook her head. "Actually, what I'd like right now is for the two of you to spend just a couple of minutes with him, no more than five, please, and then I'd like you to go home and get some rest."

"I need to stay with him, Dr. Hunnicutt," Christine said. "I—"

"I know how difficult it's been for you, Mrs. O'Mara." Dr. Hunnicutt placed a comforting hand on her arm. "But we need Caleb to rest. I imagine he'll be asleep more than awake for the next day or two, and I'd prefer he not have a lot of sensory overload, like talking and laughing and getting excited."

Christine attempted to wipe away some of her tears. "Okay."

"We'll get out of here in just a few minutes," Mr. O'Mara said. "We just want to tell him we love him."

"You can come back again tonight, if you'd like, but for ten minutes only," Dr. Hunnicutt said. "If you need or want to speak with me at any time, let one of the nurses know, and I'll give you a call."

Dr. Hunnicutt gave Mrs. O'Mara's hand a quick squeeze before leaving the room. Slowly, as if they were afraid of what they might see, Mr. and Mrs. O'Mara stepped close to Caleb's bed. Mr. O'Mara's hand shook as he grasped Caleb's fingers, holding them gently, while Christine leaned over her son and kissed his cheek.

"Hi, Mommy." Caleb's voice was soft. Barely a hoarse whisper. "Hi, Daddy. I kinda hurt."

Mrs. O'Mara's head spun around, looking at Elena in fear. "Can you do something for him? Should he still be hurting?"

Elena smiled, stepping close to Mrs. O'Mara and putting an arm around her shoulders, hoping to calm her before she frightened her son. "Dr. Hunnicutt will have orders for pain control, and I'll take care of that right away."

"And he won't hurt anymore?"

"He'll probably fall asleep right away."

Mrs. O'Mara turned back to Caleb, kissing his cheeks, brushing his hair off his brow, while Elena slipped around to the other side of the bed to check his computerized chart.

"Mommy and Daddy will be back tonight," Mrs. O'Mara whispered to Caleb. "You be a good boy, okay?"

Mr. and Mrs. O'Mara were backing away from Caleb's bed, not wanting to take their eyes off of him, when Elena saw Cesar standing in the doorway.

"Come in," she whispered.

"This is my husband, Cesar," Elena said, introducing him quickly to Mr. and Mrs. O'Mara.

"Mind if I say a quick hello to your son?" Cesar asked. "Elena's told me a lot about him . . . and you."

"Just for a moment," Mrs. O'Mara said. "Dr. Hunnicutt doesn't want him getting excited."

Cesar walked toward the bed and stood next to Elena. He wasn't all that tall, but at the moment her husband looked like the hero of fairy tales. He looked down at Caleb, tears welling in the corners of his eyes, a sight Elena hadn't seen since Isabel was born and Cesar held his granddaughter for the first time.

Cesar smiled. "How you doing, little guy?"

"Okay." Caleb smiled weakly.

A lump welled up in Elena's throat and tears filled her eyes.

Mr. O'Mara squinted at Cesar as he stepped close to the bed. "Are you the one—"

"I was lucky enough to be the one to find Caleb," Cesar said, interrupting Mr. O'Mara, not wanting any thanks. "This is a pretty special moment, seeing him awake."

"How can we ever thank you?" Christine O'Mara asked.

"I was just doing my job," Cesar said, shaking Mr. O'Mara's hand. "When Caleb's better, maybe you can bring him by the police station, and I'll take him out in the patrol car. Have a little talk with him about skipping school."

Cesar winked at Mrs. O'Mara, said a quick good-bye to Elena and disappeared from the room.

And not for the first time, Elena thanked the good Lord for blessing her with a husband like Cesar.

Chapter Sixteen

ELENA WHEELED CALEB THROUGH THE HOSPITAL corridors, red and blue helium-filled balloons tied to the back of the wheelchair waving happily above him. Doctors, nurses, administrators and other staff came out into the hallways to wave good-bye. It was a joyous occasion for everyone.

After nearly a week in a coma and two days recovering, Caleb O'Mara was going home.

"Do you think I can really ride in the police car someday?" Caleb asked, gripping Thumperina, the fuzzy blue bunny that had once been Izzy's.

"As soon as you're one hundred percent better," Elena told him, as she pushed her patient out into the sunlight.

Caleb twisted around to look at Elena. "Does that mean tomorrow?"

Elena laughed. "Maybe next week."

A black Ford Explorer sat beneath the covered portico at the back of the hospital, and Elena watched Mr. O'Mara climb out of the driver's side and rush around to open the passenger door the moment she, Caleb and Mrs. O'Mara exited through the sliding glass doors.

"Hey, buddy!" Mr. O'Mara didn't ask for permission, he just scooped his little boy up into his arms and hugged him tight. "Ready to go home?"

"Yep." Caleb grinned. "This place is okay, but they don't have Nintendo or a swing set."

"You won't be playing outside for a few more days," Mrs. O'Mara said, "but your dad bought the newest Super Mario last night, and your brothers and sisters are waiting for you to be the first one to try it out."

"Cool!"

Mr. O'Mara set his son on the backseat, covered him with a blanket and fastened his seat belt, while Elena helped Mrs. O'Mara load the backseat with balloons and other stuffed animals he'd received, but it was Thumperina Caleb held tightly.

There were hugs and promises to drop by for a visit, and then the O'Maras drove off, with Elena waving good-bye. When the vehicle turned onto Jeffries Street, Elena walked back into the hospital. It was time to turn her attention away from Caleb and back to her other patients.

It had been quiet all morning. Knowing that Marge had everything under control in the ICU, Elena headed for Quintessa's office. She hadn't heard a thing about Mr. Varner in over a week. No one seemed to know what was going on; and with Frederick Innisk still stalking the halls, the tension in the hospital could be cut with a knife.

Quintessa was staring at a spreadsheet on her computer monitor when Elena entered the oasis. "Got a minute?"

Quintessa, dressed in an ultraprofessional long-sleeved royal blue knit dress with a turtleneck that hugged her chin, spun around, smiling. "Just one. Zane's got a meeting with the board in"—she looked at her watch—"twenty-five minutes, and I've got to finish up this report for him."

"Just wanted to see if you can attend a meeting about the Harvest Festival next Wednesday."

"Let's see." Looking at her computer again, Quintessa pulled up a calendar. "Zane's heading out of town that morning. Why don't we meet in his office—around noon? I'll even get lunch for us."

"Perfect."

Not wanting to waste a moment of Quintessa's time, Elena waved a quick good-bye. She'd really wanted to ask about Mr. Varner, but she'd wait until Quintessa wasn't in such a rush.

Elena ran into Anabelle coming out of Human Resources, and considering the hard set of Anabelle's mouth, her friend wasn't happy.

"What's going on?" Elena asked, keeping up with Anabelle's clipped step as she headed for the stairwell, threw open the door and finally stopped halfway up the first flight of stairs.

"I put together another justification for the additional RN we need in CCU and Leila hemmed and hawed over the whole thing." Anabelle removed her glasses and tucked them into her pocket. "I know we have ongoing financial concerns, but I was hoping I could get Leila to see reason. At least let me talk with the head of Human Resources, but she didn't even give that question a moment's thought. She said no, absolutely not."

Elena shook her head. "When are they going to realize that they're driving the nursing staff into the ground? That the overtime we work is on our own time, because we've been told there won't be any paid overtime—but what are we supposed to do? Not write up our reports? Ignore one patient because another patient needs more care?"

"We're supposed to be miracle workers." Anabelle smiled at last. "The only good thing to come out of the meeting was that I overheard Penny Risser talking about Albert Varner."

"Anything interesting?"

"The board's meeting in private to talk about his resignation. Whether or not they should accept it and what, if anything, they should do about the proposed children's ward and pediatric intensive care unit."

Elena frowned. "I didn't know there was any question about the children's ward and PICU. I thought they were done deals. That the money was in the budget and that they were already in the planning stages."

"Apparently not," Anabelle said. "I'm sure I'm the last person on earth they want input from about any of those issues, but I'll be writing a letter to the board as soon as I get home from my quilting guild get-together tonight, letting them know how desperately I want Varner back and how much the city needs the addition to the hospital."

"Maybe a petition's in order," Elena said, knowing she really didn't have time to put something like that together, but anything that affected her job and the operation of Hope Haven was a priority and was destined for the top of her to-do list.

Phyllis Getty was draping a silky vine of autumn leaves around the nurses' station when Elena returned to the ICU. Small, feisty and eighty-four, Phyllis was one of the most delightful volunteers at Hope Haven, and the numerous service awards on her bright green volunteer jacket jangled while she worked.

"I know we can't put decorations in the ICU patients' rooms," Phyllis said, "but I thought you and Marge and the other nurses could use a bit of brightness while you're here at work."

"Thanks so much, Phyllis."

Elena pulled her hair back into a ponytail, as she sat down in front of her computer to finish up her reports on Caleb O'Mara and to see if the doctor had written any new orders for Mrs. Ackland, her patient in ICU room 3. Mrs. Ackland's daughter was traveling abroad in Europe and had been very difficult to reach when her mother was brought in by her visiting nurse. Fortunately she was already on her way back to the States. Elena's only hope was that she would get here soon.

"You seem a million miles away, Elena," Phyllis said. "Is there anything I can do for you?"

Elena could think of a bunch of things. *Take over the Harvest Festival. Create a petition to save Varner, the children's ward and PICU. Lock Frederick Innisk in a broom closet.* But she kept those thoughts to herself.

"Any chance you have time to get me a cup of hot chocolate from the cafeteria?" Elena asked, digging for her wallet. "I meant to get some while I was downstairs and totally forgot."

"You have too much on your plate, Elena. I'm surprised it's only a cup of hot chocolate that you've forgotten."

"That's why I keep lists." Elena laughed as she put a five-dollar bill in Phyllis's outstretched hand. "Get yourself a cup while you're at it."

The buzzer in Mrs. Ackland's room went off, and Elena heard a weak, "Help me. Please."

"Poor lady," Phyllis said, closing her hand around the cash. "I'll read to her this afternoon."

"Thanks, Phyllis," Elena said, pushing away from the desk and heading for Mrs. Ackland's room.

"What can I do for you?" Elena asked, gathering Mrs. Ackland's icy hands in hers. "Are you having trouble breathing again?"

Mrs. Ackland looked into Elena's face with cloudy green eyes that Elena was sure had once been bright and beautiful, full of hope and joy. "I just wanted to talk," she said, her voice soft and quavering. "Is that okay?"

"Of course it is."

"How is your granddaughter today?"

It hadn't been all that long ago, just a few hours, that Elena had talked with Mrs. Ackland about Izzy, but time had a way of expanding and contracting in the ICU. As far as Mrs. Ackland knew, she could have arrived in the hospital five minutes ago, or even five days.

Elena would never correct her. She just wanted to keep her comfortable.

"Izzy's just fine."

Elena warmed the chestpiece of her stethoscope in the palms of her hands, not wanting to shock Mrs. Ackland with the touch of something cold when she listened to her lungs, heart and intestinal tract.

"Her grandfather and I went to Peoria on Sunday and had a lovely day." It had been a spur of the moment trip, taken after Elena decided to attend a Saturday evening church service instead of two on Sunday morning, one of her attempts to renew her marriage and her husband's faith in her.

"I like Peoria," Mrs. Ackland said, closing her eyes. "Pretty place, especially this time of year, when the daffodils are blooming."

There wouldn't be any daffodils for another six months, but it didn't hurt to let Mrs. Ackland have that pretty and colorful picture in her mind.

"It's our favorite time of the year to visit," Elena said. "The tulips were all ablaze: pink ones, yellow, orange and red. What's your favorite color, Mrs. Ackland?"

"Red, I think. Yes, I like red. Does Izzy like red?"

"As a matter of fact, yes. We bought shoes while we were in Princeton. I bought some black heels, and I got her some red Mary Janes. They're special shoes to wear to church."

"I had red shoes one Christmas."

"Do you still have them?"

Mrs. Ackland shook her head, her eyes closing softly, as if she'd fallen asleep, but she spoke softly, "When my children moved me into their home I had to get rid of a lot of things. I imagine the red shoes went to a thrift shop."

"Then someone else will be able to wear them and look beautiful," Elena said, smoothing a short lock of white hair away from her eyes.

Mrs. Ackland opened her eyes again. "Any chance I could have some tea?"

"I'm afraid not. Maybe in a couple of days."

"That would be nice."

"I might even be able to bring you a cupcake in a couple of days." Elena pulled the sheet off to the side, picking up a damp tissue and dropping it into the trash. "Izzy and I made cupcakes last night, and she and her dad—my son, Rafael—took them to her preschool this morning."

"I made cupcakes for my children too. That was a long time ago, of course. Before you were born."

"Do you have a favorite kind of cake?" Elena asked, putting the chestpiece of her stethoscope on Mrs. Ackland's chest, listening carefully and not liking the quiet *whooshing* sounds she could hear coming from her heart. There was too much turbulence in her normal blood flow. Too many murmurs. "What about frosting? Do you have a favorite?" she asked, hoping to keep Mrs. Ackland calm and comfortable.

"My mother made spice cake. Lots of cinnamon and nutmeg. Too much nutmeg for me"—she wrinkled her nose at the memory—"so I cut that out of my recipe and added applesauce and a bit of pumpkin. My husband and daughter liked . . ." Mrs. Ackland frowned, as if trying to remember. "Cream cheese. I think. Yes, that's it. They liked cream cheese. I was happy with whipped cream."

"Sounds like a recipe I'd love to try."

"I know it by heart. Remind me later, and I'll write it down."

After smoothing the covers over Mrs. Ackland's chest, Elena walked to the end of the bed, lifted the covers and took a look at thin ankles and long, bony feet. She found an extra bed pillow on the recliner and propped it under Mrs. Ackland's legs. Her feet were cold, her heels irritated and beet red.

"Why don't we put some socks on your feet?" Elena suggested, rummaging through a drawer where the nurses kept extra gowns, disposable underwear and other personal needs items for their patients. The socks were rather ugly, something Marge had fought to change, but ran up against a brick wall when it came to budget restraints. Still, the ugly gray socks did the trick and patients rarely, if ever, complained.

Elena lifted one of Mrs. Ackland's feet, massaged it gently with soothing lotion, working it up her ankle and leg, before doing the same with the other foot.

"That feels nice," Mrs. Ackland said, her wheezing starting again.

"We want to keep you as comfortable as possible." Elena slipped socks onto Mrs. Ackland's still cold feet and fastened on foam heel guards before tucking in the blanket, simple tasks that an aide could do, but something Elena enjoyed.

"There," Elena said, "all snug as a bug in a rug."

Mrs. Ackland laughed, then coughed harshly.

Elena was adjusting Mrs. Ackland's oxygen when Phyllis Getty came into the room, scooting a chair up close to the bed. "I found a wonderful book in the chapel, Mrs. Ackland," Phyllis said, then turned to Elena and whispered, "Your cocoa's on the desk. Go take a quick break."

Phyllis sat down in the chair and opened the book. "'Chapter One. Thin rays of afternoon sunlight filtered through the leaves of the old maple tree that dominated the front yard of the Howard family home. Unshed tears blurred Alice Howard's vision as she squinted up at the tree's majestic canopy. How was it possible that more than fifty years had passed...'"

Phyllis's voice was soft and soothing. Mrs. Ackland's cough eased and the elderly lady closed her eyes, a smile on her face.

Elena slipped out of the room. Though there were things that troubled her about Hope Haven Hospital, like financial woes, too much paperwork and Frederick Innisk, there were many more things to be thankful for.

Phyllis Getty, for one.

Chapter Seventeen

USAN BOYLE'S BEAUTIFUL VERSION OF "I DREAMED A Dream" swirled around the inside of Candace's car as she drove past Cavendish House. Living in the 1850 Greek Revival mansion had been a dream of hers when she was little. Now she dreamed that Brooke might hold her wedding reception there someday.

Candace laughed at her thoughts. It had better be a good ten or fifteen years before Brooke walked down the aisle.

Candace hummed along with the music as she neared Lila's home. She was feeling pretty good and began to wonder why she was bothering to go to tonight's counseling session, but she was just a few blocks away and wasn't going to turn around now.

She turned off Cavendish Drive and onto Winthrop Place, slowing when a red Mercedes roadster in front of her pulled to the curb, a good distance from any of the houses on the block.

Candace's instincts kicked into gear. Was everything okay? Had the driver had a heart attack? Was someone sick?

Continuing to go slow, Candace looked through the road-ster's driver's side window, thankful the car was parked beneath a streetlight, and saw a somewhat familiar woman, her blonde hair pulled back into a tight French roll, a dark turtleneck covering a long, slender neck.

The face registered in seconds—Megan Gallagher, the woman who'd briefly visited the grief group last week.

Once a nurse, always a nurse, which meant Candace believed in helping people no matter when or where. She pulled her car to the curb and backed up a few car lengths. Turning off the engine, she climbed out and walked back to the Mercedes.

"Everything okay?" Candace asked, peering through the window.

Megan frowned for a moment, then rolled the window down when she seemed to place Candace's face.

"I'm Candace. We met briefly in Lila Adams' grief counseling class last week."

Megan smiled. "Of course. Thanks for stopping, but I'm fine. Really. No flat tires. No engine problem."

Considering how red her nose and eyes were, Candace could tell that she'd been crying. "Let me guess, you're trying to decide if you really want to go to the group counseling session or if you want to cut and run, maybe hole up in a dark movie theater somewhere?" Candace said, knowing that feeling all too well.

"Germain's Ice Cream, actually, to buy a quart of rocky road and eat the whole thing in one sitting." She sniffled then managed a grin. "Would you like to go with me?"

"Sounds fun, but... believe it or not, I felt better after last week's session than I've felt in months." The cold night air seeped through Candace's jacket, and she rubbed her arms to ward off the chill. "Once we all started talking, I realized we shared a lot in common—especially our reactions to our grief."

Megan twisted the diamond-studded wedding ring on her left hand. "I keep asking myself, Why me? Why do I get the chance to go on, to maybe even be happy again, when my husband's gone?"

"I went through that in the beginning," Candace said, "but I had my two children and a job, and I had to earn money to pay the bills. For them, I couldn't fall apart. Not completely."

Megan attempted to wipe away her tears, but there were far too many. "After the funeral," she said, her lips quivering, "everyone seemed to disappear, and when the shock wore off, when I realized I was alone, I fell apart. Since then, I haven't been able to talk with anyone but Lila."

"Let me guess," Candace said. "Your friends never mentioned your husband's name and if you brought him up, they'd change the subject or have to get off the phone or—"

"Exactly."

Why did grief have to be so tough? Candace wondered. Everyone had to go through it at some time or other, which made it seem like it should be easier.

But it was torment.

Megan reached into a purse that looked like it was worth half a small fortune and took out a pack of tissues. She dabbed at her nose then stared out the windshield, quiet for the longest time.

"We should get to Lila's," Candace said at last. "What do you say? Think you're up to going?"

"I'd prefer that quart of rocky road, but . . . okay. I'll give it a try."

"Great," Candace said. "I'll see you there."

Jazz, Verla, Olive and Lila turned and stared when Candace and Megan walked into the room fifteen minutes late. "We're glad you made it," Lila said, folding her legs beneath her in an overstuffed armchair upholstered in emerald velveteen, a new acquisition since last week. "Help yourself to some tea and have a seat."

"I'm sorry we're late." Megan bypassed the tea and sat in one of the two plum-colored corduroy chairs at Lila's right side. "It's all my fault, because once again I didn't want to be here. But Candace, bless her heart, talked me into coming."

Candace sat next to Megan, balancing a cup of orange-and-cinnamon-flavored tea on her jeans-clad lap. "She was doing the same thing the rest of us have done at one time or another."

"Sitting in the car," Jazz asked, "debating whether or not to get out?"

"Exactly, but I'm here now and I'm coping. Sort of." Megan wiped her eyes with the heel of her hand, smearing mascara over the already dark circles. "Of course, all I seem to do anymore is bake up a storm. Pastries and cakes, and I take everything to the senior center and the soup kitchens and the homeless shelters, and then I go antiquing and buy things I really don't need."

"We all cope in different ways," Lila said.

"I didn't lose a husband," Jazz said, "but I lost my mom, and I miss her. Since I no longer have her to care for, I'm trying to learn how to fill my life with other things."

"I'm going to teach her how to make pottery," Olive said, "and Jazz is going to keep me organized."

"And we'll have each other for company," Jazz added. "No more being alone."

"I'm rarely alone." Candace put her teacup on the coffee table, then stood and walked across the room, looking at all the romantic prints framed on the walls. The heroes and heroines. Princes and princesses. The lovers. "I'm with patients all day and I have my children and my mom to go home to, but—"

"But what, Candace?" Lila asked.

"I'm tired of being alone."

"That's understandable," Verla said. "My guess is that we're all tired of being alone."

Candace turned, seeing the understanding yet questioning looks on the women in the group. "But . . . I'm so tired of being alone that . . . that I'm thinking it would be nice to have a man in my life to share things with. Someone to talk with after the children are asleep, someone who'll listen to me when I rant and rave about something that rubbed me wrong at work, someone who'll laugh when I complain about the rising price of chicken breasts. I want to share those things with the man I love."

Lila leaned forward, resting her elbows on her knees, gazing at Candace. "With Dean?"

Candace shook her head. "He's not here any longer. Dean's always in my heart and even though I miss him every day and every night, I want to fall in love again; I want to be in love again with someone who's flesh and blood."

There. She'd finally had the courage to admit it.

Candace sighed heavily. She even thought about wiping the tears from her eyes, but she hadn't cried. Not this time. Not for herself.

Candace looked toward Lila for advice. "Is it wrong to want that?"

Lila shook her head. "It's just another step in the process."

"I feel like I'm betraying Dean's memory—but more than that, I want to move on. And when that dawned on me this past week, I felt a rush of relief. I felt good, and for the first time in a long time, I dreamed of a future rather than the past."

The cemetery's thick lawn had turned from a lustrous green to the color of winter wheat seemingly overnight. In the light of the moon and stars it looked like fresh snow stretching for miles, interrupted only by headstones and the mausoleum where the Cavendish family lay.

It was long past time to be home. Candace had gone for coffee with Megan Gallagher after their counseling session, and they'd talked for over two hours about baking and decorating and antiquing. They'd even talked about golf, the first time Candace had allowed herself to think about the sport since Dean had died on the back nine.

For the longest time, she'd gripped Megan's fingers as they sat across the table from each other, and she'd listened to Megan talk about her husband. She'd loved him so.

When they parted, Candace invited Megan to join her and her friends at Cuppa Coffee Wednesday morning and again for church at Riverview Chapel on Sunday. She'd balked, as Candace had imagined she would. It was hard to go from married to single, to listen to others—who weren't grieving—talk about their weekends, their daily lives, their spouses.

All the fun they were having.

But Candace knew she wouldn't have survived the worst of her days following Dean's death if it hadn't been for her family and friends, not to mention the job she'd loved. Helping to bring babies into the world had helped her make it through the many long and lonely hours each day.

The road through the cemetery curved and swirled through various sections of the memorial park, but Candace had been here so many times her car seemed to know exactly where to go; where to park. Candace opened her door and climbed out into the chilly night air. She wrapped her scarf tightly about her neck and trekked through the maze of crosses and headstones, tall trees and hedges, until she came to the hallowed place on a little bit of a rise that had been nearly a second home to her for such a long time.

"Hi, hon." She kissed her fingers and pressed them against the name etched deeply in the granite: Dean Alan Crenshaw. "Sorry I'm so late, but . . ."

For some odd reason she'd started to make an excuse for being late, then she stopped. Dean wouldn't have wanted excuses or lies. He deserved better. He deserved honesty.

The gold and burgundy chrysanthemums she'd placed on the grave last week had dried and at least half the flowers had blown away. There was a time, not so long ago, when she'd brightened Dean's grave with roses and daisies, iris and daffodils every other day. Now she came only once a week.

"Are you angry that I don't come as often as I used to?" She looked toward heaven instead of at the headstone because she knew Dean had gone to his eternal home. His body might lie beneath the earth, but his soul and his heart were with the Lord.

He didn't answer. He couldn't, but Candace knew what he would have said. "Come when you can, hon. I understand."

"I talked to a woman tonight—Megan Gallagher—who lost her husband a few months ago. I can't believe how much she reminds me of me."

Candace sat down next to the headstone, grasping one of the dead chrysanthemums, picking off petals. "Megan's so terribly lonely. And she's angry with her husband for leaving her."

A gentle wind blew across the cemetery, sending some of the petals flying.

"I was angry at you too, hon. Sometimes I'm still angry. I desperately wanted to spend my entire life with you. From the first moment we met, when my papers got caught in the wind.... Remember that? I fell in love with you that day."

Candace waited for the familiar tightness in her throat, but she didn't cry. Instead, she found herself smiling. She drew her knees up to her chest and wrapped her arms around them. It was a way of hugging herself, of feeling some bit of comfort, when there was no one else around to hold her tight.

Maybe that would change someday.

She just had to open herself up to the possibility. To let it happen.

Dragging in a deep breath, Candace looked at the stars that shone in between the clouds, and shared a little more with Dean.

"It didn't surprise me when Megan said that she doesn't want to move on. That she's nowhere near ready for that. I felt the same way for the longest time, but now ... now ... I need to, hon."

Candace stood, licking lips that were getting chapped in the cold night air. Digging into her pocket for a tube of cherry lip balm, she pulled off the lid and ran it over her lips, before clutching the top of Dean's headstone. It wasn't at all like holding him, but it was the closest she could get.

"I miss you. I realized, though, I don't feel alarm any longer when I laugh over silly things, or when a few hours go by and I realize I haven't thought about you."

It seemed as if it had happened overnight rather than happening bit by bit over three long years. The pain was going away too, replaced with only the best of memories.

Her hair blew into her face and she brushed it away.

"Oh . . . before I go," she said, stepping around the stone and tracing the cross etched into the stone. "Brooke's been asked to play 'The First Noel' at our Christmas Eve service this year. She says it's no big deal, but I know she's excited and nervous. And you know all those videos we made? Well, Brooke's been watching one of you playing carols and she plays along with you just in case the music director asks her to play even more solos."

Candace laughed. "If you were here, I know you'd be sitting alongside her on the piano bench cheering her on."

A falling star streaked across the nighttime sky. A guardian angel, maybe?

Keeping her eyes on the heavens, on the stars shining in her eyes, she offered a simple prayer. "Thank You, Lord, for helping me through my grief; for walking beside me every step of the way."

And as she walked from the cemetery, Candace blew a kiss to Dean, and for the first time, she left with a small smile on her lips and a thrill of hope for the future.

Chapter Eighteen

HE MEETING ROOM ON THE SECOND FLOOR OF
Cavendish House was the perfect place for the quilting
guild to get together. It had once been the classroom
for the Cavendish children. Even now there were a few hundred-
plus-year-old chalkboards hanging on the wall; but mostly, the
faded wallpaper was covered with quilts the women had made
over the years. Like Anabelle, most of the women in the guild
made more quilts than they could ever use or give away, and
some found their way to their meeting places.

They were always great inspiration.

Anabelle stood in front of one of the four-by-eight-foot
tables, laying out pieces of fabric she'd cut, plus pattern pieces.
On the wall, she'd pinned up a sketch of the quilt they'd
be making for the Harvest Festival, and the fourteen other
women who'd shown up tonight were already selecting pieces to
appliqué.

"When did you say the quilt needs to be finished?" Genna Hamilton, the wife of Dr. Drew Hamilton, one of Anabelle's longtime friends at Hope Haven, asked.

"Two weeks from now," Anabelle said, "which doesn't give us a lot of time."

"Once it's finished," Ainslee, Anabelle's daughter, said, "I'm going to take photos of it for the Deerford *Dispatch*. I've already written up a press release, and I hope to get photos of the quilt, and an article about our guild and, of course, the Harvest Festival in some other papers too."

"You know that the money being raised at the festival is going toward furniture and appliances for Deerford's three Habitat for Humanity homes," Anabelle said. "The more we can promote it, the better."

"And I'm sure the quilt my mom's designed is going to bring in a ton of money," Ainslee added. "So the sooner we get it completed, the sooner we can get information out to the press and start touting the auction for the quilt."

"I have an idea," Genna said. "You know I have a big quilting studio at home and I have tables for quite a few extra sewing machines. If any of you want to come to my house so we can work on the quilt together, and hopefully finish it fast, show up at eight tomorrow—or any day but Sunday—until we get it done. Just bring your own machines."

"Thank you so much," Anabelle said. "These things go so much faster when we can work on them as a group. I won't be able to take off work, but I can be there all day Saturday."

Anabelle smiled as one woman after another told Genna that they'd be there—with pastry and muffins and all sorts of other goodies to get them through the day.

If only the hospital administrators and board members could work so well together, there'd never be any problems at Hope Haven.

Once the fabric was all laid out, Anabelle set up her sewing machine next to Ainslee, who was already at work appliquéing autumn leaves onto several squares that Anabelle had pieced together in the last week.

"How are you feeling?" Anabelle asked her daughter, as she sat at her side and threaded her machine.

"Never better," Ainslee said, maneuvering the fabric around.

"No morning sickness?"

"Not a bit, Mother."

"Are you following that diet I gave you? The one I got from Candace?"

Ainslee laughed, looking up from the cranberry-colored maple leaf. "You have to stop worrying about me so much."

Anabelle pursed her lips. She stared at the blurry fabric in front of her and only then remembered to take her glasses out of her pocket and set them on her nose. "Sorry. It's been a rough couple of weeks."

Ainslee continued to stitch. "Still trying to get approval for that extra RN position?"

"I think I'm going to have to give up on that, since right now it seems absolutely impossible."

"I suppose that means you won't be cutting back on your hours anytime soon?" Ainslee asked, taking Anabelle by surprise.

"Why would I want to do that?"

"With Pop retired and no kids left at home, I was thinking the two of you might want to travel, or something."

Anabelle picked up a few squares of fabric that she'd already pinned together. "We've never talked about traveling, and I definitely haven't given any thought to retiring or even cutting back on my hours."

Ainslee laughed. "Now you know how I feel when you start questioning me about the baby and the colors for the baby's room."

Anabelle huffed. "You're not saying that I'm a buttinsky, are you?"

"You're just overly concerned, Mother." Ainslee leaned over and kissed Anabelle on the cheek. "You and Pop raised me to know right from wrong and how to take care of myself. I've got a husband watching over me like a mother hen."

"Oh, all right." Anabelle kept her eyes on the fabric she was working with. "I'll try not to interfere. Lord knows I've got enough other things to worry about."

Elena sat in the second row of pews in Holy Trinity's sanctuary, listening to the choir practice. Their voices were beautiful, something she hadn't noticed before, because she'd been standing in their midst, hearing pretty much her own voice, even though it had been drowned out by sopranos and tenors and baritones who could carry a fabulous tune.

All day she'd contemplated whether she should or shouldn't drop out of the choir. In the end, she chose to quit. She'd miss the people in the choir, but they all knew what she'd hated to admit. She couldn't carry a tune to save her life.

Now, listening to the choir, she refused to dwell on the fact that the director had graciously accepted her resignation, or the fact that she said no when he asked if she could help make new robes for the children's choir. He'd gotten a glimpse of the new Elena, and she was determined to stick to her guns and breathe new life into her marriage.

The one thing she did dwell on, though, was Albert Varner's wife, Sandy, standing at the very center of the choir, singing her heart out. But Albert wasn't there, adding his rich tenor to the hymn they were practicing. Neither Sandy nor Albert had been at practice last week. They hadn't been at church on Saturday night or, from what she'd been able to find out, at either of the Sunday services.

Elena wouldn't have stuck around throughout practice, torturing herself over the fact that she wasn't up there singing with everyone else, if she hadn't seen Sandy come in. She wanted to talk with her as soon as practice was over.

Of course, what she would say was anyone's guess. But before giving it any more thought, she got lost in the glorious music.

> *We plough the fields and scatter*
> *The good seed on the land,*
> *But it is fed and watered*
> *By God's almighty hand:*
> *He sends the snow in winter,*
> *The warmth to swell the grain,*
> *The breezes and the sunshine,*
> *And soft, refreshing rain.*
> *All good gifts around us*
> *Are sent from heaven above;*

Then thank the Lord,
O thank the Lord,
For all his love.

"Beautiful . . . and perfect," Andre Blasedale, the choir director said, applauding the men and women as they disbanded and
made a dash for the exits. Everyone was in such a hurry these
days, a feeling Elena knew well.

Sandy Varner shrugged into a red wool coat that had been
draped over the back of the first row of pews, tucked a large,
black patent-leather clutch under her arm and headed for the
narthex. Elena quickly scooted out of the pew and followed her
down the aisle.

"Sandy," Elena called out. The fiftyish woman with long
blonde hair and dark-rimmed glasses turned around. "It's so nice
to see you here tonight."

Sandy swept her hair over her shoulder, smiling uncomfortably. "I'm so sorry to hear that you've dropped out of the choir,
Elena, but I'm not surprised, considering all the other things
I know you're doing for the church and—" Sandy hesitated,
glancing down at the floor. "And for the hospital."

"I'm trying to weed my to-do list and make it more man-
ageable. And"—Elena laughed lightly—"we all know I can't
sing."

"I've always felt a lot of voices—even the ones that aren't pitch
perfect—sound wonderful, especially when they come together
to praise God."

Sandy's sentiment was nice, but Elena needed to talk about
Mr. Varner before Sandy rushed off.

"I've missed seeing you and Mr. Varner at church—and Mr. Varner's missed at the hospital."

"Life's been crazy the last couple of weeks, but we're hoping to get back on schedule," Sandy said. "We're also thinking about traveling. We've always talked about visiting the Christmas markets in Germany, and Albert would like to try out his photography skills in and around some of the old cathedrals."

"But what about—" Elena hesitated, then decided to dive right in. "What about his job at the hospital? The atmosphere at Hope Haven's been a little strained the last couple of weeks."

Sandy completely avoided Elena's questions, but tears pooled in the corners of her eyes as she took a quick peek at her watch. "I'm so sorry I have to run, Elena. Albert's meeting me for dinner and—" She smiled uncomfortably. "See you Sunday."

Elena watched Sandy's long, sleek blonde hair bounce on the back of her bright red coat as she raced out of the church. She should have told Sandy about the petition she'd be passing around, advising the hospital's board of directors that the Hope Haven staff wanted Albert Varner back as CEO. She should have told her about the petition for the PICU and children's ward—information she would have loved Sandy to pass on to her husband.

If she'd had only a few more seconds, she would have asked Sandy to tell Mr. Varner hello, but it was clear she didn't want to talk. It was obvious she was hurting.

That made it more important than ever to get a petition circulating—fast.

Chapter Nineteen

"HEY, DAD!"

James's hand tightened around his cell phone. The boys never called during the day. "What's wrong, Nelson?"

"Nothing, Dad, I just needed to talk with you before school starts."

"Hang on just a second," James muttered to his son, relieved that nothing serious was going on.

It was a little before eight o'clock Wednesday when Nelson caught his dad with a patient who'd just been admitted into the hospital, after spending a few hours in the ER. James had spent a good half hour trying to get minor details from the wife of a middle-aged man who'd gone into diabetic shock. Mr. Olmstead was stabilized now, receiving electrolytes and being rehydrated, but his wife was a basket case, which made it nearly impossible to prepare the initial assessment paperwork.

In hindsight, Nelson's call was a relief.

"I'll be back in just a moment, Mrs. Olmstead." James gave her arm a comforting squeeze. "Why don't you sit down for a moment and try to relax."

"Is my husband going to be okay?"

"He'll get the best care in the world here." James pulled a chair up close to the bed. "Please, Mrs. Olmstead, relax for a bit. If you drink coffee, I'll ask one of the aides to bring you a cup."

"That would be lovely—with sugar, no cream. Thank you."

On his way out of Mr. Olmstead's room, James caught Phyllis Getty, who had a huge amber chrysanthemum pinned on her jacket, and asked her if she could get the coffee. She was old enough to be his mother, but she hadn't slowed down in the years she'd volunteered at Hope Haven. And if there was any volunteer he could count on, it was Phyllis.

Finding a quiet place to talk, out of the hustle and bustle of Med/Surg, James slumped into a comfortable chair to take the load off his feet, and flattened his cell phone against his ear.

"What's up, Nelson?"

"Didn't Mom tell you I needed to talk to you last night?"

She had, but it was after eleven when he got home from work, and he wasn't about to wake Nelson up, not when he had to get up early in the morning for school. He'd been sure that whatever Nelson had had to tell him could wait.

But he gave his son just the facts. "Dr. Hamilton asked me to assist him in surgery last night. It went a lot longer than we expected, and I had to head for work early this morning. Sorry I didn't get a chance to talk with you."

"It wasn't all that important, but I saw Mr. Beckwith when he picked up Kirk after school yesterday, and he asked me if you'd gotten any calls about the scoutmaster job."

"Unfortunately, not one." In spite of the article he'd managed to get printed in both Saturday and Sunday's *Dispatch*, not to mention the flyers he and Nelson had posted at the YMCA, the fire and police departments and every other place they could think of. "I'll give him a call tonight and let him know what's going on."

"Thanks."

Phyllis strolled past, carrying a tall Styrofoam cup of coffee and wiggled her fingers at James, her usual way of saying hello and good-bye and everything else in between. Another volunteer walked by pushing a meal cart, but through the noise James heard the sound of a buzzer in his ear.

"By the way. You are at school, aren't you?"

"Yeah, Dad, where did you think I'd be?"

"In class."

"I've got Algebra in just a few minutes, but hoped I could catch you, just in case I run into Mr. Beckwith again. He told Kirk we'd probably have to disband the troop or join one in another town—like we talked about at the meeting. I'd rather quit than do that." Disappointment dampened Nelson's usually upbeat voice.

"You don't really want to quit."

"Nah, but—"

"But what, Nelson?"

"Are you sure you don't want to be scoutmaster?"

James hesitated, thinking of something Anabelle had said to him last week. *"Your children are only young once."*

"I haven't ruled it out," James said at last. "We set a deadline of a week from now to find a scoutmaster . . . or look at other alternatives. If no one else steps forward, I'll give it a little more thought."

"If I put together a pros and cons list for you," Nelson asked, "will that help you make your decision?"

James smiled at his son's enthusiasm. "Yeah, that might help. Now, get to class, and make sure you and your brother rake the front yard before I get home tonight."

Elena crunched through the autumn leaves scattered about the courtyard, which was undergoing a complete renovation and would include the new Wall of Hope. Cameron Scott, Anabelle's husband, was standing in the back of his Scott Landscaping truck, shoveling fine sand out of the bed and onto a deepening pile at one side of the courtyard.

With his head down, concentrating completely on his work, he didn't even notice Elena until she was just a few feet away from the truck. "Hi there," he said, digging his shovel into the sand and leaning on the handle. "Did you come out to see how things are shaping up?"

"I had a few minutes to kill before a lunchtime meeting, and I had the feeling you might be out here working."

"So what do you think?" he asked, looking around at the bare bones of the courtyard. "A lot left to do, but it's coming along."

"It's going to be beautiful," Elena said, remembering how many drawings she and Cameron had sketched out before settling on a few they liked enough to present to the hospital administrators. The Wall of Hope had been her baby, and she'd also coordinated the effort to revamp the entire courtyard. As she looked at it now—nothing more than the basic foundation—the creative side of her imagined how it would look when completed and how wonderful it would be to sit out here on spring and summer days.

"Let me show you the idea I've come up with for the water feature." Cameron climbed down from the pickup. Opening the passenger door, he reached inside and pulled out a black three-ring notebook, its edges ragged, looking like it had held many a landscape project over the years.

Tossing his dirty blue baseball cap onto the front seat, Cameron ran a hand through his gray hair. He rested a booted foot on the planter that had yet to be completed and balanced the notebook on his knee, opening it up so Elena could get a good look.

"I was in Chicago last week and checked out a large landscape supplier," he said. "I think I can get a good deal on some of their concrete patio tables, and they've got an extensive collection of water features to go in the butterfly garden."

Cameron took an envelope out of the notebook's inside pocket and handed it to Elena. "I took pictures of almost all that they had, plus some of the fountains too. Why don't you hang on to those and take a look at the pictures when you have a chance. You might want to change some of our plans once you see what's available."

"Do you have a favorite?" Elena pulled out the top photo, trying to picture the fountain mixed in with the perennials Cameron would plant in the spring.

"Yeah, but I want to see if we're both on the same page designwise."

"It's a deal." Elena tucked the envelope into one of the pockets in her scrubs. "By the way," Elena said, hoping she could talk Cameron into helping with the Harvest Festival, "we'll have a special booth set up at the Harvest Festival to sell memory blocks for the Wall of Hope."

"Great idea."

"I'm glad you agree." Elena grinned. "Think you could help man the booth? I can't imagine anyone doing a better sales job than you."

"I should have known there was a catch."

"There's more."

Cameron's eyes twinkled as he shook his head. "Of course there is."

"Do you have any pumpkins and gourds we might be able to use for decorations?"

"Close to a quarter acre. All sizes, all shapes and all colors. Want a truckload full?"

"That would be perfect! Do you think you could drop them off at Good Shepherd next week, on Thursday morning?"

"Not a problem. As a matter of fact, I've got a men's Bible study breakfast that morning. I can probably round up a couple of the guys to help me. Which reminds me . . . Anabelle said you were hoping to run into Albert Varner at church."

"Yeah, but he hasn't been there in a couple of weeks."

"Well, just in case you're interested, Albert Varner's Bible study meets at Ripley's Diner Tuesday mornings at six, and from what I hear, he never misses a meeting."

And Elena didn't plan to miss it, either.

Quintessa walked around Zane McGarry's office carrying a tray bearing cold sodas and a variety of meat and vegetarian sandwiches, deliciously made and carefully wrapped by the staff in the cafeteria. They'd made them especially for Quintessa, which meant the meat would be extra thick, the lettuce and tomatoes fresh and everything scrumptious. Not that the cafeteria's normal food was less than perfect, but everyone liked Quintessa and went out of their way to please her.

Elena felt a little odd sitting in CFO Zane McGarry's dove gray leather chair behind his upscale glass-topped desk, but she was in charge of this meeting, and Quintessa had insisted.

"Thanks so much for coming," Elena said, happy that so many of the festival's coordinators were able to make it. "I don't have a formal agenda, and I want to keep this meeting as short as possible, which I'm sure none of you will mind."

"Works for me," Quintessa said, sitting at a table in the corner where she'd set up her laptop, one of her fancy graphs already visible on the big screen that pulled down out of the ceiling in Mr. McGarry's office. "If you don't mind, I'll get all the financial details out of the way, since it's usually the most boring, then get into the logistics."

Elena took a bite of her chicken salad sandwich on thick whole grain bread, which Quintessa had ordered specifically for her, knowing that it was Elena's favorite. She listened intently to everything Quintessa had to say, although she was thoroughly familiar with the details. Quintessa had kept her aware of every detail, sending her one concise e-mail every day.

There were six women in the room. Two of them Elena didn't know, probably Quintessa's friends, but Ainslee Giffen was here, volunteering as usual, and Ginger Murphy had come too, but she was walking around the room, her hands pressed against her lower back, something resembling pain etched on her face. That wasn't good.

"Ginger Murphy, who's new to our group," Quintessa said, pointing to the very pregnant redhead, "will be coordinating the booth decorations, taking that job over from Elena. She's already lined up volunteers, including Ainslee Giffen, our own Anabelle Scott's daughter."

Quintessa introduced the rest of the ladies, then continued on, giving more details about decorations, but Elena was distracted, worried about Ginger. Trying not to attract attention, she pushed away from the desk and walked over to Ginger, putting her arm around her, trying to look like it was merely a friendly gesture, and not one of concern.

"Are you okay?" Elena whispered into Ginger's ear.

"Just feeling a little dizzy."

"Anything else?"

"A headache, but it's nothing serious."

"Why don't you sit down?"

Ginger smiled. "I'd rather lie down, but there isn't a bed in here."

"Why don't I take you upstairs and put you in Candace's care for a little while?"

Ginger might have rolled her eyes if they weren't already filled with pain. "You've got a meeting to conduct and I really need to hear everything that's going on."

"I'll update you later, but right now, let's get you out of here."

Ginger didn't argue, and she didn't fight the arm Elena placed around her back as they walked toward the door.

"I'll be right back," Elena said, when everyone looked toward her and Ginger, fear on all their faces. "I don't think Ginger's gone into labor, but this is a hospital after all, and since she's here and she's not feeling well—"

"Just go," Quintessa urged. "I'll keep everything going until you get back."

The elevator wasn't all that far a walk from Mr. McGarry's office, and Elena latched onto an empty wheelchair and had Ginger sitting down, her feet up within moments. It seemed to take forever for the elevator to come, but it probably wasn't more than thirty seconds before she pushed Ginger inside.

A hand and arm reached through the just closing elevator doors and when they opened once again, Ainslee stepped inside. "I thought Ginger might need her purse," Ainslee said, "and since I'm not really needed in that meeting and you are, Elena, I thought I'd stay with her in case she needs anything."

Ginger looked up, smiling at Ainslee, whom she'd met just before the meeting started. They had so much in common, Elena thought, and Ainslee was the first person she'd thought of when she was suggesting possible volunteers for Ginger to call. Now Ainslee was holding Ginger's hand, giving her comfort.

Elena put her palm on Ginger's forehead. She was cold and clammy and she was breathing hard—and Elena hadn't been so frightened in ages. Pregnancy wasn't her specialty and because she didn't work obstetrics or labor and delivery, she felt she knew so little.

The first chance she had, she was going to enroll in some classes. Heaven forbid this should happen to one of her friends again.

The moment the elevator doors opened, Elena pushed the wheelchair out, never more thankful that the Birthing Unit was so close or that Candace was standing in the hallway talking with Dr. Frances Carpenter, an obstetrician and gynecologist.

"Got a moment?" Elena asked, not caring who heard her. Right this moment, she'd accept help from anyone.

Candace was at Ginger's side immediately, bending down to talk with her. "What's going on, Ginger?" Candace asked, reminding Elena that Ginger was in one of Candace's birthing classes. God was definitely smiling down on Ginger, putting her in the right place at the right time when she needed help.

"I know you don't want to go back to your meeting, not yet anyway," Ainslee said, squeezing Elena's arm as Candace took Elena's place at the back of the wheelchair and pushed Ginger out of the hallway. "But you're needed in the meeting, and I can stick with Ginger."

Ainslee was right. Elena didn't want to leave.

Standing just inside the Birthing Unit, Elena watched Candace wheeling Ginger to one of the private rooms, and she knew there was nothing she could do now but worry. And she could worry anywhere. She might as well do it sitting in a Harvest Festival meeting.

"Everything okay?" Quintessa asked, when Elena walked back into Zane McGarry's office.

Elena nodded, afraid she might not be able to talk through the lump in her throat. She took a sip of her diet soda, wanting desperately to tear her thoughts away from Ginger. But as soon as she got the meeting back on track again, she folded her hands on top Zane McGarry's desk and silently prayed for her friend.

"I'm fine, Elena. Honestly."

Ginger lay on her side, a few pillows at her back while she hugged another, still looking a little pale and maybe a bit frightened. Standing at the edge of her bed, Elena glanced at the monitors. Ginger's blood pressure was low, but not dangerous; oxygen count okay. She was tempted to take her stethoscope out of her pocket and listen to Ginger's heart, but that would be taking her worry to a whole new level.

But wasn't it normal to worry, especially for a woman who'd already suffered three miscarriages?

"Has a doctor been in to see you yet?" Elena finally asked, even though she knew that emergencies were almost always responded to quickly.

"Dr. Carpenter gave me a thorough exam and a pretty good bill of health, and Candace hovered over me like a mother hen until someone else really needed her."

"Any diagnosis?" Elena asked, hoping it was strictly low blood pressure and that the severe headache combined with the dizziness hadn't been symptoms of something serious, something that could harm the baby.

"My blood pressure was low, and Dr. Carpenter's having some blood work done to check my iron level. But everything else looks good."

Elena would ask her if she was taking prenatal vitamins, if she was eating correctly, sleeping on her side instead of her back, but then she'd sound like a nagging mom. "Is Steve coming to get you?"

Ginger shook her head. "I didn't want to worry him, so Ainslee's going to take me home as soon as the doctor's seen the results of my blood work." She laughed lightly—a good sign. "She's determined to make me stay off my feet and eat healthier. You'd think we'd known each other for years instead of just a couple of hours."

"And I'm going to insist that you drop your plans to have a booth at the Harvest Festival. We can find another coordinator for the decorations too."

"Do you want me to be bored to tears throughout the rest of my pregnancy?"

"I want you to be healthy."

Ginger wiped a few tears from her face. "Me too. More than anything I've wanted in my life."

Chapter Twenty

PHYLLIS GETTY SLIPPED INTO THE ICU NURSES' station. She could have been a stealth bomber, considering how silently and almost invisibly she'd moved. Was she on a mission?

Elena had a fresh IV bag in her hands and was about to head into Mrs. Ackland's room, when Phyllis came to a halt right in front of her. "I've heard a rumor about Mr. Varner."

Elena had heard just about enough rumors. Albert Varner hadn't been at church yesterday morning and even though Sandy had been singing in the choir, she'd managed to avoid Elena.

Tomorrow morning, however, Elena planned to be at Ripley's Diner at six o'clock when the men's Bible study group met, and she hoped and prayed that Mr. Varner would be there. Even if he wouldn't tell her exactly what was going on, she hoped she could at least talk with him long enough to find a way to dispel all the rumors.

Of course, there wouldn't be rumors floating around if the hospital administrators would send out a press release or at least a notice to the staff to let them know what was going on.

Rumors piqued everyone's curiosity, and Elena figured she should hear Phyllis's tale, whether it was another rumor or the plain and simple truth.

"What's the latest, Phyllis?"

"Well"—Mrs. Getty's gravelly voice lowered—"Varner's a whistle-blower."

It was all Elena could do not to roll her eyes. What could he possibly know worth blowing the whistle on? "You've got to give me a few more details than just that, Phyllis."

"What I heard is"—she looked around, like a covert operative, and when she seemed satisfied that no one was watching or listening to her, she stepped a little closer to Elena—"there are some doctors at Hope Haven who've been implanting un-approved pacemakers and stents. Apparently Mr. Innisk is well aware of this and had allowed it to go on because it was a moneymaker, but when Mr. Varner learned the truth, he said 'stop it now, or I go to the feds.'"

Elena could only stare at Mrs. Getty in dumbfounded dis-belief. She'd obviously watched too many episodes of *Law and Order* over the years.

"From what I've heard," Mrs. Getty continued, "the board fired him so he couldn't get his hands on incriminating documents."

"There are a lot of rumors floating around," Elena said, hop-ing to put this crazy one to rest. Mrs. Getty was such a dear, but there were times when she could be a little overzealous. "I'm sure there's a more plausible explanation."

"I certainly hope so. I've been here a long time, and I love Hope Haven. I'd hate to see some kind of scandal blow up and put a black mark on the hospital."

Elena didn't want that to happen either.

Tomorrow morning she would get to the truth of the matter.

Mrs. Ackland was asleep when Elena walked into her room. There had been talk about putting her in hospice care, which her daughter had agreed to, but the doctors were having trouble getting her pneumonia under control. Her lungs were failing and the pseudomonad infection she'd contracted was putting up a stronger fight than the antibiotics.

Elena changed the elderly woman's IV bag and added morphine, working as quietly as possible. Mrs. Ackland's breathing was more labored than usual. Right now, Elena merely hoped she could control the pain.

"Is that you, Charles?"

"No, Mrs. Ackland." Elena leaned close to her patient and gently stroked white hair off her chilly brow. "It's Elena. Your nurse."

Her eyes fluttered, but she didn't open them.

Elena walked across the room, opening the blinds to let in some of the beautiful sunshine.

Mrs. Ackland licked her lips. "Could I have some water? I'm so thirsty."

Elena lifted Mrs. Ackland's glass and held the flex straw so she could put it between chapped lips.

"That tastes good."

Elena pulled back Mrs. Ackland's blankets to listen to her heart and lungs, hating the abnormal whooshing sound and the murmurs.

Mrs. Ackland opened her eyes, smiling softly at Elena. "Do you like stars?"

"I love them."

"When I close my eyes I see stars."

Mrs. Ackland struggled for breath, her face wrinkling in pain. Without asking Mrs. Ackland if she was hurting more than usual, Elena increased the morphine drip. At this point, they were doing all they could do to keep her comfortable.

And as Mrs. Ackland slipped back into sleep, Elena went out to the desk to call the elderly woman's daughter. It was probably time for her to come to the hospital so she could see her mother one last time.

Chapter Twenty-One

*J*AMES PACED THE FLOOR OF THE STAFF LOUNGE, A tall white Styrofoam cup in his right hand, the coffee he'd doctored with sweetener sloshing about, but his hands were steady, and not a drop spilled over.

"Would you sit down, James?" Elena had stretched out on a sofa, taking a short break away from the ICU, just long enough to rest her legs and eat a quick sandwich. "You look like a man in an old black-and-white movie, waiting outside the delivery room for his first child to be born."

Candace sat at one of the small tables in the lounge, a fork full of crisp green salad with some kind of creamy dressing halfway to her mouth. When Heath Carlson waved to her with a big smile on his face from the vending machine, she gave him a small nod as her cheeks flushed slightly. She cleared her throat and jumped into the conversation. "You aren't still dwelling on the Boy Scout thing, are you?"

"Yeah. Who would have thought a decision like this would cause me so much angst? I've had to make split-second decisions in my line of work, but this scoutmaster thing is driving me up a wall."

"I know what your problem is, James," Elena said.

His head spun around to look at her. "Then tell me, 'cause I'm dying to know."

"You're afraid if you take over as scoutmaster and something goes wrong—maybe you mess up when teaching the boys how to tie knots, or your archery skills aren't up to snuff or you run at the first sight of a bear—that Nelson will be upset. That he'll lose faith in you. That he'll never want you to do anything with him ever again."

James flipped one of the dinette chairs around and straddled it. "And where did this analysis come from? Are you studying psychology now, in addition to all your other projects?"

"Just a stab in the air, but I've been listening to a lot of people lately, everyone talking about family and friendship dynamics, and it just makes sense."

"Well, try this on for size." James pulled a folded piece of paper out of the pocket of his green scrubs. "Nelson told me he'd put together his own pros and cons list if I thought it would help me make a decision. Not that I haven't done that myself, but I said, 'Go for it,' and this is what I found on the car seat when I came in this morning."

James took his merry sweet time unfolding the note. He looked up at Candace and Elena. Cleared his throat.

I love you, Dad. I know you'll make the right decision.

You always do.

Nelson

James cleared his throat again. "So . . ." James pulled another folded-up piece of paper out of his scrubs, this one a colored brochure. He tossed it on the table. "How do you think I'll look in khaki Boy Scout shorts and hiking boots?"

"I'm not sure." Elena sat up on the couch, leaned forward, and, laughing, stared at James's legs tucked under the table. "Let's see how knobby your knees are."

"Have all the fun you want now, Nurse Rodriguez," James said, wadding up the brochure and tossing it at her, "'cause I'm going to be borrowing that husband of yours to help me out in the beginning."

"Have you told Nelson yet?" Candace asked, taking her plate to the sink.

"Not yet. I've got until the end of the day Thursday to see if someone else steps forward."

"Ah, James, that's the chicken's way out. You should—"

The lounge door burst open and Anabelle practically flew in, waving a piece of paper in front of them. "Have you seen this?"

James frowned. "What is it?"

"A press release," Anabelle said, her glasses firmly on the bridge of her nose, her jaw looking like it might crack from the pressure. "It isn't a notice to staff, because what could possibly make administration think we should have the details before the press?"

Anabelle wasn't facetious all that often. Whatever the press release said, it had certainly gotten under her skin.

"Does that have anything to do with Albert Varner?" Elena asked, sitting up straighter, hoping this would answer all their questions.

"It's about Varner all right. Here, let me read it to you."

Anabelle adjusted her glasses, held the piece of paper in front of her and read. "'The board of directors of Hope Haven Hospital in Deerford, Illinois, fired Chief Executive Officer Albert Varner in a unanimous vote. Board member Reverend Lark Jasperson resigned and left the meeting prior to the vote. The board voted to dismiss Mr. Varner on the grounds that he did not have enough support from the board to be "successful at the helm." Zane McGarry, Hope Haven Hospital's chief financial officer, will serve as interim CEO. Albert Varner could not be reached for comment.'"

"What on earth do they mean that he wasn't 'successful at the helm'?" The fiery temper Elena kept well hidden flared. "Albert Varner's the best CEO we've had. If it weren't for him, we might have closed several months ago."

"This isn't going to do anything to dispel rumors." Anabelle continued to shake the paper, before crumpling it and tossing it in the trash. "I hate all the stories that have been circulating about a man I've always respected. And this press release is so wishy-washy that the rumors are going to get worse."

"I have well over a hundred signatures on the petition asking the board to reinstate Mr. Varner," Elena said, pushing up off the couch and tossing the remains of her sandwich in the trash. "And tomorrow morning I plan to confront Albert Varner. We've been loyal to him, now it's his turn to return the favor. If he's happy about being fired, that's one thing. I'll accept it. If he's not, he needs to put up a fight."

And Elena was ready to lead the battle.

"Have you heard from Ginger?" Quintessa asked, when Elena stopped by her office at the end of her shift. She wanted to ask her to sign the petition to reinstate Mr. Varner, but discussing Ginger was a welcome diversion from something that could get her reprimanded . . . or worse.

"Just this morning." Elena sat in the chair next to Quintessa's desk and dropped her tote bag on the floor beside her. "She's doing great, although staying in bed is driving her crazy and she's disappointed that she can't do more for the Harvest Festival."

"Ainslee has everything under control, thank goodness." Quintessa laughed. "I keep telling myself I never again want to get involved in a project like this, but why stop after this year, especially if it's a huge success."

"Think we can get everything finished in less than two weeks?"

Quintessa frowned. "It's not like you to be anything but optimistic. Everything okay?"

"Too many things on my mind." Refusing to mention that she was exhausted, something she rarely suffered from, or the fact that she dreaded asking Quintessa to sign the petition, Elena reached into her bag and pulled out the paper that bore the signatures of 132 members of the Hope Haven staff, all of whom wanted Albert Varner reinstated to his position as CEO.

"I hear you're stirring up trouble," Quintessa said, her gaze darting to the paper in Elena's hands. She obviously knew that Elena had been circulating a petition. "Are you sure what you're doing is wise?"

Elena shrugged. "Maybe not, but I've never caved in to popular opinion. I prefer doing what I think is right, and I believe Albert Varner is the right CEO for this hospital."

Quintessa stood up, walked to one of the walls in her office, pressed a button, and a wall panel slid open, revealing a kitchenette and closet.

Elena frowned. "I didn't know that was hidden back there."

"It's one of the hospital's little secrets." Quintessa grinned. "Zane keeps a few extra suits and a tux in here, just in case a dinner engagement or an important meeting comes up and he doesn't have time to go home and change."

Quintessa lifted a pot full of coffee that smelled freshly brewed. "You look like you could use a cup."

"Thank you."

"Two sugars and a dash of cream, right?"

"Usually, but I'll have three and two right now. It's been a long day."

When the panel was completely closed, and the secret door looked like a wall again, Quintessa handed the coffee to Elena. "Are you going to ask me to sign your petition?"

"That's my plan, although I suppose I'd understand if you said no."

Quintessa reached across the desk and took the page from Elena. She printed and signed her name, included her title, and dated the petition. "Mind if I hold on to this? Zane has someone in his office, but—"

"Why would he want to sign it? He's interim CEO. Maybe he wants the job permanently."

"Don't worry, Elena." Quintessa pulled a gray legal folder out of her desk and tucked the petition inside. "We—Zane and I—weren't sure you'd bring the petition in for me to sign, let alone Zane, but I already know he supports the staff's position. Penny Risser plans to sign it too."

"You could have told me this before now," Elena teased, "instead of making me sweat, wondering what would happen if I was caught circulating a petition. I was sure I'd be reprimanded."

"There's enough craziness going on around here without—"

The door to Zane McGarry's office opened. Frederick Innisk came out, his eyebrow raising when he saw Elena sitting there, looking like he wanted to chastise her for being somewhere she didn't belong.

Another man followed, someone Elena had never seen before. He was tall, distinguished, wore a suit that looked like it had cost a zillion dollars and spit-polished-and-shined black wingtips. His hair was charcoal gray except for the silver at his temples. He was rather good-looking, but his smile screamed *Don't mess with me, or you'll be in trouble.*

The men all shook hands. "See you next Monday, Keith," Mr. McGarry said, holding the stranger's hand as if they were long-lost friends. "I'll have the contract ready to sign when you get here."

Elena might as well have been invisible when Mr. Innisk and the new guy said good-bye to Quintessa, but that was perfectly fine with her. She and Scrooge already had their problems; and she didn't want to be a blip on this new guy's radar. Because something uncomfortable rumbling around in her stomach told her that he was destined to be the next CEO.

Once Upon A Time was Elena's last stop of the day. The crystal chimes hanging above the door tinkled like delicate glass bells when she walked inside, staying focused, looking for Ainslee rather than looking at all the wonderful things she'd love to buy.

"Hi there." Anabelle's beautiful daughter peeked around a mannequin she was dressing in a pair of well-tailored men's trousers and an olive drab Eisenhower jacket, complete with a collection of gold military insignia. "Have you come to buy, or talk about the festival or the quilt?"

"Actually, none of those things, but you can fill me in on the quilt, if you want."

Stepping out from behind the World War II mannequin, Ainslee couldn't have looked prettier, her mahogany hair waving over her shoulders in a similar style to the Veronica Lake look-alike who'd been in the store a couple of weeks ago. Her chocolate eyes were as big and bright as her mom's. She wore black-and-white vertical-striped pants, black-and-white espadrilles, a black peplum jacket that wouldn't fit much longer and a fat red silk chrysanthemum over her left breast pocket. The lucky lady was also wearing to-die-for chunky red Bakelite bracelets and earrings.

If she didn't love her job so much, Elena thought, she just might quit and ask for a job working with Ainslee. She would absolutely love to wear all the wonderfully retro clothes and accessories.

"I'm sure Mother's filled you in on almost everything about the quilt, which is gorgeous. Just wait until you see it."

"Another few days, right?"

"We're meeting at Dr. Hamilton's tomorrow to finish it up, and a photographer from the *Dispatch* is coming over to take photos." Ainslee walked across the shop, stopping behind the counter. "The photos and article about the auction and the festival should definitely be in Saturday's paper."

"The press release looked great," Elena said, unable to resist a kitschy yellow and white polka dot bracelet on the counter. She slid it on her left wrist and held it up to the light to see if it sparkled, then took it off when she realized it was really much too far-out for her taste.

"Everything else is under control for the Harvest Festival," Elena said, "and you do have the meeting for next Tuesday—a week from tomorrow—down on your calendar?"

Ainslee reached under the counter, pulled out her purse and dug inside for her Blackberry. "Four o'clock next Tuesday. Right?"

"Right, but there's a little something else I'd like to add to the agenda I already sent."

"What's that?"

"A surprise baby shower for Ginger, right after the meeting. Not a big one—just the people at the hospital who've spent time with her and the ladies from our Bible study."

Ainslee smiled. "I can make that work. But how are you going to get Ginger there, when she's supposed to be on bed rest?"

"I've already gotten an okay from her doctor." Elena held a pair of sparkly purple rhinestone earrings up to her ears and checked them out in the mirror, twisting her head this way and that. "And she's bored at home. I was hoping you might talk her into coming to the meeting and—"

"Your wish is my command," Ainslee said. "Anything else I can do?"

"I think you've volunteered more than enough. Your mom will have my head if I ask you to do too much."

"She worries too much. She's given me a mile-long list of foods to eat, foods not to eat, foods that will cause gas, you name it."

Elena heard the frustration in Ainslee's voice. Anabelle could be a little, well, domineering on occasion. "Your mom just wants you to be healthy. Goodness knows she's taken care of enough pregnant women in her years as a nurse, that she knows what's good and what's not so good."

"She doesn't like my choice of colors for the nursery. I e-mailed her a picture of the crib and changing table Doug and I have ordered, and she said a Jenny Lind–style, with all those fussy spindles, would be better than the sleek, ultramodern crib Doug and I fell in love with. And last night she called to tell me she'd ordered a book for me on HypnoBirthing. She's sure it's something I'll want to try, all about using mind over matter to erase pain. For some reason, she's not happy with any of my decisions and—"

Ainslee sighed heavily, then laughed. "Once a little girl, always a little girl, I guess."

"And once a mom, always a mom." Elena smiled. "Just you wait and see."

Chapter Twenty-Two

ELENA SPRINKLED HOT SAUCE ON HER SCRAMBLED eggs as she sat in the booth at Ripley's Diner. She would have preferred chorizo in her eggs, the way she made them for Cesar, but she hadn't come into the restaurant at six o'clock because she was dying for a delicious breakfast. She was here to talk with Albert Varner as soon as his Bible study group ended.

Picking up a piece of thick, crispy bacon, she took a bite, chewing it slowly as she watched the doors at the back of the restaurant slide open. There had to be a good fifteen or twenty men inside the meeting room, some in business suits, others in jeans and T-shirts, slacks and golf shirts and one in a Chicago Bulls sweatshirt. Definitely a mixed bunch, with their faith in the Lord in common.

Albert Varner was in the middle of the group, shaking hands, talking, laughing, everyone taking forever to leave.

Elena wiped grease off her fingers and took a sip of freshly squeezed orange juice as the men finally started filing out. Albert Varner was one of the last, and the moment he got close, Elena pushed out of her booth and walked up to him, trying to look casual, quite a feat when she felt like she was spying on an old friend.

"Mr. Varner," she said, smiling her best guilty smile, "good morning."

Elena hated the look of his frown, wondering if he was going to blow past her, head right out the door, get in his car and take off. But slowly the frown eased, he said good-bye to the men he was with and held out his hand to Elena.

"Hello, Elena." His handshake was warm and strong. "I should be surprised to see you here, but Sandy told me the two of you had talked at choir practice the other night, so my guess is you've come here hoping to talk about the rumors floating around the hospital."

"Good guess." Elena laughed lightly. "If you have a moment—"

"Do you have a table already?"

He didn't waste much time, Elena thought, glad she didn't have to convince him to sit down for a talk. She scooted back into her booth and pushed her plate off to the side of the table. When the waitress walked by, Mr. Varner asked for a cup of coffee then folded his forearms on top of the table. "You know, Elena, you're the last person I ever expected would track me down and try to find out if the rumors running rampant at the hospital are true."

"The rumors have nothing to do with me being here this morning or trying to talk with Sandy the other night.

But"—Elena grinned as she lifted her cup of coffee—"do you have spies inside the hospital telling you what's going on?"

"I had the best assistant imaginable." He stirred sugar into the cup of coffee the waitress set in front of him. "Penny has kept me informed of just about everything, at the risk of her own job."

"The rumors are ridiculous. Whistle-blower I might be able to believe, but insider trading?" Elena shook her head. "Never."

She took a sip of her coffee, watching Mr. Varner closely, hoping to read his face, to figure out what he was thinking, but he didn't reveal a thing physically, or verbally either.

"But the rumors aren't the reason I wanted to speak with you. And even though I'd love to know why you left the hospital and why there's a press release out saying you were fired because you didn't have enough support from the board to be successful at the helm of Hope Haven—which is absolutely ridiculous—I don't expect you to tell me what was behind the whole thing."

"Then what do you want?" he asked, taking a sip of his coffee and watching her over the rim.

"I want you to come back to the hospital."

"The board already has a replacement in mind, so that's a moot point."

"Only if you let it be a moot point." Elena held her coffee cup out when the waitress walked by, let her fill it to the brim, then emptied three packets of sugar inside. "Nearly every person working at the hospital has signed a petition stating that you should be reinstated."

"Or what?" Mr. Varner asked, as Elena stirred the sugar into her coffee. "Petitions are all well and good for stating your case, for letting the government or some other entity see how many people support a cause. Unfortunately, the board doesn't have to look at your petition or even recognize its existence."

"Considering that they haven't even responded to individual letters," Elena said, "that doesn't surprise me. But don't you feel that once the board sees how the staff, and I'm including Zane McGarry, feel about you, how much everyone respects you and how much we want you back, they might reconsider?"

"It's a business decision, Elena. Unfortunately, my stance on a couple of issues—"

"The PICU and a new children's ward?" Elena asked. Both had been on her mind since Anabelle had overheard the discussion in human resources.

"I'm for a PICU and a children's ward. Unfortunately, the majority of the board members feel it's frivolous to include those items in our budget, when there are perfectly good ones in Peoria and Chicago."

"Well, they're out of their minds."

Mr. Varner laughed. "Maybe, but they make the final decisions."

"What about all the arguments that were presented at the board meeting last year, that many new families are moving to Deerford and that many of those families have children who could benefit from a PICU and children's ward? That must have had some impression on the board."

"It did at the time, Elena, but the financial woes we had a few months ago caused the board to take another look at a new five-year plan, and they didn't feel the need for either unit."

"And you tried to change their minds?"

"Actually, I told them I'd quit if they took those two items out of the budget." He laughed. "They didn't even blink an eye. I was fired. End of story."

"It doesn't have to be the end of the story," Elena said, folding her arms atop the table and looking Mr. Varner straight in the eye. "Just tell me one thing. Are you happy being away from Hope Haven, or do you want your job back?"

"Retirement's not my cup of tea, and Hope Haven's been my life for a long time. I miss it. I miss the people."

"Good, because there are a bunch of us who are ready to fight. And—good Lord willing—we're going to win."

At noon that day, when Elena was officially at lunch, so no one could accuse her of interfering in hospital business when she was supposed to be working, she typed a quick e-mail note to Anabelle, Candace and James.

> *Cuppa Coffee*
> *6:00 AM Wednesday*
> *Important!*

She hit Send just as Frederick Innisk and Keith, the man she'd seen in Zane McGarry's office, the man who might be in line for the CEO job, walked around the corner. Elena quickly made a wish for them to keep on going. She didn't want them stopping in the ICU. She not only had too much to do—even though it was her official lunch hour, a lunch hour she rarely, if ever, took—but she was in a fighting mood, and she might make some wisecrack to Scrooge if he looked at her funny.

"And this is the ICU . . ."

So much for wishes coming true.

"Keith Bancroft, I'd like to introduce you to Elena Rodriguez, one of our registered nurses."

Elena was sure the words "and a thorn in my side" were on the tip of his tongue.

"It's nice to meet you, Mr. Bancroft." Somehow Elena managed to smile, then wondered if she might be all wrong about Keith Bancroft. She didn't know for sure if he was the man who might take Albert Varner's job. "I'm sorry—is it Mr. Bancroft or Dr. Bancroft?"

"Mister," Innisk said, frowning at Elena as usual. "You'll probably see a lot of him in the next week or two as we discuss his coming to work as our new CEO."

She should have trusted her instincts. "Hope Haven's a wonderful hospital, Mr. Bancroft."

"Did I see you in Zane McGarry's office yesterday?" he asked, offering her a quick, very perfunctory handshake.

Elena nodded. "Mr. McGarry's assistant, Quintessa Smith, is a friend of mine."

"If there's a cause to be fought for," Mr. Innisk said, grinning at Keith Bancroft, "Elena's your go-to girl and Quintessa is often her backup."

There was obviously a backhanded slap behind Mr. Innisk's words, but Elena refused to let him get to her.

"I'll keep that in mind." Mr. Bancroft took a quick walk around the already cramped nurses' station. "I'll be back next Monday. If you're here, perhaps you could show me around the ICU. I'd like to get to know the hospital inside and out."

Smile, Elena. Keep smiling. "I'd be happy to."

Without another word, Frederick Innisk and Keith Bancroft moved on, heading for some other department to make someone else uncomfortable.

She'd always considered herself a good judge of character. She couldn't pinpoint exactly what it was about Keith Bancroft that put her on edge. Maybe it was the fact that he was not just good-looking, but too good-looking.

Superficial. That sounded about right. A man of very little substance.

If he became CEO, she hoped she'd be proven wrong, because that could be very bad for Hope Haven Hospital.

Phyllis Getty was sitting at Mrs. Ackland's bedside when Elena came into the room. She had a Bible propped up against Mrs. Ackland's side and was holding one of the elderly woman's frail hands, reading a Psalm Elena knew well. Psalm 96 had always made Elena smile, and she did now, as she checked Mrs. Ackland's vitals.

> *Let the heavens rejoice, let the earth be glad;*
> *let the sea resound, and all that is in it;*
> *let the fields be jubilant, and everything in them.*
> *Then all the trees of the forest will sing for joy. . . .*

Mrs. Ackland had slipped in and out of consciousness all morning, barely aware of her surroundings. With each passing hour she grew more and more weak. Her daughter had been with her all night, afraid to leave, to not be with her mother when she closed her eyes for the final time.

Elena listened to her heart and lungs, even though she doubted there'd been any change in the past hour. Now she only hoped that Mrs. Ackland's daughter had received the voice mail message Elena had left and that she'd return to the hospital in time to say good-bye.

Phyllis closed her Bible, gave Mrs. Ackland's fingers a little squeeze and whispered, "See you later, Mrs. Ackland," then offered a knowing smile to Elena. Phyllis Getty had been volunteering at Hope Haven longer than Elena had worked there. She might not be a doctor or nurse, but she knew how to comfort the patients, knew when it was time to whisper a few last words.

Mrs. Ackland turned her head, her cloudy eyes following Phyllis out of the room, then turning them to Elena. "I was hoping you'd come by."

"You're my favorite patient," Elena said, smiling as she held Mrs. Ackland's hand. "Coming by to see you and taking care of you is a pleasure."

Mrs. Ackland gasped for air. Her oxygen count was low; her blood pressure much lower than it should be. At this point, all they could do was keep her comfortable. Mrs. Ackland winced in pain, and Elena increased her morphine drip. There was no need for her to suffer. Not now.

"Would you like me to call the chaplain?" Elena asked, as she opened one of the drawers in a cabinet next to Mrs. Ackland's bed and took out a soft hairbrush.

"Pastor Tom was here not long ago." Mrs. Ackland grasped for Elena's hand. "If I go, you won't resuscitate me, will you?"

They had a Do Not Resuscitate order on Mrs. Ackland, and when she'd signed it, she'd been very adamant that her time had come and she didn't want to be kept alive only to prolong the inevitable. There was no way to sugarcoat the answer. "No, Mrs. Ackland. We just want to keep you comfortable."

She smiled weakly. "I'm going to see my Charles, you know."

Elena brushed a bit of snowy white hair away from Mrs. Ackland's face. "Yes, I know."

For the past two days she'd wanted to go home, wanted to see her husband—her Charles. She'd missed him so. That was one of the blessings of faith—knowing that you'd see your loved ones. Elena hadn't always believed it was possible. Not that she'd disbelieved, she simply hadn't had enough faith.

Finding it again had made moments like this so much easier to accept.

"Would you like me to put the oxygen mask on you, Mrs. Ackland?" Elena upped the concentration of oxygen. "I know it isn't all that comfortable to wear, but it'll make it easier for you to breathe."

"No. I just want to see my daughter again, and then I want to be with Charles." Mrs. Ackland struggled to swallow. It became increasingly difficult for her to breathe.

Please, Lord, let Mrs. Ackland's daughter get here soon.

Again Elena upped the morphine drip, and within moments, Mrs. Ackland's breathing seemed to ease.

"What do you think heaven is like?" Mrs. Ackland's eyes closed, the thin, almost translucent lids fluttering.

"What was it the Apostle John wrote in Revelations?" Elena said, remembering the verses so well. "One of the angels came... 'And he carried me away in the Spirit to a mountain great and high, and showed me the Holy City, Jerusalem, coming down out of heaven from God. It shone with the glory of God, and its brilliance was like that of a very precious jewel, like a jasper, clear as crystal.' That's how I see heaven."

Mrs. Ackland attempted a feeble smile. Her chest rose and fell heavily, and then . . . *Thank heaven!* Mrs. Ackland's daughter came into the room, looking harried and worn.

"Mama." She walked slowly to the side of the bed, taking her mother's hand. "I'm here, Mama."

Mrs. Ackland drew her daughter's hand to her mouth and kissed it. "I love you, so much," she whispered. "So much."

"I love you, too, Mama."

And Mrs. Ackland closed her eyes, peacefully letting go.

Chapter Twenty-Three

ANABELLE FLEXED HER FINGERS, DESPERATELY trying to work out the pain as she got up from the quilting machine and let Genna Hamilton take over. Another hour, maybe even less, and the art quilt for the Harvest Festival auction would be finished. It had already been decided that Genna, Anabelle and Ainslee would pose with the quilt when the photographer from the *Dispatch* came to snap pictures.

"Looks terrific," Ainslee said, taking a photo of Anabelle with her own digital camera.

"That picture you just took of me isn't going to look all that terrific." Anabelle scowled at her daughter. "My hair's a mess, I don't have any lipstick on and I don't want people seeing me massaging my hands. Someone might get the wrong impression, think I'm getting old."

"Oh, Mother, if anyone's thinking that, it's you. And you're the last person on earth who needs lipstick. You were blessed with perfect skin, great hair, and I think I heard Pop saying more than once that he liked your lips just the way they are."

Anabelle rolled her eyes at her daughter's ridiculous comments and tucked her hands into the pockets of the wine-colored sweater she was wearing with jeans and tennis shoes. They were warm there and hopefully the pain would ease up.

"What are you going to do with all the photos you've been taking?"

"Didn't Elena tell you? We're going to have a page on the Harvest Festival Web site showing the creation of the quilt, from your initial design, to you cutting fabric, the women from the guild working together that first night, picking out the pieces they wanted to appliqué . . . right up to the auction. A picture of the winner, a picture of the check that's going to help pay for the Habitat for Humanity furnishings and then the quilt hanging on the new owner's wall."

Anabelle smiled at last. She loved everything about quilting. The stacks of fabric, the spools of colorful thread, learning a new technique or discovering an old one written down in an antique quilter's diary. But most of all, she loved seeing the finished pieces hanging on a wall, spread out over someone's bed or tossed over a chair or couch. There were so many memories in quilts, especially the time spent making them, especially when you had a loved one at your side, as she'd had Ainslee.

"We are going to teach your child—my grandchild—how to quilt, aren't we?"

Ainslee laughed. "If I have a girl, definitely; if I have a boy, Doug would have my head."

"Well, of course, I was thinking about a little girl. Your father would have had a conniption fit if he'd seen your brother sitting at a quilting frame with a needle and thread in his hand. Of course, Evan was all boy, and I would have had to drag him kicking and screaming to even touch a sewing machine."

"Aren't you glad you had two girls?"

Anabelle smiled. "I thank the good Lord every day."

"Done!" Genna's shout of joy echoed around the room, as she stepped back from the longarm quilting machine. "I don't know about the rest of you, but I'm anxious to get this off the frame and hung up in the living room where it'll look beautiful for the newspaper photos."

"I'm thinking we should hang it in here," Anabelle said. "Your living room is gorgeous, but don't you think it would be nice for the people in Deerford to see where this was created?"

"I don't know, Mother." Ainslee crossed the room and snapped a photo of Genna with the newly finished quilt. "I think Genna's right. It will look beautiful in the living room, and there won't be stacks of fabrics, tables and sewing machines around to distract the reader. We want them to see the quilt in all its glory."

Anabelle shrugged, moving to the frame to start unrolling the quilt. "Sure, that'll be good."

Of course, it would have looked really good hanging in Genna's workshop, but it seemed that she and Ainslee were at odds all the time lately. Where a quilt should be hung, whether or not she should wear lipstick, the colors for the baby's room and even whether or not she should retire from the job she loved.

Maybe she was overreacting, but lately she just didn't feel like she was part of her daughter's life anymore.

And she was afraid of being pushed away.

Of course, as Cameron often reminded her, she was the one who'd taught her children to stand up for themselves, to be strong, assertive and independent.

It wasn't long before the quilt was off the machine and six women from the guild were heading down the stairs to hang the finished product in Genna's elegant living room.

"Slow down just a bit," Ainslee called out from the top landing. "Turn around and smile up at me so I can take your picture."

Anabelle stood at the front of the group, her hair mussed, lipstick long ago chewed off and her hands aching, but still she managed to smile for Ainslee's camera. "Be careful up there, Ainslee," she called out, being a fussbudget once again, something she just couldn't help.

It was a mother's prerogative.

"Oh, Mother. I'm not three years old any longer. Just smile for the picture." Ainslee aimed the camera. "Say cheese!"

It seemed as if it took forever for the flash to go off, and once it did, the women were heading off to the living room.

"Should we drape it over the sofa?" Genna asked. "Or figure out a way to hang it above the fireplace?"

Glass shattered somewhere in the house, the crash reverberating through Anabelle's ears. Her heart raced.

"Ainslee!"

Anabelle ran back to the home's massive entryway. Ainslee lay on the floor at the bottom of the stairs, her hands clasping her belly. All around her were the broken remains of a tall crystal vase, water, flowers, a camera and the overturned console table that had once sat against a wall near the bottom of the stairs.

Anabelle went to Ainslee's side, not worried in the least about stepping on shards of glass. Ainslee was all that mattered.

"I'm okay, Mother. Really I am," Ainslee said, sitting up. "I'm just embarrassed."

Anabelle knelt down beside her daughter. "There's no need to feel embarrassed. Accidents happen."

"I think the bottoms of these shoes are a little too slippery for skipping down stairs." Ainslee was laughing lightly, while Genna picked up pieces of glass and Jane DeVol cleaned up water with a roll of paper towels, but Anabelle's concern hadn't ebbed.

"Did you stumble? Slip? Or what?" Anabelle asked, worried by the way Ainslee was holding her stomach, afraid that Ainslee might be in shock, not yet realizing what had happened.

"I think I slipped, landed on my bottom and slid all the way down. Probably a very mortifying picture if someone had caught it on camera."

"Does anything hurt?" Anabelle asked, trying not to come right out and ask if she had any abdominal pain. The last thing she wanted to do was frighten her daughter.

"I'm fine, Mother. But . . ." Ainslee reached out and stroked a tear away from Anabelle's face. "Don't cry. Please."

Anabelle bit her lip. She hadn't even realized she'd been crying. "You just scared me."

"It was just a little fall, on my bottom, not my abdomen. My ankles don't hurt. My knees are fine." Ainslee smiled. "My pride's a bit bruised, but that'll go away, and that vase had to be horribly expensive—"

"I was getting tired of it anyway." Genna grinned as she held a hand out to help Anabelle up. "Now I have an excuse to go out shopping tomorrow."

"The only thing I want to do right now," Anabelle said, "is take Ainslee to the hospital and get her checked out."

"We don't need to do that, Mother." Ainslee was adamant. "Besides, the photographer will be here pretty quick, and you worked too hard on that quilt not to have your picture taken with it."

"I have hundreds of photos of me with hundreds of quilts. I only have one pregnant daughter."

Ainslee smiled and Anabelle was sure she was going to laugh at her, tell her she was a silly old fool for worrying so much.

Instead, a tear slid down Ainslee's cheek. "Do you want to take your car or mine?"

Elena was right. He was a chicken.

James sat on a barstool at the kitchen counter, watching Fern move slowly from refrigerator to counter to stove, fixing dinner herself for the second time in a week. It took her longer than it would take him and dinner had been an hour later than usual last night, but she'd been not only proud of herself, but exhilarated too.

"Cooking dinner—no matter how long it takes me—is a heck of a lot better than sitting around being bored," she'd said, and then she'd kissed him. It had been a very good night.

And he had to admit, he liked watching her. He'd married one really pretty woman, and, man, how he loved her.

Which made the decision he was about to reveal a whole lot easier.

"The brisket's been cooking on low almost all day," Fern said, resting her arms on the countertop, taking a deep breath. "I cooked up a Bobby Flay barbeque sauce, the yams are baked and ready to be doused with butter and cinnamon and I've got honey butter for the rolls that'll be ready to take out of the oven any minute. Not quite the Deerford Roadhouse, but close."

"Need some help with any of it?" James asked, getting more and more antsy by the minute. He wasn't sure how to break the news, but he wasn't going to wait. Nelson needed to know tonight—not a few days from now.

"I've got it all under control," Fern said, "but I'll let you say grace."

"I'll say it as long as we still have plates left to eat on," James said, listening to the clattering and clanging of dishes, silverware and knives being set on the table. "Gideon and Nelson seem to be vying for the 'who can make the most noise' award."

Fern chuckled. "Gideon couldn't hit a basket to save his life during practice this afternoon and Nelson got a B— on his algebra test. Neither one of them is happy, but I'm sure they'll give you the lowdown over dinner."

Great. He had been hoping for peace and quiet or a few laughs before he spilled the beans, but he guessed he'd have to listen to grumbling first.

It was one of the special things that came with fatherhood.

James laughed to himself as he put the basket of rolls on the table, asked Nelson to pour milk and asked Gideon to help his mom with the meat and potatoes. Gideon moaned; Nelson's complaints were more of a whine. Nothing new.

Yet.

At long last they were all gathered around the table. James reached for Fern's hand and squeezed it, knowing that she'd done the cooking for him, so he could have a few extra hours a week for himself, or to spend with the boys. But it had been good for her too, and that made everyone happy.

"Your dad's going to say grace tonight," Fern announced, resting her folded hands on the table.

"Oh, good." Gideon took his baseball cap off and dropped it on the floor next to his chair. "It was supposed to be my night and I've spent the last couple of hours trying to think of something clever, since there wasn't much to be thankful for at basketball practice."

"I heard," James said. "Not even one single basket?"

Gideon shook his head. "It's pretty darn lousy when the best slam dunker and the best shooter can't hit the basket to save his life."

"After you and Nelson do the dishes—"

"I had to do the dishes all by myself last night," Nelson whined. "Why do I have to help tonight?"

"Because the sooner you get them done the sooner Gideon and I can go outside and shoot hoops."

"What's in it for me?" Nelson asked. "Sitting around while you help me understand distributive, associative and commutative properties so I get a better grade on my next algebra test doesn't sound all that exciting."

James cleared his throat. "Couldn't we stop grumbling for a bit and thank God for the dinner your mom made?"

Nelson rolled his eyes. Gideon was already eyeing the brisket. Fern was ready to burst out laughing.

James bent his head and folded his hands. "Heavenly Father, thank You for the bounty before us. Thank You for our health and for the doctors and therapists who are helping Fern become stronger. And thank You for taking an overwhelming burden off my shoulders, allowing me to realize just how much I want to be Nelson's new scoutmaster, so I can take him camping out in the woods with bears and spiders and things that go bump in the night. Help me to be the best scoutmaster I can be, and thank You for giving me a family that I dearly love."

James cracked open one eye to see the huge grin on Nelson's face.

"Amen."

Anabelle walked into one of the private rooms in the Birthing Unit where Ainslee had been for the past half hour, being checked out by Dr. Carpenter and Candace. They'd planned to go to the ER, but when Candace ran into them in the parking lot, after she'd finished teaching one of her birthing classes—which met on Tuesdays in November because of Thanksgiving—she insisted they go up to Labor and Delivery.

"Everything okay?" Anabelle asked.

"Perfect." Ainslee smiled.

"But that doesn't mean it wasn't a good idea for you to bring her in," Dr. Carpenter said. Except for wearing a white lab coat that had Dr. Frances Carpenter embroidered over the pocket, no one would picture her as a doctor, not with her corkscrew black hair sticking out wildly about her head. But she was a great obstetrician, and Anabelle was glad she was the one who'd examined Ainslee.

"You've been a nurse long enough to know that most falls like Ainslee took can't hurt the baby. She knows that too. And you both know that the womb is pretty shock resistant, and the baby is cradled in the amniotic fluid and muscles and fat, which is designed to keep the baby safe. *But*"—she faced Ainslee—"for peace of mind, it never hurts to have an exam, at least to check the baby's heartbeat. And your baby sounds absolutely fine."

Ainslee and Anabelle both sighed with relief.

"I have another patient to check on, but call me—or your regular obstetrician—if you experience anything out of the ordinary in the next few days."

The doctor shook both their hands, and Anabelle was more than ready to get out of the hospital and head back to Genna Hamilton's home to see if the photographer was still there. But Candace didn't move. Instead, she stared down at Ainslee's shoes.

"Those ballerina flats are lovely," Candace said, "but don't ever again skip in them. Low heels are great, but you might consider getting some that aren't slippery on the bottom. And no more high heels."

Ainslee looked indignant. "You're sounding like my mother."

"I've learned a lot from your mother." Candace winked. "You might try listening to her a little more. Moms really do know best."

Chapter Twenty-Four

ELENA WARMED HER HANDS AROUND THE PAPER coffee cup, filled to the brim with Cuppa Coffee's best steaming cocoa, topped with a dollop of whipped cream and shaved dark chocolate. It was decadent and very much a necessity this morning. The last few weeks had been a bear, and things weren't going to calm down until after the Harvest Festival.

Candace sat across from Elena, taking a sip of mocha latte. "I'm sure Anabelle will tell you this later, but Ainslee fell down the stairs at Genna Hamilton's last night."

Elena felt a cold shiver run up her spine. "Please tell me she's okay."

Candace nodded. "Dr. Carpenter examined her and, thank heavens, she's fine. It was a much better outcome than Ginger's scare last week."

Elena sighed. "I wish I knew she was going to be okay. After three miscarriages, Ginger's baby has to be healthy."

"She came to my birthing class last night with Steve, her husband," Candace stated. "She said she was feeling good and she'd been to the doctor and everything was looking fine."

Elena frowned. "You say that as if there should be a 'but' attached to the end."

"She's taking it easy. No stress. Staying in bed most of the day. Not sitting at the sewing machine." Candace took another drink of coffee. "I'm still praying for her. I won't stop until the baby's born."

"Our Bible study group has taken meals to her so she doesn't have to fix anything. And if you knew my Bible study group, you'd know that a lot of praying has been going on."

"Which reminds me," Candace said, "Megan, a friend of mine, said she'd meet us here this morning, since she couldn't make it Friday. Hope that won't interfere with what you wanted to talk about."

The front door of Cuppa Coffee blew open, and James and Anabelle came in together, both bundled up good and warm.

"Six o'clock right on the nose." James stripped out of his coat and threw it over the back of a chair. "Punctuality is one of the top ten qualifications of a good scoutmaster."

Anabelle stiffened. "You didn't."

"I most certainly did," James said, slinging his arm around Anabelle's shoulders. "You're looking at the new scoutmaster of Deerford's one and only and most esteemed Boy Scout troop."

"Congratulations," Elena and Candace said.

"I suppose this calls for a cup of coffee on me to celebrate your new status." Anabelle tossed James a quick grin. "In truth,

I'm just glad you finally made up your mind. Your pacing was starting to drive me crazy."

"It's not that I didn't want to do it." James pulled an extra chair over to the table and sat down. "With work, helping out in surgery every once in a while, worrying about Fern and trying so hard to take care of her, I think I got overwhelmed at the thought of one more big responsibility being added to my plate."

Anabelle set a cup of plain black coffee in front of James and sat down without taking off her coat and immediately blew on her own coffee to cool it off a bit before taking a sip.

"Now that you're all here," Elena started, catching everyone's immediate attention, "you should know that I spoke with Albert Varner yesterday. Anabelle was right. He was fired for arguing with the board about the hatchet job on the PICU and children's ward." She filled them in on the rest of the discussion she'd had with Mr. Varner.

"Somehow we have to get him rehired," Elena continued. "I wanted to think that the petition and our letters to the board would do some good, but they won't look at them. Not that they're all bad people—"

"They're businesspeople," Anabelle stated. "The hospital has to make money to survive, to keep us working, which means they have to look at the big picture."

"But are they looking at the whole picture?" James asked. "You have to wonder if they ever look outside the box."

"Well, they've looked outside the hospital for the new CEO," Elena said, again thinking how much Keith Bancroft disturbed her. "If you haven't met him, you will. He and Frederick Innisk are making the rounds."

"Tall guy? Handsome?" Candace asked, getting up from the table as she usually did to order a pastry for all of them to share.

"That could be me," James teased, "but I've seen Innisk walking around with a guy fitting that description too. Fortunately they haven't stopped by to say hello."

"This is no time for silliness," Anabelle said, putting on her motherly frown. "Do you know anything about him, Elena?"

"Not much. His name's Keith Bancroft."

It was James's turn to frown. "That's it?"

"No one wants to show me his résumé, and I found several Keith Bancrofts on the Internet, but none of them looked anything like the man I met. I do know, however, that there's something about him that bothers me."

"Using your female intuition?" James asked, grinning as usual.

"Wait until you meet him, and you'll see what I mean. Of course, whether I like him or not wouldn't mean a hill of beans to the board. And Frederick Innisk seems to like him. That counts for a lot at Hope Haven."

Candace set one large cinnamon roll on the table between them along with five forks. "Don't dig in yet. My friend Megan Gallagher is on her way in, and she's going to join us, so be nice. She was really interested in the Harvest Festival when I told her about it."

Megan Gallagher breezed in a few minutes later. She was tall and pretty, and with long blonde hair pulled back into an elegant French braid, she looked just about perfect. The rock half the size of Illinois on the ring finger of her left hand shouted wealth. She carried a handbag that must have cost a good four figures, definitely not something Elena would ever own, and her coat had the distinct look of cashmere. But she didn't seem the least bit pretentious, Elena thought. She had a warm smile.

James pulled up a chair for Megan while Candace got her a tall cup of straight black coffee, the same thing James drank: dark Colombian, with two packets of sweetener.

They talked about next to nothing for the first couple of minutes, then Megan touched on something near and dear to Elena's heart. "Candace tells me you're coordinating a Harvest Festival for three churches, which seems like an unbelievable task to me."

"I have a lot of volunteers," Elena said.

"You can never have enough volunteers," Megan stated, and Elena knew she was going to love this woman. "I have an attic full of harvest decorations that I've used in the past. They're going to waste shoved away in boxes, so I'll dig them out and see if you can use them."

Elena laughed. "At this stage of the game, and because we're trying to keep our expenses to a minimum, we'll take any free decorations we can get. By the way, we're having a last-minute planning meeting next Tuesday at four at the hospital. Any chance you could be there?"

"I'll do anything to get out of the house, so sign me up for whatever you want," Megan said. "Candace tells me you're planning a cake walk, amongst other things."

Elena nodded, hoping she'd just met Wonder Woman. "Cake walk, face painting—"

"I can do that with my eyes closed." Megan pulled her wallet out of her million-dollar purse and opened it up to show off her pictures. "My son and daughter wanted face painters at all their birthday parties so I took a class to learn how to do it just right. I do balloon animals too. As for the cakes—running a cake walk isn't my thing—"

"You mean there's something you don't do?" Anabelle asked. It might have sounded snippy coming from anyone else, and even though Anabelle could be a bit judgmental and straight-forward, Elena knew that she didn't mean anything the least bit negative.

"I don't jog. I'm the world's lousiest dancer. I can't sing to save my life, but I'm a whiz at planning parties and charity balls."

"She decorates cakes too," Candace said. "In fact, I hope you don't mind, Elena, but I've already told her about the baby shower for Ginger, and she's going to make the cake."

Elena was beginning to think she'd died and gone to heaven. She had just met someone who topped her in the energy department.

Thank You, Lord!

"I know you all have to get to work," Megan said, "but I was wondering. If someone were to open a bakery here in Deerford, where would be the best place for it?"

"A bakery that does everything, like breads, pastries and cakes?" James asked. "Or what?"

"I'm thinking a bistro-type bakery," Megan said. "Fresh quiche with fruit on the side. Muffins. Cookies. Brownies. That type of thing, with coffee service, quaint tables, open strictly for brunch and lunch. And then, of course, the cakes. That's where my heart lies. After my husband died, I went into a decorating frenzy, buying how-to DVDs, making gum-paste flowers and experimenting with designs. I might as well put it all to good use."

"I've heard one of the shops up the street might be closing," Anabelle said.

"Demarest Hardware?" James asked.

Anabelle nodded. "There's not all that much business in small hardware stores these days, not when you can walk into a big-box store and find pretty much anything you need, at a smaller price, so Demarest is sadly closing its doors."

"That could be a pretty good location," James added. "It's got great windows looking out on the street and it's close to the hospital."

"It sounds perfect. I'll check it out—" Megan's sentence not only came to a sudden halt, but her eyes widened as she stared out the window. Elena turned around in her seat to see what Megan was gawking at.

"You don't know him, do you?" Candace asked, as she, James and Anabelle glanced out the window at Keith Bancroft looking at the menu posted on the door.

"Oh, I know all about Keith Bancroft."

Elena wasn't too thrilled with the tone of Megan's statement. "Mr. Bancroft is in the running for our hospital's CEO position."

Megan frowned. "Well, if he gets the job, you'd better look out."

This was getting interesting. Elena needed ammunition for the battle she aimed to wage in order to get Albert Varner back. This just might be the thing.

"You're saying he's not the most upstanding man on the face of the earth?" Elena asked.

"Not exactly." Megan shook her head. "I've known two companies that hired him to restructure their organization. Heads rolled at both places. Policies were stripped and rewritten. Both companies became top-heavy with lawyers and, well, let's just say the whole thing was troublesome from the beginning."

James frowned. "Are the companies still operating?"

Megan nodded. "Yes, but under new management and new ownership—mine."

"Yours?" Candace looked like she might choke on her coffee.

"It was my husband who took them over. He's the one who got rid of Bancroft. Then he rehired most of the original staff and executives and spent months going over policies with a fine-tooth comb while bringing in experts to revamp the revamped mess."

"I think we need to keep this guy far away from Hope Haven. Of course, we'd need proof of his misadventures and"—Anabelle turned her gaze on Elena—"someone brave enough to go to the board with the information."

Chapter Twenty-Five

WITH A FAIRLY USELESS PETITION IN HAND AND A little incriminating evidence in her pocket, Elena walked into Innisk Securities and asked to see Frederick Innisk. She should have made an appointment, but it was highly doubtful he would have allowed his secretary to put the Hope Haven Troublemaker on his calendar.

He might not want to see her now, either, but surprisingly enough, after his secretary lifted her phone, dialed a number and said, "There's a Mrs. Elena Rodriguez here to see you," a door opened and Frederick Innisk said, "Come in, Elena."

Why did she feel like he was the spider and she was the fly?

"Good afternoon, Mr. Innisk. Thank you for seeing me without an appointment."

He offered her the chair in front of his desk. For some reason she'd expected a straight-backed chair without any cushions, but she sank into plush, creamy leather. She'd also expected stark gray or white walls, but they were painted a pale blue with rich mahogany wainscoting.

"You've caused a lot of unrest at the hospital." He sat behind his desk, resting his elbows on a glass blotter that had photos of children beneath it, fingers steepled. His beady eyes glared at her from behind his acrimonious pose.

Elena's nerves started to jitter, but she couldn't let him get the best of her. "I don't consider anything I've done troublemaking, Mr. Innisk. What I've done has all been in the interest of bringing Mr. Varner back to Hope Haven."

"That isn't going to happen."

"Mr. Varner has always been loyal to Hope Haven. He was instrumental in saving the hospital from closure a few months ago. And, as you can see from this petition"—Elena took the stapled sheets of paper out of the notebook she'd been carrying and placed them on his desk, pushing them across to where his elbows rested—"a large percentage of Hope Haven's staff strongly believes that Mr. Varner should be reinstated."

"Releasing him was a board decision. It was not done without great thought."

"From what I've heard, it was done when the board told him to cut the children's ward and Pediatrics Intensive Care Unit from the hospital's budget."

Elena opened her folder again and drew out an inch-thick stack of legal-sized white paper with even more names written on them. "This petition was circulated over a year ago and presented to the board at that time. All 2,833 names on the petition belong to citizens of Deerford who believe a PICU and children's ward would be beneficial to Deerford."

"You don't know all that much about business, do you, Mrs. Rodriguez?"

"I know enough."

"But not enough to realize that businesses operate on careful analysis of present and future economics, on long-term business plans, on the power of the dollar. Hope Haven is not operated on the power of a few petitions. It's a business. In fact, it's a corporation and as such, operates under the auspices of its board of directors."

"Perhaps you don't know why Hope Haven was founded."

"I know the exact reasons, Mrs. Rodriguez."

"Well, let me remind you, Mr. Innisk. Winthrop Jeffries believed a man's soul should be nurtured and cared for as much as his body. He instilled in the people who worked for him, who built Hope Haven, the words from I Peter 5:2 that say, 'Be shepherds of God's flock that is under your care, serving as overseers—not because you must, but because you are willing, as God wants you to be; not greedy for money, but eager to serve.'"

The edge in Innisk's voice softened. "This is not the world that Winthrop Jeffries lived in, Elena. A hospital can no longer operate on that premise."

Elena was struck by how genuine he sounded. And how tired he looked. "Before I go, Mr. Innisk," Elena said, pushing back the chair and standing. She leaned across Frederick Innisk's desk and set a neatly typed piece of paper in front of him. "Perhaps you should contact the CEOs of these two companies that were 'reorganized' by your Mr. Bancroft. Or you might want to talk with the new owner of the companies, who stepped in and purchased them before they went bankrupt."

"I haven't heard anything about this." Innisk ran his hand over his face. "I expected our vetting of him to check out."

"Call them, Mr. Innisk. And I suggest you do it soon, before Mr. Varner has a chance to accept another job with another hospital. There are others who have looked at his record from Hope Haven, and they've been amazed to see the earnings curve the hospital had for quite a number of years. They're also aware that Mr. Varner helped save Hope Haven from financial disaster a few months ago."

"He wasn't alone in saving the hospital."

"Maybe not, but he was the CEO of Hope Haven at the time. You may not have recognized his importance during that crisis, but other hospitals have. He is in demand, Mr. Innisk. Surely the board of directors of Hope Haven won't want to lose him completely."

With that, Elena turned on her heel and walked out of Frederick Innisk's office. Heart beating a mile a minute, she slid into her car, closed the door and nearly collapsed.

But she'd never felt so good in her life.

Chapter Twenty-Six

ELENA SAT ACROSS FROM CESAR INSIDE GERMAIN'S Ice Cream, the place on Deerford Square where they had gone on their first real date. She sipped on an extra large double chocolate malt; Cesar had a root beer float. Just like old times, except that they were a little older.

Maybe a little wiser.

"You look awfully tired tonight," Cesar said, reaching across the table to hold her hand, as he had all those years ago.

"I've had a lot on my mind lately. Church. Work. The Harvest Festival. You." She smiled. "Not necessarily in that order."

"Do you miss the choir?"

"I've only missed one week of practice, but no, I didn't miss it at all."

Cesar stirred the ice cream around in the tall, opaque glass, staring at the swirling drink, as if there were something troubling him.

"Something wrong?" Elena asked.

He looked up slowly. "What is it about going to church that you like so much?"

In her wildest dreams, she hadn't expected that question. "I suppose if I put a list of reasons on paper there'd be a lot of them. Mostly, going to church, believing in the Lord, gives me a great sense of peace that I can't explain. When I walk into church—not just Holy Trinity, but any church—I'm filled with wonder and hope and joy. It's like someone breathed new life into my lungs and made me stronger."

Elena took a sip of her malt, thinking about the many reasons. "You know, when I sit here with you, I remember falling in love. The feeling that I was invincible. That my heart was ten times larger than it had ever been before and it beat faster. When you touched me, when you first told me you loved me, I thought I could never be happier."

Cesar grinned. "Do you still feel that way?"

"I'm more in love with you today than I've ever been. When we're together, I feel fulfilled, like every wish I could have ever wanted has been granted. And the more I'm with you, the more I want to be with you. And that's the way I feel about going to church. The more I go, the closer I am to God, and that makes me want to go even more."

"You can't have that feeling just with me? That fulfillment?"

"If you weren't in my life, I'd feel like half of me was missing. I wouldn't be able to walk or talk or function at all. I've always felt that way."

"But?" Cesar asked.

"I can't say that loving God has made me love you more, but I believe that knowing God has made my heart bigger, which gives me even more room for the love I feel for you." Elena laughed. "And now I'm sure I'm not making sense."

"I think you are." He slurped the last of his root beer float. "At least you've made me see that you're not making a choice— God or me. You've shown me that having one makes the love for the other stronger."

"That sounds pretty good."

Cesar dug into his pocket for his wallet, put a couple of dollars down for a tip, and took out a couple more bills to take up to the cashier. "I've got to get back to work."

Elena sipped on her malt until Cesar had finished paying the cashier, then slipped into her coat and they walked together out to her Jeep, parked next to his patrol car.

Standing at her car door, he put his arms around her. "Do you have a lot to do for the Harvest Festival this weekend?"

"I have some costumes to make for me and Izzy and you."

"Me?"

Elena nodded. "An old-fashioned striped bathing suit."

Cesar laughed. "There is no way I'm wearing anything like that."

"Only in the dunk tank." She grinned. "I was thinking you could dress as a scarecrow the rest of the time."

"I'm beginning to think you should rejoin the choir and spend more time at practice—anything to keep you from drumming up ideas to torment me."

"I'm spending my time tormenting others lately."

"Who?"

"I paid Frederick Innisk an office visit today."

Cesar's eyes narrowed into a deep frown. "You did what?"

"Went to his office and gave him a piece of my mind about firing Albert Varner and tossed a piece of information at him that really threw him for a loop."

"Something you want to share with me?"

"It's a long story. I'll tell you later. But, there was something different about him today. Not that he was any nicer, but I expected him to have oil paintings of the guillotine or a hangman's noose on his walls. But, no, he had a Chicago Cubs poster, another one of the Chicago Bulls, and both looked like they'd been autographed. He even had a photo of himself with Michael Jordan on his desk."

"You're not starting to think that he's halfway human, are you?"

Elena shrugged. "I'd like to think that somewhere deep down inside the old buzzard there's a heart of gold. But if it's there, he doesn't want anyone to know. And why that would be is anyone's guess."

Cesar laughed. "We can come up with some guesses when I get home tonight, but here's something to think about." He had a Cheshire cat grin on his face, which meant he was thinking something she might not like.

"Okay, hit me with it."

"I've decided I'll wear that old-fashioned swimsuit at the festival. But . . . you're wearing one too. I think you'll look awfully cute."

"Do you have any more big ideas you want to share with me? I thought I was supposed to stop coming up with ideas. That I was supposed to cut my to-do list in half."

Cesar kissed any further words away. "When it's over, you'll come up with another project, and I'll probably get irritated. But I knew when I married you that I wasn't going to be settling down with a couch potato. I married you because of who you are, a woman with a huge heart, and I don't want you any other way."

Chapter Twenty-Seven

*I*T WAS TUESDAY, A MERE FOUR DAYS BEFORE THE Bread of Life Harvest Festival, and because God was obviously smiling down on everyone involved, all plans were going without a hitch.

"Did you see the *Dispatch* over the weekend?" Ainslee asked, her smile even more brilliant than normal. "Granted it's not the biggest paper in Illinois, but the quilt got front-page coverage—in full color, and there was only one typo. They misspelled my name, but I can live with it."

There was a round of applause from everyone in Zane McGarry's office—Elena, Quintessa, Ainslee, Ginger and even Megan, who'd become a Harvest Festival volunteer extraordinaire right out of the chute.

"All donors have been given receipts for their auction items." Quintessa jotted down a few notes, as if something new had just dawned on her. "Rafael Rodriguez, Elena's son, will be at the

237

festival with his band and will act as our emcee. He'll also be our auctioneer."

"I have everything under control for the face painting and balloon animal booth," Megan said, "and as discussed, children under thirteen will be treated to balloons and face painting free of charge. Everything else I make will go toward the Habitat for Humanity fund."

"I can't believe how much you ladies have done in just a few days," Elena said, her diet soda in hand. "Thank you so much for stepping up to help."

"I'd apologize for dropping all my duties," Ginger said, "but I'm just thrilled the doctors said I can go—as long as I don't stand on my feet too long. And Steve's off duty that day, so it's going to be extra special."

Ginger didn't know just how special things really were, Elena thought, looking forward to surprising Ginger in just a few minutes.

"Any last questions about the festival?" Elena asked, looking around the room, but no hands were raised, no one said a word. "Okay, then, I guess we're good to go."

"Oh, wait, Elena, there is one more thing," Ainslee said. "Megan and I put a bunch of decorations in the conference room that we'd like you and Quintessa to look at—and Ginger too, if you're interested."

"Of course I'm interested," Ginger said. "Just don't let me get overexcited about them or start volunteering to decorate. I'm trying my hardest to be good, but it's been a chore."

"Let's go look at them now," Quintessa said. "I need to get Zane's office cleaned up and get back to work, so I'll need to make this fast."

Ginger held her back as she walked, as if she could be in pain, but Elena kept an eye on her, looking for any signs of exhaustion. All she saw was a smile.

Hallelujah!

"I'm getting to know this hospital so well I could find my way around in the dark," Ginger said, as they walked out into the hall.

"Don't mention dark and hospital in the same sentence, not around here," Quintessa said. "We went through that a couple of months ago when the big storm hit. I hope we never, ever experience something like that again."

"The whole thing was such a surprise," Elena added. "It was like one moment the skies were quiet, then bam!"

Elena opened the door to the conference room for Ginger, and she stepped inside just as Quintessa flipped on the light switch.

"Surprise!"

Ginger's hands flew to her chest. "Oh. My. Goodness."

Candace rushed toward Ginger with a wheelchair and insisted she sit down. "Doctor's orders. Mine too." Candace helped Ginger put her feet up on the footrests and stuffed a skinny pillow behind her back. "There. That should keep you comfortable."

"You really didn't have to do this," Ginger said, "but thank you so much."

Pink balloons floated like clouds against the ceiling. The tables were draped with pink-striped tablecloths made from fabric Anabelle had at home, and Megan provided the pink polka-dot bows that hung all around the conference room in loops and scallops. And the ladies from the prayer group had arrived early to help decorate.

"Want to see the cake?" Ainslee grabbed the back of the wheelchair from Candace. "It's gorgeous, made by our newest friend, Megan."

It was three tiers tall, each pink-and-white-flowered, striped and polka-dotted tier separated by cuddly looking white plastic teddy bears. It was too gorgeous for words, so Ginger just laughed and cried.

"As much as I'd love to tell you that we have hours and hours to spend here having fun," Quintessa said, trying to keep everything running on schedule, "some of us really do have to get back to work in"—she looked at her watch—"half an hour. So let's open presents."

"I'll cut the cake," Megan said, picking up the sterling silver cake knife she'd brought with her. She'd also brought gorgeous china that was stark white with a small pink-and-white-striped border around the edge.

"I'm beginning to think I might have gone a little overboard with the pink," Megan said as she slipped the first piece of cake onto a plate.

"What made you think I'm having a little girl?" Ginger asked, smiling.

"I could have sworn someone told me that," Megan said. "I can't imagine doing pink when I have blue at home, unless someone told me 'Girl.'"

"I brought the pink tablecloths," Anabelle said. "For some reason I thought you were having a girl too."

"So what *are* you having?" Elena asked, handing a piece of cake to Ginger and taking one for herself.

"To be perfectly honest, I don't have a clue. Steve and I decided we didn't want to know, although I admit I've probably called the baby she or her more than once."

"That should make unwrapping gifts interesting," Ainslee said, laughing. "I wonder just how many of us went pink when we picked out our gifts?"

Elena had. She knew Megan and Quintessa had too. This should prove to be very interesting. Even more interesting if Ginger and Steve ended up with a little boy.

Oh well, that was something to dwell on later. Right now, it was party time!

Ribbon and wrapping paper began to fly as Ginger opened gifts of onesies, "Our Little Girl" picture frames, blankets, dresses, bottles, night-lights, more than Elena had expected, and almost everything was some shade of pink.

"You can always exchange things," Quintessa, ever practical, said, as she ate a piece of cake. "But if it were me, I'd just hope and pray for a little girl."

"I'll be happy with either," Ginger said, and once again she teared up. "Steve is going to be so surprised by all of this. I really can't thank you all enough."

Elena was on her second piece of cake, carbs she'd no doubt work off before the day was over, when one of the conference room doors opened, and Phyllis Getty walked in carrying a huge bouquet—at least three dozen, if not more—of red and white roses. Someone obviously hadn't heard about the party's surprise color theme: pink.

"They're beautiful," Elena said, helping Phyllis carry them to the table, wondering who they could be from. She was sure all the people who'd been invited were here and that their gifts had already been opened.

"Would you like me to open the card for you, Ginger?" Elena asked.

"But they're not for Ginger, Elena. The card says they're for you."

Elena frowned. "Me?"

"That's what it says."

"*Hmm*." Cesar rarely if ever sent flowers. It just wasn't his thing.

Candace handed Phyllis a large piece of cake while Elena took the envelope out of the forked holder and opened it, pulling out the card. A smile widened on her face, and then she read:

> *I can't possibly know who all was involved in saving my job, so please share these flowers and my thanks.*
>
> > *Albert Varner*
> > *Chief Executive Officer*
> > *Hope Haven Hospital*

The party couldn't have ended on a better note. Everything was going according to plan.

Now if the Bread of Life Harvest Festival could go off in the same way—without a hitch.

Chapter Twenty-Eight

A MASS OF PEOPLE STOOD IN LINE TO THROW balls at the poor saps who were on the verge of getting dunked. Police Chief Brian O'Hanlon had been the first to go. He had a half-hour slot, starting just a few minutes after the festival opened, and so far he'd brought in eighty-five bucks.

"Think I can't knock you in, Chief?" Cesar shouted. He was standing in his old-fashioned striped bathing suit with a boater hat tied with a bright orange ribbon, and because it was cold, he had on a pair of gray wool socks and combat boots. It was a crazy outfit, but the folks at the festival loved it, taking his picture, one of which was bound to end up on the front page of the *Dispatch*.

Elena planned to put it on the Web site too. What a kick that would be.

"You're all talk, Rodriguez," the chief shouted back, egging Cesar on.

"I've got nine balls here," Cesar said, winding up his pitching arm, "and I say at least eight of them knock you in."

"I'm not a betting man, Rodriguez, but if you're right, I'll work your shift one day. If you're wrong—"

"If I'm wrong, I'll rake your yard one day next week."

"Not just my yard, Rodriguez. Let's say mine and Sergeant McDaniels'—and he's got five acres."

"It's a deal."

Cesar wound up, putting on a show. The crowd grew. And grew.

Cesar launched his pitch and hit the target dead on.

The chief made a huge splash, and the crowd roared.

"All right, Chief," Cesar shouted, the moment Brian came up for air. "Up and at 'em. That's one out of nine. Eight more to go—and in case no one ever told you, I was the number one pitcher at Deerford High three years running. They nicknamed me Nolan Ryan, and you don't get that moniker unless you're good."

Elena just stood there in her own old-fashioned striped swimming suit, boater hat and pigtails laughing at the two grown men who'd grumbled about taking a turn in the dunk tank, but were suddenly having the time of their lives.

The Bread of Life Harvest Festival was a success.

Elena wanted to shout for joy, but she'd wait and do that when she bought nine balls and tried to dunk her husband. Of course, she knew turnabout would be fair play, and that she was bound to go in more than a time or two or three.

She left the dunk tank, walking around the booths.

"Any sales yet?" she asked Cameron Scott, who sat inside his pumpkin- and gourd-decorated booth, selling bricks for the Wall of Hope.

"Six, and that's in just the first half hour."

Cameron stood, doing some deep knee bends, those very same knees cracking as he went down then back up again.

"So, what do you think of my sales chart?" He pointed to the screaming yellow poster board with Support Hope Haven's Wall of Hope printed at the top, sitting on an easel. "Each ear of Indian corn on the money scale signifies one brick at fifty bucks," he said. "Just don't look too close, 'cause I'm the one who bought the first one, something no one else needs to know."

Elena gave her friend a hug. "Keep up the good work, Cameron. Just don't go broke in the process."

A few booths down, Elena found Brooke, Howie and Izzy, supervised by Anabelle, since Candace had been asked to work, collecting Pennies for Habitat for Humanity. Heath Carlson stood at the booth rummaging through his wallet.

"*Buela!*" Izzy ran out from behind the booth and launched herself into Elena's arms. "We've made five hundred seventy pennies so far."

"That's five dollars and seventy cents, Izzy," Anabelle said, leaning against the counter of the booth, wearing a scarecrow costume, while Izzy was dressed as harvest princesses in gold, green and amber satin and tulle, wearing crowns Anabelle had supplied from her days as high school prom and homecoming queen.

"Put your pennies here," Howie called out to a couple passing by. "Put your pennies here. Buy a stove for Habitat for Humanity."

"I think we should hook him up with Cesar. They make a pretty good sales team." Elena set Isabel back down so she could go into salesperson mode too.

"Pennies, please. Pennies, please," Izzy yelled, trying to outshout Howie, and one couple after another stopped by, emptying the pennies out of their pockets.

"How many pennies would this be?" Heath asked the children handing them a ten-dollar bill.

Isabel's and Howie's eyes widened.

"Like a million!" Izzy squealed.

"More like a thousand," Elena said with a laugh.

Heath smiled and winked at Elena and Isabel as he continued to the next booth.

Elena watched for a moment, noticing that poor Brooke was standing at the back of the booth, picking at a hangnail, bored to tears. Typical eleven-year-old girl.

"Any idea what time the auction's going to be?" Anabelle asked. "I'd like to see how it goes."

"Three thirty. Just close up shop whenever you need to take a break. And make sure you take Brooke, Izzy and Howie to see how beautiful the quilt looks hanging up inside the auction booth."

"Are people looking at it?"

"Along with the dunk tank, it's the biggest hit of the festival."

Anabelle smiled. "You know, you spend so much time on a project like that, and you love it yourself, but you never know what others will think."

"You don't need to worry, Anabelle. It's going to make a fortune."

They chatted for a few more minutes before Elena took off, needing to tour the rest of the festival. The weather had turned out so beautiful that the booths had been set up both inside and out; and everywhere Elena walked, she could smell the aroma of hot dogs, corn dogs, cinnamon rolls, deep fried Snickers and hamburgers.

With her stomach growling, Elena picked up a funnel cake, munching on its sugary sweetness when she stopped at the face painting and balloon animal booth.

Elena laughed out loud. "I don't believe it."

"Don't believe what?" James asked, as he sat on the stool in front of Megan—who was dressed as a pumpkin queen—having a fire-breathing dragon painted on his cheek. "This is the real me."

"Yeah, that's you all right. The bad boy."

"I paid good money for this," James said. "If you're not careful, I'll buy ten bucks worth of balls to knock you into the dunk tank."

"You wouldn't."

James's brow rose good and high. "I would, Mrs. Rodriguez, and I'm nearly as good as your husband."

"Where's Fern?" Elena asked, once the teasing was over and she had a chance to worry about James's wife.

"Keeping Ainslee and Kirstie company at the quilt booth."

"Hey, Dad!" Nelson ran across the church activity center, his tennis shoes squeaking on the floor. He had a hot dog in one hand and a chocolate-covered banana in the other. "Can I bum another five bucks? I want to knock Officer Rodriguez in the dunk tank."

"I thought that was just a dollar for three throws," James said.

"Yeah, it is just a dollar, but I might not get him on the first three. I'm not all that good a shot, you know."

James dug into his pocket, pulled out his wallet and sorted through the bills for a five.

"Have you seen your brother?" he asked.

"He's shooting hoops in the gym, trying to impress some girls. You know how it is, Dad, at Gideon's age kids aren't all that keen on harvest festivals."

"No, I guess not." James laughed and handed the five to Nelson. "Here you go. But why are you so anxious to dunk Officer Rodriguez?"

"Do I have to have a reason? It just sounds like fun."

He had a point. Megan painted a quick butterfly on Elena's cheek before she said good-bye and headed back to the dunk tank. If it was Cesar's turn, she needed to get in line.

Cesar was dry as could be sitting on the bench in the collapsible cage, but Nelson was up and determined to get him.

"Hey, Nelson," Cesar shouted, "I'll give you five dollars if you wait a while and try to dunk my wife instead of me."

Elena indignantly put her hands on her hips. "No fair, Rodriguez!" she hollered. "You can't bribe the customers."

Nelson wound up his pitching arm. "And it's you I'm interested in, Officer Rodriguez."

"Why me? I never did anything to you."

"Just because." Nelson threw, his ball ending up a good ten feet from the dunk tank.

"You know, Nelson," Elena said, taking hold of his shoulders, "I think someone forgot to tell you that guys who are thirteen years old and terrific at science get to stand closer to the dunk tank when they throw."

"That's a pretty good rule, Mrs. Rodriguez. How much closer do I get to go?"

"Well, let's just start walking and figure out where we should stop."

They were about ten feet away when Elena finally let go of Nelson's shoulders. "Give that a shot."

Nelson did.

Cesar went down.

The crowd roared again.

And Elena's cell phone rang.

Every person who'd paid for a booth had Elena's number. All the coordinators and volunteers had her number. Hopefully nothing had gone wrong.

"Hello."

"Elena, it's Candace."

"But you're at the—" Elena's stomach clenched. Candace wouldn't have called from the hospital unless something was wrong. But she tried to remain calm.

"Is everything okay?" Elena asked.

"It's Ginger."

When Ginger had called early this morning to say she didn't feel up to coming to the festival, Elena wondered if the baby had decided to come a few days early. "Please tell me she's okay. She hasn't gone into labor already, has she?"

"I don't know how to say this, Elena, but...she's lost the baby."

A horrid knot settled in Elena's throat. "No. Please, no."

Elena looked toward Cesar. She was a nurse and she dealt with death all the time, but right this moment, she needed her husband. And as if he could sense her need, he climbed out of the dunk tank and ran toward her.

"Hey, everyone, give me a shot," Chief O'Hanlon called out. There was something about cops. They always knew when something was wrong, and they took charge. Brian was taking charge now, turning the attention back to him, and away from Cesar and Elena, who moved away from the crowd so she could talk.

"Is Steve with her?" Elena asked.

"He was out on a fire when she went into labor and got here as soon as he could. We hoped we could save the baby, but..." Candace's voice, a near whisper, trailed off.

Hot tears washed down Elena's face. Cesar's arm went around her waist, holding her close.

"I didn't want to bother you, Elena. Ginger didn't want me to call, either, but I knew you'd want to be here for her. At least for a little while."

"I'll be there in a few minutes. Cesar's here. He'll let Quintessa know what's going on and...and I'll be there."

"Why don't you let me take you?" Cesar said, when Elena hung up the phone.

"No, stay here. Please." Elena wiped tears from her eyes. "Go make money in the dunk tank and help Rafael get big bucks for the quilt—just in case I'm not back."

"You don't have to come back, hon."

"Yes I do." She kissed him softly. "The last thing I need right now is to have free time on my hands. I'd just try to understand why this happened." Elena struggled to push the thought from her mind but she couldn't. How could God take another baby away from Ginger and Steve? Such kind people who loved that baby so much and wanted nothing more than to meet her?

And for the first time in a long time, Elena couldn't put words together into a prayer.

Elena stood at the side of Ginger's hospital bed, holding her hand, wishing she could find something comforting to say. But it was Ginger who did the talking.

"She's beautiful. She *was* beautiful, so tiny, with red hair, just like mine."

"Don't do this to yourself," Steve said, sitting in a chair beneath the room's window. His eyes were red. He looked like he wanted to scream. "You can't talk about her like she—" Steve dragged in a deep breath. "I've got to get out of here for a little while."

"Don't go," Elena called after him, but he'd already gone from the room.

"It's okay, Elena," Ginger said, squeezing her hand. "This has really hit him hard."

"What about you?"

"Someone has to be strong," Ginger said. "Steve stayed tough the last three times. This time I have to hang on, because he can't deal with losing another baby and watching me go out of my mind with grief."

How could she be so strong? Elena wondered. Or was she in shock? Too numb to scream or cry.

"Can I get you anything?" Elena asked, wishing there was something she could do, but feeling helpless.

Ginger shook her head. "Pastor Tom was here and he prayed with Steve and me. I talked with my mom and she said she could be here in a couple of days." Her voice began to quiver. "And I know Steve and I will get through this okay, but . . . " Her tears began to flow and Elena took her into her arms and let her cry.

Elena felt her own tears stinging her eyes and she wanted to pray, wanted to talk with God about what had happened, but the only words that came were "Why, Lord? Why?"

Chapter Twenty-Nine

THAT NIGHT, ELENA WAS SITTING ALONE IN THE hospital chapel when Cesar entered.

He slid into the pew beside her and took hold of her hand. "We made $4,702 on the quilt, and Anabelle couldn't have been happier."

Elena turned to Cesar. She wanted to smile, but she couldn't find the strength.

"I'm glad you came to be with Ginger and Steve," he said. "They needed you."

"I thought about trying to be there for the auction, but for some strange reason, I just wanted to sit here after I saw them."

"I can understand that," Cesar said, caressing a tear away from her cheek. "This is where you feel closer to God."

Elena shook her head. "I don't feel close to Him at all right now. I don't even feel Him in this chapel, and I sure didn't feel Him anywhere near when I was upstairs with Ginger."

"You're just upset."

"I prayed so many times over the last few weeks. We all did, asking God to bring that baby into the world for Steve and Ginger. They'd already lost three babies. Why did they have to lose this one too?"

"My mother used to cry when she lost someone she loved, and she'd pray. And when I'd ask her how she could keep on praying when God had let someone die, she'd just say, 'He moves in mysterious ways. We must have faith in Him.' When my mom was dying, I wanted to believe with all my heart. I wanted God to save her. I begged Him for a miracle, and when He let her die, I just became less of a believer. But you . . . you can't lose your faith, Elena. You need it now to get you through this."

They sat in silence for several minutes.

Cesar swallowed hard, squeezing Elena's hand tighter. "You know, I've been thinking a lot about God since I found Caleb. I wasn't even on duty in that area. If I hadn't been there for a call that turned out to be false, I wouldn't have been close to the creek. I wouldn't have gotten to Caleb as fast as I did. But because of that false call—I *was* there. Because of that false call, I *was* able to save Caleb. I think my mother was right. God does move in mysterious ways."

Elena bowed her head. Once again she tried to pray, but it was like she'd forgotten how.

"I have a little something for you," Cesar said. "Something I hope will help with what you're going through right now."

Elena tilted her head toward her husband as he opened a small black box. He unfolded the tissue paper inside that looked like it had once been white, but was now yellowed with age. There inside rested a beautiful gold filigree cross on a delicate chain.

"This was my mother's," he said. "You never met her, but she would've loved you, and she would have told me I was a very lucky man to have found such a special lady."

"I'm sure I would have loved her too." Elena attempted a smile. "After all, she raised you."

"My mother believed in God with all her heart and all her soul. She wore this cross always, and I remember her reaching up to her chest and holding on to it when she was troubled or in pain. Even as she died, she held on to it. We were in the hospital and I was holding her hand and she told me that God was with her. I didn't believe it then, but I think I'm starting to believe it now."

Cesar pushed up from the pew and slipped the cross and chain around Elena's neck, latching it at the back.

"My mother would have wanted you to have this. She'd want you to hold on to it. She'd want you to regain that solid faith of yours again." Cesar gently kissed Elena's brow. "*I* want you to find your faith again."

It was nearly freezing outside when Elena pulled into the parking lot on Wednesday, the day before Thanksgiving. In spite of the cold, the sky was blue and cloudless. She couldn't have asked for a better day to stand with the people from Habitat for Humanity to watch three new homeowners step inside their furnished homes for the first time.

They'd cried and laughed, and Elena had cried and laughed right along with them.

As she walked past the leafless floribundas, she found herself mentally making a list of all the things she had to do before the celebration she and Cesar would be holding at their home tomorrow for a houseload of family. Cesar wanted peanut butter fudge. Rafael wanted yams, mashed potatoes and stuffing. Izzy wanted everyone to watch the Macy's Thanksgiving Day Parade with her.

Elena had invited Ginger and Steve to spend the day. Whether they'd come or not, she didn't know. She could only hope and pray.

As she neared the hospital, Elena felt the sudden need to clutch the cross she wore around her neck. It had given her strength over the last few days, calmed her when she was feeling down.

She wanted so desperately to feel the peace in her heart, the wholeness that had come to her after she'd begun to believe, to have faith. It was returning slowly, but something else was holding her back.

Please, Lord, restore my faith. Help me to believe in You again.

"Ma'am?"

The voice was so soft that Elena thought for a moment that she might have imagined it, that the wind had whispered through the naked branches of the trees, sounding so much like a young girl.

"Could you help me? Please?"

Elena followed the voice to the nearby cluster of trees and found a teenage girl shivering on the ground. Her jeans were dirty and ragged. She wore tennis shoes without socks. Her face was smudged, her hair slick with oil, looking as though she hadn't had a bath in weeks. And she had to be at least nine months pregnant.

"We need to get you inside right away," Elena said urgently as she positioned her arms under the girl's to help her up.

"My water broke a couple of hours ago and I've been having contractions. A lot of them. I couldn't walk any further."

"Do you need assistance, Mrs. Rodriguez?"

Elena looked up to see who was offering to help.

It was Scrooge.

"Yes. Please."

Mr. Innisk seemed to know exactly where extra wheelchairs were kept, and he ran inside to get one, returning moments later wheeling it toward Elena and the young girl. She was shivering. Her body temperature had to be plummeting.

Mr. Innisk took off his coat and draped it over the girl, who looked at him with expressionless eyes.

"Let's get her up to the Birthing Unit," Mr. Innisk said, moving quickly with the wheelchair, heading inside, then toward a bank of elevators. As if it had known they were coming and that they were in a hurry, the doors opened and Mr. Innisk pushed the wheelchair inside.

The girl winced in pain. "I'm scared. Help me. Please."

Mr. Innisk frowned, and Elena was afraid he'd say something abrupt. Ask her what she was doing out in the freezing cold. Tell her that if she didn't have insurance, they'd send her to some other hospital. But he didn't.

"This is a good hospital," he said. "We've got wonderful nurses to take care of you."

"I can't have this baby. I just can't. It doesn't matter if the nurses are good or not, I have no way to take care of it."

"What's your name?" he asked.

"Tracy. Tracy Givens."

"Well, Tracy," Mr. Innisk said, "let's worry about all of that later."

The elevator opened again and Mr. Innisk pushed her straight to the Birthing Unit, calling out orders and getting attention.

Fast.

Candace was there, reacting like the expert she was, and in no time at all they had Tracy in a room by herself, isolated from the rest of the women.

"I don't have any money," Tracy said, beginning to cry. "I don't know where the baby's father is. I haven't seen my parents since my eighteenth birthday. If they knew I was here—"

"Would you like me to call your parents?" Elena asked. "I'm sure they'd—"

"No. Please don't."

"It's okay, Tracy," Mr. Innisk said. "You don't have to see your parents or talk with them if you don't want to."

In between contractions, Tracy attempted to sniff back her tears. "If it hadn't been so cold, I was going to deliver the baby myself and just leave her here at the hospital. You take care of babies when they're abandoned like that, don't you?"

"You're not abandoning your baby," Elena said. "You're here in a warm hospital. We're going to get you all cleaned up, and we're going to make sure you have a healthy baby."

"But I can't keep her. I'd be a lousy mom, just like my mom." She swiped her hand across her face to wipe away tears. "Can I give the baby up for adoption?"

"Is that what you want, Tracy?" Elena asked gently.

She nodded. "I can't let my baby live on the street. Not like me."

Dr. Carpenter came into the room, her hair a mass of black curls flying every which way. "Hi, Tracy. I'm Dr. Carpenter. I'm going to check you out and—"

"If I'm no longer needed, I'll be on my way." Frederick Innisk said, interrupting the doctor. "No need to return the coat."

"Please don't go," Tracy said, looking up at Mr. Innisk. "Couldn't you just wait a little longer?"

The hard lines on his face calmed as he resigned himself with a nod. "I'll be right outside the door."

"Thank you," Elena said, following Mr. Innisk out to the hallway and taking hold of his hand, as if they were the best of friends, instead of sworn enemies. "I'm glad you were there for her."

"You would have done okay without me."

"She seems to trust you. She didn't warm up to me the way she did you."

"I have that affect on some people—not you, of course." Then he actually winked. *The* Frederick Innisk, previously known as Scrooge, had winked at *her.*

Elena reached up and wrapped her fingers around the cross Cesar had given her, the cross his mother had believed in, and for the first time in days, she prayed, really and truly prayed.

Heavenly Father, I believe we're in need of a miracle today. Amen.

"Hi, Elena."

She spun around when she heard Ginger's voice. She hadn't seen Ginger since she had been released from the hospital early on Sunday and insisted Elena go to church with her; and for some reason, she looked more beautiful than she ever had before.

Steve had his arm tucked through Ginger's, but he released her long enough to give Elena a hug.

"Mr. Innisk, I'd like you to meet Ginger and Steve Murphy. Steve works for the Deerford Fire Department." Elena looked at Steve and Ginger. "Frederick Innisk is one of the board members here at Hope Haven."

After the introductions were made and everyone shook hands, Ginger turned to Elena.

"We've been making the rounds, stopping by to see everyone who's been so kind to us in the past few days, and we were on the way to see you next. We want you to be the first to know our good news." Ginger's smile brightened her face. "We've decided to adopt. It's probably going to take forever, but—"

"I have a good friend," Innisk said, powering right into the conversation, "who does a lot of pro bono adoption work. Perhaps I could introduce you to him."

Steve frowned. "Why would you do that for us?"

"Because the good Lord moves in mysterious ways," Elena stated, taking hold of her cross again and squeezing it tightly. Could Mr. Innisk be thinking the same thing she was, that there might be a baby available for adoption sooner than they could ever imagine?

Mr. Innisk paced back and forth for a moment or two, then stopped again in front of Steve and Ginger. "As it happens, there is a young woman in the hospital right this moment who's about to give birth. She has said she'd like to put the baby up for adoption."

Both Ginger and Steve stared at Mr. Innisk, too overwhelmed to say anything.

"Do you think you might be interested?"

A scream came from the birthing room, and Elena squeezed her cross even tighter.

Ginger looked at her husband and then smiled at Mr. Innisk. "Please, do whatever it is you have to do, and we'll just wait here and put the decision in the Lord's hands."

Another scream came from Tracy's room.

Without another word, Frederick Innisk punched a number on his cell phone.

And Ginger, Steve and Elena held hands and prayed.

"Heavenly Father, we thank You for the gift You have given us today. A beautiful baby girl."

Pastor Tom stood with the proud adoptive-parents-to-be. Ginger and Steve cried, finding it hard to believe that they were finally blessed with a child, a miraculously healthy baby swaddled in pastel pink.

Elena, Candace, Anabelle and James all peered anxiously through the nursery window, smiling at the bounty of this beautiful Thanksgiving.

"In Jesus' name we pray. Amen."

About the Author

USA Today best-selling author Patti Berg began penning stories while in elementary school, when she wrote the script for a puppet show that she and her friends put on at a local hospital. Thirty years later, one of her dreams came true when the first of her many warm and lighthearted novels appeared in bookstores.

Scared of dogs until the age of fifty, Patti now goes out of her way to pet every dog she gets close to and would happily bring home all of the puppies in the pound if her less impulsive husband would only let her. He's had less success keeping her from saying *yes* when family, friends and others ask her to volunteer. A past president, secretary and newsletter editor of the Sacramento Valley Rose chapter of Romance Writers of America as well as past president, Web site and conference coordinator for RWA's Published Authors' Special Interest Chapter, Patti is currently volunteering with the Ada County Idaho Sheriff's Department.

She lives in southwestern Idaho with her husband of thirty-three years and a huggable Bernese mountain dog named Barkley.

Read on for a sneak peek of the next exciting and heartfelt book in *Stories from Hope Haven*.

Available through Guideposts' direct mail program by calling Customer Service at (800) 932–2145.

Strength IN *Numbers*
by
Charlotte Carter

*J*AMES BELL WALKED ACROSS THE PARKING LOT TO the entrance of Hope Haven Hospital, the chill morning air clouding his breath. The Lord had blessed this early December morning, as the sun was just beginning to rise into the beautiful clear sky. The cold front moving in from Canada nipped at his cheeks, so he picked up the pace with each step he took. As a registered nurse, he was eager to do his bit to help others heal their bodies as well as their spirits.

The automatic door swished open and the warm air struck him.

James took the stairs to the staff lounge and locker room on the third floor. Inside the lounge, the bulletin board was draped with silver garland for the holidays. Various notices were posted, most of them old and faded.

He spotted an envelope in his employee mailbox. Shrugging out of his jacket, he opened the envelope and read a memo addressed to all employees.

Due to a continuing financial shortfall, salaries of all Hope Haven Hospital employees will be reduced by ten percent (10%), effective January 1.

The administration regrets the necessity . . .

James's knees went weak. His mouth dropped open, and his heart sank to his stomach, turning into a painful knot.

He'd known for some time that the hospital was struggling financially, but he'd thought the problem had been solved. He hadn't imagined the hospital CEO Albert Varner would take such a drastic step.

A 10 percent cut in salary meant James would earn several thousand dollars less per year to support his two teenage sons and wife. Fern suffered from multiple sclerosis. Their insurance didn't cover all the necessary medications for her MS, and the excess came out of their pockets.

In time, that expense was likely to grow.

Same thing with his boys, Gideon and Nelson. Each year their expenses for clothes, cell phones and school activities increased. Sometimes exponentially.

A 10 percent cut would be disastrous.

What would he do?

His mind in a fog and a sick feeling in his stomach, he went into the locker room and changed into green hospital scrubs. He left and slowly descended the stairs to the second floor to the General Medicine and Surgery Units. Still a half hour until his shift officially started, he was in no rush to get to work.

The quiet of early morning on the nursing floor would soon be replaced by the hurried footsteps of doctors and technicians coming and going, meds being administered and patients leaning on their call buttons.

A pair of poinsettia plants sat on the counter of the nurses' station, supplied by the families of grateful patients.

Anabelle Scott and Candace Crenshaw, his nursing colleagues, were behind the counter, their expressions as grim as he felt.

"You look like you heard the bad news too," James said.

Anabelle, the nurse supervisor for Cardiac Care, gave him a sympathetic smile. "Not exactly good news right before Christmas, is it? Particularly for those of you with young families."

Candace, who worked in the Birthing Unit, shook her head. "I've already bought most of the presents for Brooke and Howie." Her forehead furrowed and she bit her lip. "Now I'm wondering if I should take some of them back."

As a young widow and single mother, Candace was understandably worried about the impact of a salary cut on her family's finances.

From force of habit, James checked the automated computer system to see how many patients he had—a pneumonia on oxygen and a hand surgery. He skimmed the rest. He really needed to pull himself together. His patients deserved his best efforts and all of his concentration.

"For months the hospital has been teetering on the brink of disaster," Anabelle said, "and somehow Albert Varner has pulled us out. Maybe he'll find another way again."

James wasn't all that optimistic. The news had really shaken him. Maybe that was because Fern was going through a rough patch with her MS and he was worried about her.

The stairwell door burst open and Elena Rodriguez, a nurse from the Intensive Care Unit, hurried across the floor to the nurses' station, planting herself in front of the small group.

"What I want to know," Elena started as she waved the letter, "is what we're supposed to do."

"That's what we were just trying to figure out as well," James said.

"And with Christmas right around the corner," Candace added with a sigh.

"It's just I'm so close to having enough for the trip to Spain."

James rubbed his hand across the back of his neck. He knew Elena had said she'd been planning and saving for the trip for years, dreaming of the day when she could visit the ancestral land of her great-grandfather.

"Just yesterday I got a brochure about festivals in the Andalusia region, and I was trying to figure out the best time of year to go." She pulled her lips back to a discouraged angle. "Now I don't know if I'll be able to go at all."

Anabelle spoke up. "I'm afraid the pay cut will cause employees to look for work elsewhere. That could impact all of us."

James exhaled, bent his head and studied the toes of his white work shoes. "Maybe we ought to do what we always do when things get tough—leave it in God's hands and have faith everything will work out for the best."

His co-workers murmured their agreement, though he still saw concern in their eyes.

As though a starting bell had been rung, the activity on the second floor picked up. Graveyard-shift nurses updated the day-shift nurses on patients, reviewed medications and added insights about the patients' health and morale as needed.

The hospital loudspeaker paged doctors. Meal service carts rumbled through the hallway bringing breakfast to waiting patients.

James settled into the sudden change in pace as he checked in with patients from the previous day. This was what he did. He was good at his job. He'd learned as a medic in the first Gulf War that this was what he wanted to do with his life.

About nine o'clock, he received word a transfer patient from Springfield was being moved into his unit later in the morning. An amputee who had lost his leg in a motorcycle accident. The kid was only seventeen.

James's heart broke for the youngster. Losing a limb was a tough adversity to handle for someone so young.

As the morning progressed, James made sure a room was ready for the new amputee patient. According to the computer system, the boy's name was Theodore Townsend.

A soft *ping* announced the arrival of the elevator on the floor.

The boy lay on a gurney being pushed by the hospital orderly, Becker. The boy's mother held his hand while Dad stood stoically looking straight ahead. Both parents were simply dressed, the dad a muscular guy who looked like he might be a plumber or in the construction business.

"Room 207," James told Becker.

The stocky orderly expertly rolled the gurney down the hallway and made the turn into the room.

James picked up the paperwork to make sure everything was in order.

"Hi, Theodore," he said as he entered, flipping quickly through the printed pages.

"Ted," the boy replied in a monosyllabic grunt.

"Okay, Ted, how're you doing?"

"Great. I'm having a blast." The young man's sarcasm fell flat against the pain etched in his face and the fear visible in his hazel eyes.

James rested his hand on the young man's shoulder for a moment, speaking in a low voice meant to both soothe and reassure. "I'm James, your nurse. We'll get you settled in a minute, then you can get some rest."

Ted's eyes cut toward James, but Ted didn't speak. His mother still had a death grip on her son's hand, her complexion almost as white as her knuckles. Worry lined her face.

"Mr. and Mrs. Townsend, if you'd like to step outside, it'll take me just a few minutes to make your son comfortable. Then you can come back in and visit."

Having an injured child was probably harder on the parents than it was on the kid. Mothers, in particular, often didn't want to leave their child's bedside for even a few minutes.

"Come on, Cynthia." Mr. Townsend hooked his hand through his wife's arm. "I saw a waiting room down the hall. We can wait there."

Bending down, Cynthia kissed her son's cheek. "We'll be right back, Teddy, I promise."

"It's okay, Mom. I'm not going anywhere."

As the mother turned to leave, James saw tears welling in her eyes. Tough business, being a mom.

When the parents left, James and Becker positioned them-selves to shift the boy onto the regular bed. Physically fit with good muscular development, the young man probably weighed about 170 pounds.

"We're going to lift you up and place you on the bed," James said. "This may hurt, son, but we'll make it quick." He slid his hands under Ted's arms; Becker had the patient's hips.

Ted visibly gritted his teeth.

James gave Becker a one, two, three count. Together they hefted the boy. Ted sucked in a quick breath and then was safely on the bed.

Becker adjusted the IV pole and pulled the gurney away. "He's all yours, James. I promised you'd take real good care of him."

Becker left, and James went to work adjusting the boy's po-sition in the bed and checking the dressing on his wound. The kid had lost his right leg just above the knee, leaving him with nothing but a stump.

"How's your pain level?" The doctor's orders included pain medication as needed.

"I can handle it." He squared his jaw tough-guy style.

"How'd you mess up your leg?" James asked.

"I hit a patch of gravel. The bike slid and took me with it." Ted turned his head away. "It would've been better if it had killed me instead of turning me into a stupid cripple."

James's breath caught in his lungs and he felt a stab of sympa-thy. Depression and grief for a physical loss weren't unusual, and Ted was experiencing both.

"They're doing a lot of good things with prosthetics these days, Ted. You'll be surprised how quickly you'll be up and walking under your own steam again."

The boy's head whipped back, and he glared up at James with a combination of anger and regret. "I'm a soccer player, man. Soccer players don't walk. *They run!*"

James had vaguely recognized the Townsend name, and now he realized he'd read about Ted in the local paper—a star high school athlete with a great future ahead of him.

A future that a single moment of carelessness had suddenly reshaped.

"Maybe you'll be the first soccer player at your school with a prosthesis," James said in an effort to provide encouragement.

The boy hissed out an expletive. "Get outta here, man. You don't know anything about me or soccer or anything else." Awkwardly, he rolled onto his side, presenting James with his back.

Knowing further conversation was useless, James left and went to the small lounge where the Townsends were waiting. Sitting together on a love seat holding hands, they looked as forlorn as their son, but less angry.

Mrs. Townsend hopped to her feet. "Can we go back to his room now?"

"In just a minute," James said. "He's grieving for his lost leg and he'll go through all the stages of grief just as he would if he'd lost a loved one. He'll be angry at everyone—probably including you, himself and even God."

"Oh, dear." Cynthia covered her mouth with her hand and more tears welled in her eyes.

Mr. Townsend looped his arm around his wife's shoulders. "I wish I'd never given him permission to ride that bike. It's all my fault."

"Blaming yourselves won't be productive," James said gently.

"Hard not to," Mr. Townsend said.

James nodded that he understood.

"Rest assured, I'm not going to let my boy out of my sight ever again," Cynthia announced.

A smile tugged at James's lips. *Typical mom reaction.* But it was still going to be a rocky road for the entire family over the next several months, long after Ted was discharged from Hope Haven.

He didn't envy them the ride.

Before James could take a break for lunch, his cell phone vibrated in his pocket. Because of his wife's illness and the fear that she might need him, he always carried the phone with him.

He checked the number. *Fern.* His chest tightened with anxiety as he brought the phone to his ear. "Hi, sweetheart. Are you all right?"

"I'm just leaving Dr. Chopra's office. She's calling in a new prescription for me." Fern audibly took a breath—simply talking had become an effort for her. He was glad her mother went with her to appointments. "Could you pick it up on your way home?"

"Of course. Sure you don't need it sooner? I can run out on my lunch break."

"No, she gave me a couple of samples. I'll be fine 'til evening."

"Okay, but get some rest this afternoon. Don't overdo it."

After telling Fern good bye, James slipped the cell back into his pocket and closed his eyes. What were they going to do when the pay cut kicked in? How was he going to tell Fern? Then he remembered what he had told his friends that morning about leaving things in God's hands.

Please, God, help my wife.

A Note from the Editors

Guideposts, a nonprofit organization, touches millions of lives every day through products and services that inspire, encourage and uplift. Our magazines, books, prayer network and outreach programs help people connect their faith-filled values to their daily lives.

Your purchase of *Stories from Hope Haven* does make a difference! To comfort hospitalized children, Guideposts Outreach has created Comfort Kits for free distribution. A hospital can be a very scary place for sick children. With all the hustle and bustle going on around them, the strange surroundings, and the pain they're experiencing, is it any wonder kids need a little relief?

Inside each easy-to-carry Comfort Kit is a prayer card, a journal, a pack of crayons, an "I'm Special" wristband to wear alongside the hospital-issued one and a plush golden star pillow to cuddle. It's a welcome gift and has a powerful effect in helping to soothe a child's fears.

To learn more about our many nonprofit outreach programs, please visit www.guidepostsfoundation.org.